Nick J. Brown was born in Salford sometime between the death of Elvis Presley and the release of *Never Mind the Bollocks, Here's the Sex Pistols*. He lives in Manchester with his partner. This is his first book.

to rise

in

the dark

Nick J. Brown

Іncendiary Books

Copyright @ 2024 by Nick J. Brown

Independently published.

The moral right of the author has been asserted.

All characters and events in this publication, other than those clearly in the public domain, are fictitious and any resemblance to real persons, living or dead, is purely coincidental.

All rights reserved.

No part of this publication may be reproduced, stored in a retrieval system, or transmitted, in any form of by any means, without the prior permission in writing of the publisher, nor be otherwise circulated in any form of binding or cover than that in which it is published and without a similar condition including this condition being imposed on the subsequent purchaser.

ISBN: 979-8-335-87821-0

Cover design by Nick J. Brown

Cover image by Patrick Strattner/fStop Images GmbH via Getty Images

Quote on page 31 from 'Night', William Blake, 1789

For Nicola

When my mother died I was very young,
And my father sold me while yet my tongue
Could scarcely cry " 'weep! 'weep! 'weep! 'weep!"
So your chimneys I sweep & in soot I sleep.

There's little Tom Dacre, who cried when his head
That curled like a lamb's back, was shaved, so I said,
"Hush, Tom! never mind it, for when your head's bare,
You know that the soot cannot spoil your white hair."

And so he was quiet, & that very night,
As Tom was a-sleeping he had such a sight!
That thousands of sweepers, Dick, Joe, Ned, & Jack,
Were all of them locked up in coffins of black;

And by came an Angel who had a bright key,
And he opened the coffins & set them all free;
Then down a green plain, leaping, laughing they run,
And wash in a river and shine in the Sun.

Then naked & white, all their bags left behind,
They rise upon clouds, and sport in the wind.
And the Angel told Tom, if he'd be a good boy,
He'd have God for his father & never want joy.

And so Tom awoke; and we rose in the dark
And got with our bags & our brushes to work.
Though the morning was cold, Tom was happy & warm;
So if all do their duty, they need not fear harm.

The Chimney Sweeper, William Blake (1789)

You know, I've heard a lot of stories about myself over the years. Not all of 'em pleasant, not all of 'em true. One that pops up quite a bit is from when I worked at the garden centre in Swinton. I'm supposed to have serenaded Tony Wilson over a stack of cut-price fence panels.

Well, I'll tell you now, it's complete bollocks. A colossal untruth.

They were trellises and they were top of the fucking line.

Pete Moran, 2022

1

August 2022

'Your mate's dead.'

Joe tells me this right as my teeth sink into a butty, which is unfortunate because, like many folk, I find death tricky enough to speak about as it is. The onus on sombre respect. The tight leash on wit and recriminations. It's trickier still when your mouth is stuffed, cheek to cheek and roof to tongue, with corn beef and brown loaf and you aren't even sure who's passed on.

Your mate's dead.

Despite the graveness of his message, Joe's bombshell is delivered in the easy tone you might use to note another day of sun and blue skies beyond the canteen window and now he waits, looming over the table, the aforementioned butty, and my dinner break. This cryptic doom monger, tall and almost bald, though how tall, or how bald is impossible to say. Dark, foreboding wisps are visible way up there but, as with mountain peaks obscured by cloud form, it's difficult to know what, if anything, is going on at the top.

Joe is no close and trusted colleague, he's the type you give a wide berth. This distance measured preferably in the less orthodox span of weeks and months rather than the standard feet and inches.

Your mate's dead.

Deep within me, something begins to stir, a power terrible and unrelenting: my teenage self. The mischievous James Edwards. Joker, piss-taker, General Smart Arse. This youthful immaturity rarely slips its chains without the lubricating help of booze, but here we are on a Tuesday afternoon, and I feel the General marching to the surface, barging his way centre stage. As curious as I am to discover who's died, I also wonder how much time Joe will waste expecting a reply while I chew on in ignorance.

The adult Jim Edwards, however, is insufficiently fuelled for such hijinks. It's my first week back in and I've neither the alcohol nor enthusiasm inside me. General Smart Arse is forced to make a tactical withdrawal.

Deprived of speech, unable to emit so much as a grunt to spur Joe into explanation, I gesture with my butty-laden hand for him to continue, but Joe does no more than echo his previous statement. 'Your mate's dead.'

I perform several unpleasant gulps. 'What mate?' I ask.

'I said,' he says, 'your mate's dead.'

Frustrated at both my lapse in grammar and the futility of our exchange, my entire being slumps, right from the tips of my steel-capped boots up to my thinning, greying hairline.

'Ok,' I say, 'which mate?'

'You know,' is as much as Joe feels the need to part with. He seems confident this brief remark will suffice and eyeballs me as if the answer should be obvious. This certainty doesn't last. His expression gives way first to doubt, then growing confusion before settling on a shocked fluster. Joe stoops down at me. 'Don't you know?' he asks.

I sigh, and slump once more. With any luck I've fallen asleep, my snoring head on a Formica pillow, and this is all a dream, albeit an incredibly dull dream lacking even the smallest flight of fancy or surrealist visitation. I would've hoped my imagination was up to conjuring more unusual sights. A shiny bowtie, perhaps, for my towering tormentor. Or troupe of workmates performing the slapping, jumping dance from New Order's 'True Faith' video. Maybe an alternate version of Lewis Carroll's White Rabbit, attired in management shirt and tie, whipping out his pocket watch to inform me *I'm* the one who's late and I need to get back to my post sharpish.

I clear my throat and prepare the voice normally reserved for extracting confessions from my two kids. A voice of authority and assurance perfected after a spell at home watching vintage detective shows.

'Joe,' I say, 'if I knew who you meant I wouldn't be wasting the precious seconds of my life this conversation is eating away at. I'd be eating away at *this*, instead.' My diagonally cut sandwich is brandished like a wholemeal flick knife and Joe moves back a step. 'Now,' I say, 'who's dead?'

'Peemorah.' The words emerge so quickly they blend into an unintelligible compound, which I ask him to repeat. He does so with marginally less haste, but just enough clarity. 'Pete Moran'.

It's a name that stops time. Again, I'm unable to speak, also unable to move. I no longer feel the body I know to be mine. Even the wall clock seems frozen as I wait for its mechanism to push on.

Pete Moran. A name from my past and now a name with no future. But Moran can't be dead, he's younger than I am. Next month, I'll turn forty-eight and Moran should do likewise three weeks later.

The clock finally moves and as it does the canteen's motion-sensor illumination flickers on, back-lighting Joe, throwing his immense shadow over my stricken form. Pale-skulled, dark of eye and sunken of cheek, he could easily pass for a mundane version of the Grim Reaper. A humdrum apparition wearing not rough, dark robes, but fluorescent yellow hi-visibility vest.

No black cowl, just the washing instructions label askew at the back of his neck and the remaining strands of once lustrous locks whipping overhead.

Death, stalking deserted warehouse dining spots.

Death, indifferent to clothing care labels.

Death, desperately clinging to follicles which don't feel quite so strongly toward him.

I don't usually require such wanton symbolism, but then I'm not the usual me. This is my second day back in the warehouse after more than a month on the sick and if day one was a smooth half-shift of easing myself in to a chorus of 'are you better now?', today is the bursting of the bubble. The fall and crash to Earth.

I drag myself back to the present, to this bright August afternoon, but focusing on my dinner I'm met only with decay.

Beige bread filled with the mottled purple of a once-living creature. Salad wilting under my gaze. A banana, fresh enough this morning but now bruised and past its best and frowning up at me from a Tupperware coffin.

As eerily as the lights flickered on, they flicker off and leave Joe as Joe once more. Not Death, but still a massive inconvenience on my day. I watch his lips move but struggle to pick out what he's saying. I do my best to listen, though my mind won't cooperate. I catch words which might be 'news' and 'radio'. Those I hear for sure are the last Joe utters before shuffling away. 'He's dead.'

Not everyone's demise is reported in solemn tones on local radio news, but then not everyone is Pete Moran. Not everyone has co-written a Top Ten single or recorded and released five albums. Not everyone has been a constant irritant to the music industry and associated press while enjoying modest success on their own increasingly stubborn terms.

To his loyal flock, Moran was a character, a distinctive voice – think John Cooper Clarke with a heavy cold. For those who went unconverted, Moran was more than a false prophet. He was also a bit of a prick.

To me, Moran was Moran or plain old Pete. We'd met at fifteen and become inseparable. By seventeen, formed our own group. Then, Christmas 1992, came the split. The events of our fourth and final gig tore not just the band apart, but also dealt our friendship a blow from which it never truly recovered. And now he's gone.

The idea his life could be over seems unreal. Almost as unreal as the idea Moran could rise to where he did in the first place. That someone from round our way, someone I knew, might make it, still amazes me.

Time ticks on, and my shift ends. I'm about to leave the warehouse when Amrita, my section manager, stops me.

'Can I have a quick word before you head off?' she asks. 'It won't take long.'

We step from the main floor into a side office, the walls of which are crammed with graphs and flow charts. Amrita offers me a chair.

'So,' she says when we're both seated, 'how're you getting on?'

'Fine, really,' I tell her. 'Everything's much the same as when I went off.'

'Well, good.' Amrita glances down at her hands causing a loose strand of black hair to fall over her face. She pushes it behind an ear and returns her attention to me. 'That's good.'

In her actions is a nervousness I don't recognise. Amrita isn't new to management; she's been doing it a good while now. She's mid-thirties, a sarcastic confident woman adept at keeping her mostly older, mostly male workforce in check. What "quick word" can get her this agitated?

'I wanted to let you know beforehand that…' she stops and glances down again and that strand of hair falls, and once more she readjusts it. 'On Friday, you're gonna get called in for another meeting.'

'Why? I thought we sorted everything yesterday.'

On Monday we'd been in this exact office, in these exact chairs having a chat about managing my return. The rehab hours, the workload, the occasional joke between two people who've known each other for years. It was an easy ten to fifteen minutes and left me feeling positive about working again.

'I know, Jim. But this will be more formal, and it'll be with upstairs. You'll want Karl in there with you.'

Karl is our union rep. I can't think why upstairs would want a formal meeting unless Joe has reported me for threatening him with a sandwich. 'What are they after?' I ask.

'Well, firstly, it'll be about your attendance standards. There's a new policy about flagging up patterns.'

'What sort of patterns?'

Amrita turns to the desk next to her and picks up a sheet of paper which she passes to me. At the top is my name and payroll number, followed by a list of dates going back about twelve years. Highlighted in red ink are a trio of recent Julys;

July 2022 – five weeks sick, back issue.
July 2019 – six weeks sick, back issue.
July 2018 – one-week special leave.

I have to read this last date twice because I can't believe it's there. July 2018 sets something off inside me that isn't a sarcastic teen. 'They can't be serious?' I ask.

'I'm sorry, Jim. It's either a computer or someone in an office somewhere just looking at the basic facts and sending memos out. It's new and I don't agree with it, so I wanted to give you a heads up.'

There's a very good reason why work classing my week off in 2018 as just another absence riles me so much. I wasn't off with my back – I didn't even have a problem with it then. I wasn't off with a cold or the flu. I was off because my dad had died. Seven months after a terminal cancer diagnosis, he was buried on what would've been his sixty-seventh birthday.

I want to screw this bit of paper into a ball and launch it somewhere but know it won't do any good. The thing will not get far before it hits a wall and tumbles limply to the ground, my situation changed not one bit.

'Also,' Amrita begins, 'they'll want to talk to you about increasing your hours and workload. They'll want you on your normal duty in a month.'

My anger doubles. I feel like swearing, loudly and repeatedly. 'And if I'm not ready for that?'

Amrita pauses, glances down and the hair falls and this time she leaves it across her face. She doesn't look up. 'They'll push for medical severance.'

I don't know how to respond.

'They'll say,' she continues, 'if you're not up to the job, they'll have nothing for you.'

This isn't a "quick word" at all. Unless you hear medical severance in its simplest terms, that of "bullet".

'And they've told you this?' is all I can think to say.

'Not in so many words.'

'How do you know then?'

Amrita looks up, her eyes meet mine and she takes a breath. 'Because it's exactly what they did with my dad.'

Rahul. Nearly ten years my senior and with an accent that still bore traces of the India he'd left as a child, Rahul had started at the warehouse the same day as me. We'd learned the ropes together and played on the works five-a-side team; him in goal and me as an energetic defensive force. His daughter had joined the firm about a decade afterward and made the move to management around four years in.

'Where is your dad?' I ask.

As I hadn't seen Rahul about the building the last day or so, I'd assumed him to be on leave or a different shift. This has always been the way of the warehouse. Familiar faces can disappear overnight having changed hours. Sometimes, it can take months to realise a person no longer even works there.

'They finished him,' she says, 'because of his shoulder.'

Rahul never had a problem with his shoulder right up until the day he damaged it moving house. It'd remained an issue for him, and he'd been moved to a less strenuous section so as not to aggravate it further.

'When was this?'

'Last few weeks. The paperwork's going through now.'

I don't know what to say other than ask how he is.

'Still in shock,' Amrita tells me. 'It's all happened a bit fast. The last time he was off with it they offered him physio, not the door. But then that was a while ago, pre-pandemic.'

'The good old days?' I say, not hiding my sarcasm.

'The not quite so overtly crap old days,' she counters.

During lockdown the warehouse had been deemed a vital cog in the supply chain of anything and everything. There would be no working remotely. No subsidised spell waiting it out at home. Anything and everything came through our doors, and so must we. I rode empty trams, walked through a deserted central Manchester, but once inside our warehouse, bar distancing measures and the later introduction of masks, it was as if nothing had happened.

To see and speak with people as before – Rahul and Amrita, union Karl, even Joe – was a comfort. As was the security of knowing that if I went into the warehouse, money would still arrive in my account. The extreme juxtaposition, however, felt weird. Civilization had apparently ended, the apocalypse begun, but our work wouldn't perform itself.

In time, normal service resumed for the wider world. Masks were discarded. Trams became as full as ever. So too, everywhere else. The warehouse, though, hadn't changed; there was no baseline state to which it could return. Instead, it began to proceed backwards and downwards.

New practices were implemented without union approval on a Monday and ditched by Friday following pushback. There were overworded technicalities around sick pay, a sterner disciplinary process, and price hikes in the staff canteen. None of it a reward for fattening the company share price during the pandemic, and none of it much help in getting the job done. I was glad to have a spell at home. A spell of not having to trouble myself daily with the forces of incompetent posturing. Unless, of course, I switched on the news.

'I told my dad you were coming back in,' Amrita tells me. 'He said to say hello.'

'Tell him…' My mind is a void. Even if I knew the right words for the situation, I can't seem to find them. 'What's he gonna do?'

'About all he can do, look for another job. Try and find someone who'll take on a fifty-six-year-old with a dodgy shoulder. I told him to have a look for me while he's at it.'

I ask her if she's serious.

'No. Yes. I dunno. I see how they treat people now. How they expect me to treat people. It's not right and it's only gonna get worse.'

There's a knock at the door and Joe ducks in. Amrita is needed for the handover of shifts. She stands and I feel the urge to plead my case.

'But the doctor's referred me on,' I tell her. 'I'm on a waiting list.'

'I know, Jim. I know. But this lot upstairs, they don't wait anymore.'

Amrita leaves and I'm alone in the office. Beyond the open door, the warehouse grinds on.

2

I force past and future from my thoughts, Moran and medical severance will have to wait. It's rush hour and I'm heading for the tram. The streets are busy, the pavements teeming, and the air baking hot. It's early August but the summer seems to have lasted for an age. As I walk, sweat gathers under ruck sack straps, my cotton work shirt sticks to my skin.

When I pass the bus station at Shudehill something strange happens. I see a tram pull up in the distance and, squinting to decode its yellow digital array, make out the words Manchester Airport, the very line I need to take me home to Chorlton. This, of course, is not the strange part. The strange part is what happens next. I begin to run.

Not that running is strange – unless (a) you want to get into its adoption as a lifestyle choice or (b) you look at the act itself, the continuous falling forward, the swimming through air, the flailing against the inevitable – but it's strange for me. I'm no longer one of life's runners.

No longer a fixture at the gym near work before or after my shift. No longer charging about on a five-a-side pitch. No longer having kickabouts in the park with my son. Those days are behind me. I'm a walker, nowadays, ambling along at a relaxed pace with the chance to observe and spot that which others might miss.

The glint of a quid on the ground.

A clandestine heron hunched in its topcoat.

The well above eye level sign for some intriguingly named thoroughfare.

Despite all this, so I can spend an extra twelve minutes at home rather than at a tram stop, I am running.

The sudden exercise is alien to my body and my legs feel unreliable. Rather than limbs of flesh and bone, I'm moving on a pair of pipe cleaners, ready to bend or sag at any moment. I feel a jarring at the bottom of my spine, and a twinge in my right hip, but on I press, ruck sack slapping my back in twisted encouragement. A stride or two more and I'm betrayed, my left foot clips the kerb, and no longer am I running.

Questions present themselves as I fall forward. Which part of me will strike the pavement first?

As I swim through the air. Will I end up back on the sick?

As I flail against the inevitable. Balloon Street, why?

The world blurs around me, the ground rises in greeting, and my hands thrust out scraping across the rough surface as I land. I look up to see the Metrolink, packed with commuters who've witnessed my fall, glide away. A young woman helps me up, and I splutter thanks between ragged breaths.

Masses bustle past me, shoulders nudging mine. The humid air blends laughter and voices with harsh sounds from the road nearby. Revving engines, animalistic horns. My equilibrium is off, my heart racing. I feel harried, under siege. I need quiet and a sit down and, most of all, I need a pint.

When the sun is bright in the sky, a powerful lust grips the populace. Some primal impulse must be assuaged, a pagan right fulfilled. People are compelled to gather in its path and worship. Tables outside bars are crowded beyond reasonable standards of safety or personal space. The day's final glimpses of the fiery orb are chased down as if we'll never see it's like again.

But as a non-believer, a solar heretic, I much prefer the shadowy confines of an ale house and so take up residence in a wood-lined recess of The Lower Turk's Head with a beer and two packets of crisps. Efforts to clean my hands of dirt and grit in the toilet sink prove a waste of time. Dark red oozes from both palms. As I fill my mouth with booze, the stigmata of an ill-advised dash for public transport leaves a scarlet print on the glass.

The phone in my shirt pocket weighs heavy, tempting me to go online and type in Pete Moran's name, but I resist. I've no desire to read an obituary, some strangers take on a person I once knew so well. I do take out the mobile though only with the intention of texting Katie, my wife. I tap out a message, telling her I'll be home later than usual, and press send. I wonder if she's heard about Moran and as her reply is quick and short with no question about the delay, but an extra couple of kisses,

I take this to mean she has. I put the phone away, lift my bag of crisps and sink deep into the cushioned bench.

The longer I sit and crunch, the more difficult it is to escape thoughts of work or Pete Moran, but given a choice of unpleasant problems, I prefer to think about someone else's.

Sunlight through a window illuminates the chair across from me, hitting the seat like a spotlight, giving otherwise unseen dust motes their chance to shine. They converge into a shape I convince myself is Moran. Only rather than a single form, this presence morphs between two distinct versions. From the lad I grew up with into the cult figure he'd later become. A 3D lenticular image only I can see.

It's the teenage Pete, the kid from Swinton searching through records and books in his bedroom. Then I tilt my head, change the angle, and there's Moran on late-night television playing up to the audience, operating on the edge of full-blown parody. I observe this alternating vision play with a cigarette, shift it from finger to finger and then get up, to head out for a smoke from which he'll never return.

Once the band had gone to shit, it took over a decade for our paths to cross again, but prior to the pandemic we'd run into each other every few years. I try not to replay these memories, I'd rather remain in the here and now, but the pull of the past is strong. It's all I can do to hold these thoughts to recent times and the last I saw of Moran.

It was less than twelve months ago and no more than a five-minute walk from where I now sit. September or October, one of our birthday months, summer and autumn in the middle of their handover, and the world back to business as usual.

I'd left the warehouse on my break for an hour of fresh air and pounding the concrete, roving between shops. With my dinner nearing its end, I was heading back up Tib Street when I spotted a character who wasn't difficult to recognise. There were the scruffy jeans and Doc Martens boots. The battered old olive drab combat jacket. His distinctive bird's nest hair was particularly disordered that day. I only saw him from behind, but knew it was Moran.

He was running the gauntlet between the army and navy surplus on one side of the road and the sex shops on the other. Mannequins dressed in fatigues faced off against those in barely-there lingerie, the latter armed with an array of carnal weaponry. Moran strutted between the two as if he was on New York's Bowery and not a Manchester backstreet.

I was tempted to shout his name. I knew a get-together would've followed full of handshaking and backslapping and talk of a drink or two which might easily become six or seven. We could've caught up, asked after each other's families – was he still with Kelly? How was his daughter, Lauren? – then reminisced about the old days.

I was tempted to shout, though I didn't. Something held me back. Instead, I tailed him at a distance as he carried on past the newsagents and the chippy, then crossed over to stop outside a hairdresser's window. I hid myself in a doorway, peering out around the brickwork.

I thought Moran was lingering to wave hello to someone inside, the giver or receiver of a half-price cut and blow, but as he lifted his shades, I realised it was himself he was checking out. Preening and posing, testing out his best smile in the glass.

An abrupt blast came from up ahead, the cough of a vehicle turning off the ring road, and I shrunk further into the alcove to avoid detection. I was lurking in the shadows like a voyeur. What if Moran saw me? What if somebody else saw me? How would I explain away my actions? I may've confessed to playing a prank on an old pal or being a starstruck fan, stalking my celebrity hero and too shy to approach. It was cringeworthy, but it beat the hell out of the truth.

As the car moved past, I peered out again and found Moran nowhere to be seen. I'd only looked away for a second, and he was gone.

I finish my pint and pour what remains of the crisps into my mouth, getting ready to face the world. Rather than return the blood-encrusted glass to the bar I leave it on the table, pick up my rucksack and walk out into the sun.

The area is quieter now and soon I'm on a tram bound for Chorlton and home. The chatter of passengers begins to grate so I slip my headphones on and zip up a protective bubble for the journey back to south Manchester. I lean my head on the window and close my eyes, but in seconds I'm hit with a feeling which forces me upright to focus on my surroundings.

The music in my ears is loud and abrasive, however that's just personal taste. There's something else I hear though, and it's not the rumble and squeak of the tram. It sounds like the throb of a ceiling fan but on a larger scale. I feel odd. At forty-seven I've a proud record of never having made a show of myself on public transport, and don't wish to break that today.

On the edges of my vision central Manchester is hazy, and I realise my mistake only when it's too late. I'm in a seat facing the rear of the carriage. I'm travelling backwards. The past isn't somewhere I like to revisit, but before I can move to stop this, I've been taken.

3

Friday 18th December 1992

It was not simple fear I felt, but dread. Dry-mouthed, cold-skinned, damp-palmed dread. On the verge of our finest hour, I saw only doom. This feeling born not deep in my bones or down in the gut, but overhead. Pale fire ablaze against darkening heavens. An ancient fear with a modern face.

We heard it first, rotors thrumming as they sliced the air, and looking up there it was. A lone Greater Manchester Police helicopter, moving with slow purpose, its single light fixed on a distant point.

Fifteen days was all it had been since two IRA detonations within a single Thursday morning. Twin forces shattering windows, flying glass piercing winter flesh. Was it about to happen again? Had there been another phone call, a coded message predicting further chaos, or was this something else? A bullet, perhaps. One more nightclub bouncer shot as gangs spoiled for control of the city's doors. Different, but the same. Still terror. Still dread.

At the rear of the Academy, our orange and white rented van was parked, half-unloaded and fully forgotten. We had become distracted from our task, no longer ferrying equipment into the venue through grey double doors, the entrance for staff and talent. This was to be our fourth gig and none of us had more than eighteen months playing experience. We were talent in its most abstract form. Second-hand amps and instruments we had yet to master dotted the ground as we tracked the chopper's journey.

In the days of Rome, of emperors and augurs, the pattern of its flight would have been analysed, an act of sacrifice performed, a decision made on whether to pursue a chosen course. But this was not Rome, and we had neither emperor nor augur nor live animal to bleed – so close to Christmas, finding even a dead turkey would prove difficult. All we had was Rob Moran.

The elder of our party, and driver for the evening, removed a part-smoked cigarette from his lips to share a short statement: 'it's kicking off, again.'

Hardly a rival for "beware the Ides of March", but then this was December and Rob did not have much of a reputation for prophecy. The chances were high his pockets contained a betting slip for the weekends football matches. The chances any of those picks might come true was considerably less.

Far more predictable was the source of the eventual reply. Pete Moran, our singer and the closest we had to a Caesar, never could pass up the opportunity to aim a sly dig at his older brother.

'Cheers for that, Nostra-dumbarse,' was his latest effort.

'Shut up, shit,' Rob's quickfire response.

There were four of us in the band. Devon Bradshaw was our drummer. Short and quiet and never more at home than when creating a racket behind cymbals and snares.

Steve Williamson played guitar. Lanky and arrogant, his towering frame made for an overbearing presence on stage as well as most everywhere else.

Which left me, James Edwards. Average of height and calm of temperament, my duties those of co-songwriter, bassist, and keeper of the peace. This latter burden had kept me far too occupied of late.

We were moments away from something truly special, a support slot for the Ramones, an act we all adored, so why did destruction feel so close at hand? Our once tight-knit group was in danger of coming apart. Loose threads dangled from us. Pull hard on any and the whole enterprise might unravel. Over the past week we had scarcely been in the same room together, had barely exchanged a word. Even meeting each other's gaze was beyond us, so instead we focused on the helicopter, following the craft as it moved farther and farther away.

With our attention on the sky overhead, Pete slipped past his brother to steal the cigarette out from Rob's lips and received a size twelve Doctor Martens boot to his backside in return. Welcome laughter spread amongst us as Pete danced a sore-arsed jig.

This skit felt so smoothly executed, its separate movements blending into a single whole, that it could have been borrowed from a black and white screen. Some slice of Three Stooges slapstick repeated and honed in secret, then trotted out for public amusement. The Two Morans, a ready-made double act. Interchangeable as straight man and comic foil, almost interchangeable as people. Their resemblance so uncanny it was often joked the shorter Pete was merely a squashed-down version of his elder sibling. They shared the same surname and musical taste. The same sense of humour, personality, even the same bedroom. They were close, but Pete and I were closer or had been until recently.

I glanced towards our frontman, hoping he might do likewise, hoping for a nod or wink, an indication everything would be OK, that the evening would play out without incident. I watched him as he took a last slow drag on the cig then flicked what remained to the ground, extinguishing its glow beneath his heel.

Without a look or remark for any of us, Pete slipped through the doors and into the Academy. I knew then our fate was sealed. We would not last the night.

4

Home is a three-bed terrace on a quiet Chorlton street and as I walk in the front door, Katie is coming down the stairs with an expression you don't need to be a television detective to interpret. Head inclined, blue eyes wide, melancholy smile. It all confirms my earlier thought: she's heard about Moran.

My wife sees the dried blood on my hands, and leads me through to the kitchen, seating me at the table and fetching our first aid kit from under the sink. As she begins to clean my wounds, I hear our children in the front room. Voices from the TV and sounds from their tablets. Katie picks up a cotton ball and presses it to a bottle of foul-smelling liquid.

'There's a chance this might sting.'

'Do you think anyone ever falls for the "might" part?'

She laughs and her attention moves from my wound to my face. 'Only the very young and the very drunk. You don't seem to be either.' The disinfectant-smeared wool sears my open flesh and I grimace. 'How're you feeling?' she asks.

'Wasn't so bad. "Sting" is probably underselling it a bit, though.'

'Not your hands,' she says. As a nail technician at a local salon, Katie's used to dealing with strange paws, not that I imagine it's always such a bloody business. 'I meant about Pete.'

My wife watches me, awaiting an answer. Her ginger hair hangs loose at her shoulders, she wears light blue jeans and striped cotton shirt.

'I dunno,' I tell her. 'I mean, it just doesn't seem real.'

'I bet. We heard it on the radio. They played one of his songs and I had to explain to some of the younger staff who he was. I never said we knew him.'

Katie covers my grazes with plasters in different colours and sizes, shapes and designs. Pink oblongs and squares criss-cross my left palm. The face of a dazed owl peers up at me from my right. 'This is the last thing you needed your first week back.'

I nod and think about the other news I didn't need. Medical fucking severance. I want to tell her but know she'll worry. She already worries. About the kids. About money. I'm not sure I want to add to that, so I hold it in. It's what I do.

'Have you heard from Devon?' she asks.

'Not yet. I'll message him later.'

'Do you know what happened? They never said on the news.'

Over the years I've been guilty of pondering the final moments of the great and good, indulging morbid celebrity fascinations, but with Moran I feel no urge to speculate over his death. He wasn't some distant star living an alien existence, he was an old mate.

After tea, we're on the sofa; our two children, ten-year-old Ella and almost thirteen Jack, are in their rooms. An episode of *Columbo* is about to finish, another homicide investigation soon to be neatly tied up. On the coffee table, my mobile phone shakes and beeps with a text. I look at the screen and see the name I've been expecting to hear from, the only member of our band I'm still in contact with, Devon Bradshaw.

His message is one I've been unable to send:

Have you heard?

Three words. A simple sentence I didn't know how to form.

I try to construct a reply but can't do this either. Peter Falk is questioning a suspect. The washing machine is spinning in the kitchen. My wife is voicing her own theory about how to get away with murder. I stare at my mobile and read Devon's message again.

Have you heard?

Yeah, mate. It's a shocker, is all I manage in return.

Devon asks me to let him know if I hear anything about the funeral and I tell him the same.

I'm awake when I shouldn't be. When no one should be, save for insomniacs, night prowlers and Americans. I can't get comfortable. My lower back and hips feel sore. I try various positions, stick a pillow between my knees, but nothing works. I give up and go downstairs.

I can't recall when I first noticed the pain. There was no single incident of feeling something go, no theatrical grabbing at my lumbar region as if I'd just been struck. Maybe I was sat on a tram after a shift and aching, but then it's a manual job and being knackered at the end of a day is nothing new. This ache, though, was in a specific spot above my arse and while it seemed alright the next morning, it appeared more and more often before it seemed to spread into my right hip. Eventually, I went on the sick.

In the kitchen, I get a drink of water and pace slowly through the rooms.

That first time, I was off for six weeks. I saw a doctor who thought it might be hip bursitis, and when I returned to the warehouse, work arranged for me to have physio sessions as part of my rehab. Any other ailment I'd had over the years had just sorted itself out and I fully expected this to as well.

In the front room, I peer out the curtains for something to do.

Every so often my back would flare up and I'd find myself off work again, visiting the doctors to be given a list of YouTube videos of stretches and exercises, then having an MRI which showed no structural damage. I'd return to work and the cycle would begin anew.

And here I am, three years on and still stuck in that cycle. I lie down on the front room carpet, there are times being flat on the ground is the only comfortable position. I close my eyes and try not to think about anything and what seems barely a minute later, a hand is on my shoulder, a figure looming above me. Katie, my angel in silk pyjamas, waking me to tell me it's morning.

*

Around midday, I'm back at the warehouse before my half shift. I sit beyond the loading bay with the union rep Karl. The sun has cooked the stacks of pallets, long out of use, on which we rest. The baked wood is like a fire under my arse. Karl has confirmed what Amrita told me yesterday about the warehouse's plans.

'I'd have mentioned all this Monday,' he tells me, 'but didn't want to dump it on you your first day back. They can't sack you, though they can pay you off and shunt you out the door.'

He holds a machine coffee, switching it hand to hand with each sip, waiting for the plastic container and liquid to cool. Karl's a similar age to me, his hair short and dark, the last knockings of a recent holiday tan clinging to his skin.

'And that's what they did with Rahul?' I ask.

'That's exactly what they did. Quite a few have gone lately.' Karl takes another sip, performs a further container juggle. 'Us old guard have all been here too long; upstairs see our terms and conditions as too generous. They'd prefer we were all new-starters on zero-hours.'

I bring my feet up onto the pallet. With the direction of this conversation added to the heat and my interrupted night's sleep, all I want to do is lie down again and close my eyes.

'We shouldn't be surprised,' continues Karl, 'this is the way every industry is going. Profit for the top and fuck all for those at the bottom. It's the default mindset of a country run by glorified spivs.' He takes a mouthful of coffee. 'Can you believe we've had twelve years of this shite?'

'Seems more like thirty,' I reply.

'Tell me about it. Sometimes I wonder if it'll ever end. Charlie was lucky he won't have to see it get any worse.'

'Charlie?' I say. 'Do I know Charlie?'

'My greyhound. He died the other month.'

'Shit, sorry mate.'

'The poor sod. From birth to death under this shower.'

In my brain, long unused synapses flicker. 'Under spiv rule this, one long dog's life.'

Karl gives me a furrowed look. 'Is that an old Fall lyric?'

'No. I mean, I hope not.'

Karl takes another drink and swallows with no real enthusiasm. 'While we're talking music, it's a shame about your mate.'

Moran, Christ.

'I used to like some of his stuff. The early stuff, anyhow.'

When you have fourteen years between albums, the bulk of your work can be classed as "early". Unsure which of these conversations I'd rather not be having, I switch the subject back to the warehouse. 'What did Rahul get?'

'Six months' pay and any outstanding leave. Course, he's at an age where he can officially take part of his pension. That'd be a bit more complicated for you.'

'Because of my excess of youth and vitality?'

Karl's smile is weaker than the coffee in his hands. 'It's nice you've still got your sense of humour.'

The ability to make sarcastic comments from a reclining position is one of the few joys I have left.

'Anyhow, try not to worry about it, Jim. It's all a way off yet, but if it comes to it, we'll do what we can for you. There's a possibility you could make a claim for RSI, though we'd have to prove this place was at fault, because they won't admit It. They don't admit responsibility anymore, they contest everything. They're a hard-faced lot. We had to fight to get what we did for Rahul.'

'Cheers, mate. I just... I dunno, expected more, I suppose. I mean, I'm back in. I'm showing them some fucking loyalty. Don't I get any in return?'

Why am I working again? I'm certainly not fully fit. Is it because I'm tired of explaining myself to doctors and the warehouse, tired of the constant rehashing of it all, the letters and phone calls? Or is it a search for some version of myself who now feels lost, from before all this started, who I can barely even recall?

The last time I was on the sick I'd been brought in for a meeting after a fortnight and asked about my current condition. When I told them I was not in a state to fulfil my role, they'd replied, 'Well, if that's the case, we've got nothing for you.' And this after only two weeks. There was no mention of recovery, no offer of physio, just a cold hard statement as if fear of unemployment might miraculously sort my back out.

Karl stands and moves to a nearby drain down which he pours the last of his coffee. 'I think if you were still on the sick, they'd have had you in for a meeting. It's just how things are now. There's no loyalty in this place. No empathy, no patience, no hope.' He crushes his plastic cup and throws it in the bin. 'All that died round here with old George.'

George Cartwright. When I started at the warehouse, Cartwright and Sons had been a family-run operation overseen by the white-bearded, Santa Claus figure of George Cartwright.

'You are all my sons,' George liked to inform us, pointing at the signage. 'My sons and the odd daughter, and this door,' gesturing to his office entrance, 'this door is always open to you.'

And it had been as well, until one day about five years ago it was shut.

George's secretary had returned from her dinner hour to a door not just closed but locked. Or so she'd thought, having tried the handle with no success. The landline in his office rang unanswered and his car was still parked in its usual place at the side of the building. She assumed he'd simply nipped out for a walk or gone for a liquid lunch in some city centre pub.

I'd been in the canteen on a break with Karl and Rahul when Amrita came in.

'Have any of you seen George about?' she asked.

We hadn't and she left to carry on her search, but when we headed back to the floor, we spotted her stood in the car park, head leaning back as she stared upwards. We went outside to see what was happening, and Amrita told us George's mobile had been called and the ringtone sounded from inside his office. A ladder resting against the brickwork led up to the locked room. One of us would have to go up it.

Rahul couldn't because of his shoulder. 'What if it locks up on me?' he'd said. 'Who'll come and get me? It won't be Karl, will it?'

'Not with my fear of ageing shop floor equipment used in an uninsured context, no.'

Amrita had turned to me and raised her eyebrows.

'Well, I can't go up there,' I told her.

'Why not?'

'Because I'm a worrier.'

'A worrier?'

'Yeah. I worry what lasting effects the sight of an unexplained head outside an upstairs window might have on George. Look what happened to William Blake.'

'He ended up on nights, didn't he?' Karl or Rahul had offered.

'"If they see any weeping, that should have been sleeping".'

'Can one of you stop arsing about and get up that ladder?'

A passing Joe, tall in height and short on both seniority and a ready reason not to do as he was told, was given the task and, minutes later, the rest of us were back inside and forcing open the office door, behind which lay our fallen leader, dead long before Joe peered in at him.

Within months the warehouse had been sold to a larger rival, George's sons no longer seen around the building or even on its signage. Cartwright and Sons had become Cartwright & Co. and the place began to change. It wasn't just the death of George or the speedy departure of his children. It wasn't even the appearance of an ampersand in the company's name. We were now part of a larger conglomerate with shareholders to satisfy.

It's Saturday morning. My first week back in work done, I'm still under the duvet when my mobile starts to ring. I turn to the bedside table and see the alarm clock and my device next to it. I stretch for the phone and as my fingers curl round it, the thing slips from my grasp to bounce away on the bedroom carpet.

'For fuck's sake,' I announce and await a reply which never comes. I'm home alone. Slowly a conversation with Katie from an hour ago comes back to me. Her and the kids heading out to do the weekly shop and leaving me to doze. I didn't have a great night's sleep again, which the events of Friday no doubt had a lot to do with.

My end of week meeting at the warehouse had gone much as Amrita predicted. Upstairs had sat me down and given the spiel about how glad they were I was back; they'd offered cursory support for my recovery only to follow that by informing me about the increase in hours.

With Karl next to me, I'd stood my ground, citing occupational health recommendations and it was agreed I could stay on 50% for another week. With that battle won, I was then "made aware" of what the future might bring.

Medical severance.

I've told Katie about the hours and my firm stance. 'Good for you,' was what she'd said. I've yet to tell her about the rest.

After work I went for a drink with Karl, and Rahul came out to join us. We reminisced about better times, compared ailments and then Rahul shared some advice as regards the warehouse. 'Fuck 'em,' being his exact words.

In bed, I manoeuvre myself to recover the still ringing mobile; on its screen is an unknown number. I never used to answer unknown numbers, but as this one starts with the local prefix, there's a chance it might be something more than a nuisance call.

'Hi, is that James Edwards?' a female voice asks. Nobody has called me James in a long while.

'Yeah,' I reply, beginning to regret pressing accept, 'I'm James, well, Jim. Who's this?'

The use of my full first name implies a level of importance I didn't much expect from a weekend phone enquiry. I start to think it might be news of my NHS referral, or then again it could be the bank. Have I had some unforeseen expense; a payment gone awry? I know I've money in my account, but every so often I'm struck by a fear that suddenly it's there no longer and I've slid into the red. The red of high blood pressure and soaring body heat. It's an old fear, one I've never been able to outgrow.

'It's Lauren,' the voice says, nervously, 'Pete's daughter.'

This does not cause me to relax, and I push myself upright.

'Pete Moran?' I ask, knowing full well which Pete she means. I only know a couple and only one of those has a daughter named Lauren. But this doesn't stop me from saying his name out loud. I can't recall the last time I did.

With everything else going on, I've pushed thoughts of Moran to the back of my mind. I've not heard from Devon about the funeral, and I haven't gone searching for details. As close as we'd been in our youth, I'd hardly seen Moran over the last couple of decades. Out of his forty-seven years of life, I'd shared no more than two and a half.

I know I should go to the funeral but knowing and doing are two very different concepts.

I know there are jobs that need taking care of round the house, but it's all too easy to put them off until some unspecified tomorrow.

I know I should open up to Katie about what's happening at work, but well...

'I'm really sorry about your dad,' I tell Lauren. 'I still can't believe it.'

'Thanks. I hope you don't mind me calling, like. My Uncle Rob gave me your number.'

Rob Moran. I've neither seen nor spoken to him in ages and didn't even know he had my number. Perhaps he got it from Devon.

'I don't mind, at all,' I say. 'I'm glad you rang. I mean, I wanted to pass on my condolences somehow.' I've become as nervous as she is and have started to babble.

'Thanks, I just called about the funeral. It's on Tuesday.'

I ask where the service will be held because this would seem the correct response in such a situation.

'The crematorium at Southern Cemetery,' Lauren replies, which throws me as I'd imagined the answer to be Swinton, the town where we grew up, where Moran had still been living and where, since my father passed, I've felt less and less inclined to return. 'Will you be able to attend?' she asks.

I stare about me, looking for inspiration and an easily available excuse, but my tired, sparkless mind comes up empty. The truth, the simple, selfish truth, is I don't want to go. I feel I've already attended too many funerals, those of both parents not to mention a growing number of former colleagues, and the thought of this new send-off being for someone from my own era fills me with dread.

But with Southern Cemetery only down the road from me, and Lauren having taken the time to call with all she must be going through, I feel I can do nothing other than tell her yes.

5

Obituary

Manchester Evening News

Pete Moran, a staple of this city's music scene since the mid-nineties, died at his home in Swinton yesterday. He was 47.
An early claim to have been present at the Sex Pistols' infamous Lesser Free Trade Hall concert, albeit as a foetus in the womb of his mother, proved to be erroneous. By that evening in June nineteen seventy-six he had already been out in the world for the better part of two years. Creative, yet unreliable, such a tale would set the tone for much of his career.

Moran's brief tenure with the Liverpool/Manchester collective We, Ignoramuses was a case in point. Despite jointly penning their breakthrough hit, 'Holding Me Down'

(1995), he and the band had already parted ways before the song entered the Top Ten.

Although a well-known sight on the local music landscape, Moran remained little more than a footnote in the wider industry. His naturally combative character, dislike of compromise and staunch refusal to relocate closer to London were often cited as prime hindrances to greater acclaim. As was his perpetual war of words with much of the country's music press which would see him title his second album, Pound Shop Iggy Pop (1998), in a direct quote from an NME review of his debut, Sound Escape (1996).

Not that Moran was without his admirers. A loyal fanbase, both at home and abroad, welcomed every tour and new release. Gigs in his native city were always lively affairs, as were interviews with this newspaper.

There were further albums, Lucky Idiot (2001) and the controversial Northern B****** (2007), before Moran began an extended hiatus, returning in 2021 with In Jest, a collection of darker and more personal acoustic songs referencing his struggles with addiction, fame and the creative process.

The son of Martin and Joan Moran, he was born in Salford but spent his early years in Withington, south Manchester, before the family finally settled in Swinton, a place Moran would call home for the rest of his days. He attended Moorside High School and, briefly, Eccles

College. His time before success was spent working at a local garden centre.

He is survived by his parents, brother, Robert, wife, Kelly, and daughter, Lauren.

6

"Am I holding this job down or is it holding me?"

We, Ignoramuses, 'Holding Me Down', 1995
Words: Pete Moran/Johnny Sheedy

The weekend disappears all too quickly, even my Monday half-shift passes in a flash. The highlight of the latter is the granting of two days leave. Two whole days off work again, even if the first does involve an old mate's funeral.

On Tuesday morning, I set off early and walk not so much as the crow flies but as a blind tortoise might meander. I avoid main roads, hoping to steer clear of beeping horns from vehicles stopping to beckon me inside. I take tangents, veer down side streets and alleyways, in no hurry to reach my destination.

Katie offered to come with me, but I prefer to do this alone, and the walk gives me solitude and an opportunity to clear my mind, neither of which I suspect I'll get much chance for until this task is over. Not that I intend to be out all that long. My aim is the acceptable minimum: service, fleeting appearance at the wake, then wave goodbye and exit.

My pace is an easy one, even so the hot weather invites beads of sweat to gather under my clothes. I wear my only suit, rescued from the back of the wardrobe, sponged and shaken, given an airing at formal occasions.

Despite taking the scenic route, Southern Cemetery's grounds appear far too soon as do the assembled mourners. It's a decent crowd, a couple of hundred, the number of whom I'd wish to speak to being somewhere in the low single digits. I'm tempted to do a lap of the graveyard, to walk among the dead and hope none are feeling talkative. Instead I head for the Old Chapel, slip between the hordes without meeting their eyes and, once inside, find a space halfway back on the right among strangers.

Between the stained-glass window at the head of the building and the huge, gothic organ to the rear, I see many people I can identify, but only one I know personally. Amid select musicians, journalists and industry types, figures I've seen on album sleeves, posing and writhing on stages or from their nipples upwards on television, is Rob Moran.

I spot him on the front row, his head in constant swivelling motion as he speaks to those around him. The elderly couple he's sat with I now recognise as his parents, Joan and Martin. I've not seen Rob in so long it's easy to forget just how much he and his late brother resembled one another, how intertwined their lives were back then. Some part of me wants to reach for those memories, to pluck out a random evening of teenage camaraderie and wrap myself in the hijinks and cheap beer, the music and girls, but any rush of nostalgia is tempered by the occasion and an abrupt movement from the row behind me.

I hear the shuffling of feet, and polyester slide across polished wood, then a chorus of tuts twinned with low repetitious apologies. I feel a breath on my neck followed by a voice I know all too well.

'Well, we've finally made it to Manchester music's inner sanctum. The promised land, man. Never thought it'd be a fucking crem', though.'

I turn to find a grey-haired lady bristling over this foul language and rubbing the Christ on her cross. I turn further and find the copper-toned shaven head of Devon Bradshaw, brow crinkling as he repents his sins.

As a teenager, Devon kept his hair short as something of a nod to fashion. Now pushing fifty and with a hairline whose retreat began even before his thirtieth birthday, the choice has returned out of sheer necessity. Not that I'm much better off, but at least my losses are restricted to an area at the back of my head, a section I never see and can deny all knowledge of, though which offers the possibility I'll soon look like a fourteenth century Franciscan monk.

'It's a full house,' I tell Devon, 'I'm surprised you found me.'

'Don't be daft, man. I'd recognise that barmcake anywhere. I've been having a wander round the yard. Tony Wilson's out there. And Gretton and Hannett.'

The Factory Records mafia, Moran liked to call them. He adored their ethos, their bloody-mindedness, their Northern pride. If we'd had a demo tape, he was convinced they'd sign us, but the label went bust before we even made it into a studio.

There was an urban myth from around the years after the band ended. Moran was working at a garden centre and our former singer is said to have performed an impromptu audition for Wilson, in the hope of securing a prime spot on Granada News. How much was fact and how much fiction about this tale, I never knew.

'Anthony H?' I say to Devon. 'Out there, queueing to get in? How quickly people forget.'

'Nah, you twat. They're buried in the cemetery.' Of the original Factory cabal, only Alan Erasmus and Peter Saville were not currently at rest close by.

Devon's elderly neighbour is unimpressed with our chat and makes a dramatic show of clearing her throat.

'Sorry,' we offer in unison. As our band's rhythm section, we're used to being in time with one another. It almost feels like we've been living the same lives only a few towns apart.

Our wives are best friends – it was through Devon dating Sandra that I met Katie – and we both have two children, one boy and one girl. The pair of us have been doing the same jobs since the nineties: me at the warehouse and Devon as a plumber. A few years prior to Covid, we each lost a parent within the same six-month spell, his mum passing only a short while before my old man. Today, even our outfits are a match. Standard funeral attire. Black suit and tie, white shirt, best shoes.

About the only difference is our family backgrounds. Mine is very much Swinton and Salford, but Devon's is more of a mix. His late mother was a dinner lady in Bolton originally from North Wales while his dad was a south Manchester postal worker who'd left Jamaica in the sixties. She was white and he was black. After their marriage the two had moved to Swinton where Devon's upbringing was more Welsh than West Indian. When I met him as a teenager, the closest he'd been to the Caribbean was Rhyl Sun Centre.

'How're things, mate?' I ask him.

'Same old, same old. How about you?'

Funerals not being the place to air your woes – it could, after all, be worse – I tell him I'm alright.

'You look well,' he says, and I nod.

That this short exchange will represent our lone foray into the personal is just how we are. Nights out run along similar lines as pleasantries are dealt with early and quickly. I'd enquire after his sister, Louise, and his father, Clyde.

Devon might then ask if I'd heard much lately from my cousin, Lee. It was the routine housekeeping of an age-old friendship, and once out of the way we'd switch to music, films, and sport.

Then, when enough beer had been drunk, our attention would drift from the trivial to the nonsensical, recalling vague fragments from our shared youth.

'I wonder what happened to that bloke with the crab sticks?' Devon could ask.

'What bloke with the crab sticks?' I'd then reply.

'The one who was always in The Swan.'

'Oh, aye yeah, I'd forgotten about him.'

'Well?'

'Well, what, mate?'

'Well, whatever happened to him?'

'The bloke with the crab sticks?'

'Yeah.'

'I heard he had them removed. Some revolutionary procedure on the continent. First of its kind. Was a complete success and he now lives a perfectly normal life.'

'Thanks for clearing that up for me.'

'Of course,' I might add, 'there's plenty from back then you just don't find around these days, isn't there? I mean, look at pornography.'

'I don't think Sandra would approve.'

'There were always pages ripped from dirty mags in ditches and dells or snagged among rhododendrons back then.'

'I blame the digital age, man.'

'You just don't see random snatches in a bush anymore, do you?'

'You rarely see a bush.'

On and on these exchanges would ramble until hours later we'd emerge into the murky air for a taxi and a tram.

Then the pandemic struck, and these nights were put on hold. Our wives would have long phone calls whereas we'd communicate via short texts.

That twat across the road has been over again.

Devon had a low-level dispute running with a local busybody.

I hope he stayed two metres away. What was it this time?

The list of grievances ran from placement of Devon's van to the mere existence of Devon's van.

Wanted to know why I wasn't out for the NHS clap.

And why weren't you out for the NHS clap? Does Sandra know?!?

Sandra Bradshaw worked long shifts as a nurse at a local hospital.

Because I'd used up all the pots and pans cooking Sandra her favourite meal.

Sandra's favourite meal was a macaroni cheese prepared to her own exact specifications. The type of milk had to be whole. The mustard, English. It required two types of pasta, macaroni and penne. Some fried pancetta was mixed in before the whole thing was topped with extra cheddar and placed under the grill. It was the nicest version of a simple meal I'd ever tasted, if a notoriously cookware-heavy undertaking.

And what did he say to that?

Maybe next time just make her a sandwich.

We've finally got back to our regular meet ups and fallen into our old ways again. Recent gatherings have taken advantage of the good weather. Devon and Sandra bringing their kids round and us all sat out in our back garden.

'Did you see his obituary in the *Evening News*?' I ask.

'Yeah, not a single word about us, the bastards.' Once more, the old lady next to him coughs at his use of an expletive and Devon apologises before continuing. 'They called him a footnote. A footnote, man! What does that make us?'

I ponder for a second. 'A footnote to a footnote?'

'So, what, a toe, then?'

'Yeah, and a rotten one, at that. Amputated for the greater good.'

With the grim reality of our position in Moran's story settled, Devon's attention begins to stray. He scans the chapel, settling on the grieving family at the front.

'There's Rob and his mum and dad,' he says. 'Have you spoken to them?'

'Not had a chance, mate.'

'What about Kelly?'

A reunion with Moran's widow is not high on my list for today. I've yet to spot her and tell Devon so.

'Have you seen the daughter?' he asks. 'Lauren, isn't it?'

'I dunno what she looks like, mate.'

'Me neither. I know what she sounds like, though.'

With my neck aching from twisting to talk, I've incrementally been returning to a forward-facing position, but hearing this I spin back to him. 'What do you mean?' I ask.

'Well, I got a call off her over the weekend, telling me about the funeral and asking if I was coming.'

'She called me, an' all.'

'I know. I'd already given Rob your number to pass on.'

'I thought you might've,' I tell him. 'When did you talk to Rob?'

Devon shrugs. 'Last week, sometime. I had him in my work phone, did a job for him a few months back. His kitchen looked like someone had diverted the Irwell through it. Forty-seven,' he muses. 'Who dies at forty-seven?'

I could mention my mum died at forty-three, but we both know this and it doesn't seem the time.

'Makes you think, doesn't it?' he adds.

'I'm trying not to think about it, actually.'

'Can't say I blame you, man. At your advanced age, you'll probably be the next to go.'

'I'm not that much older than you, Devon.'

'You say that, but I'm not sure mathematics would agree. Think of all those days, Jim, the hours and minutes.'

Seven and a half months is the difference, a sizeable gap as far as he's concerned and one that he's lorded over me for almost twenty years, ever since I approached the so-called foreboding milestone of the big 3-0, while he'd only just turned twenty-nine. Normally, this sort of talk would continue with my bringing up Devon's lack of height, but I decide to save that in case I need it later.

'Mate, months are nothing in the grand scheme of human history. Just the blink of an eye.'

'Really?' he says. 'Well, how about you start blinking on your birthday and come May, we'll see if you still don't think it's a long time. Before that, though, are you coming to the do afterwards?'

'For a bit, yeah. I want to chat to Rob, and we need to say hello to the daughter. And Kelly, maybe. Pay our respects.'

'It's the done thing,' says Devon.

Our conversation is interrupted by deep rumbling. A bass line I recognise within a couple of beats as one of the first I learned many years ago. Pews creak as we begin to rise. A heartbeat-like double pump of a drum plays through hidden speakers, joined by lilting piano as Moran's coffin is carried slowly through the chapel, towards the heavy dark curtains and whatever lies beyond.

7

I like Johnny Sheedy, even if he is from the wrong end of the East Lancs Road, but, you know, some things just don't last. You see, as far as I'm concerned Manchester and Liverpool are brothers. Now, the problem with some brothers is they don't get along so well in close proximity, and I should know I shared a room with our kid for what felt like a lifetime, and it got to the point where one of us had to move out. That's why me and Johnny don't work together anymore.

Pete Moran, 1995

I stand on my own outside the chapel, by alcoves of inscriptions to departed loved ones. With eyesight that is some way off 20/20, I'm at a distance where the letters on the plaques are just a blur to me and don't feel like getting any closer. My lack of visual sharpness is no help in searching the crowd for Devon either, having lost sight of him after the service. But unable to see one old friend, I do spy another. Rob Moran is out front of the chapel receiving condolences from mourners as they pass.

In the years since I left Swinton we've only bumped into each other a few times, at gigs or pubs in town, but barring the addition of glasses and a sprinkling of grey, he's barely changed since I knew him as a teenager. I hold back until the numbers round him thin out and then approach.

'Rob, mate, I'm so sorry for your loss.'

Up close he looks exactly what he is, a man who's had a tough week. Hands unable to maintain the same position for very long, and eyes struggling with the opposite.

'Cheers, pal,' he says, 'and thanks for coming.'

'No worries, it's the least I could do.' Already I feel myself at a loss for conversation and reach for one of death's easy platitudes. 'It was a lovely service.'

'Yeah, it was. I'm glad it's done now, though. I've been dreading it, I tell you.'

'I'll bet. Well, you've earned yourself a pint.'

'Right now, pal, I'd settle for a cig, but I've given the bloody things up.'

His hands burrow deep in his pockets, an effort to keep them still or dig about searching for his lighter and a stray Silk Cut.

'You've done your Pete proud,' I tell him. 'The music choices were down to you, I take it.'

'The Eternal' by Joy Division had accompanied the coffin into the chapel. The Stone Roses' 'I am the Resurrection' playing as we all filed out.

Rob nods. 'Choosing stuff I knew our kid would like wasn't so difficult. It was picking songs our mam thought acceptable that was the hard part. I only got her to agree to 'Resurrection' because I told her it was about Jesus. I wanted to use 'New Face in Hell'.'

A flash of mischief appears in Rob's expression, a look I saw many times in his brother.

'Pete would've loved that,' I say.

'Well, our mam never. She said it wasn't right.'

'Never a big Fall fan, your mum, if I remember rightly.'

'Nah, Jim. Not one bit.'

'How're they holding up, your folks?'

Rob shrugs and stares down before answering, his hands back out in the warm air and reaching for the right words.

'They're quiet, you know. In shock at having to attend their youngest's funeral. Parents aren't supposed to bury their kids, are they? Or see them cremated.'

'I was surprised it was down this end and not up at Agecroft.' South Manchester did seem a bit out of the way for a family from Swinton.

'Anywhere round Agecroft has enough bad memories for the old man already. What with the mine and that.'

Martin Moran was still working at the town's colliery when I first met Pete, but it would close in the months afterward.

'Also,' Rob adds, 'our mam grew up round here.'

'I don't think I knew that.'

'Yeah, most of her lot are buried in the cemetery, not that it mattered with Pete insisting on cremation.'

'He left a will?' I've yet to begin putting that kind of thing in place. Though with two kids and a wife, it's something I should investigate. But it feels too official, like acknowledging I'm on the final stretch and the end could arrive any minute.

'Strict instructions,' says Rob. 'No religious ceremony and no burial. Neither of which impressed our mam.'

According to Rob, there'd been an episode in recent years. One his brother never felt the need to share with anyone, except his solicitor. It must've scared him enough to put his affairs in order, but not enough to slow down. In the days after the heart attack that caused his death, the term "lifestyle" had been bandied about as a contributing factor, Pete Moran's being more at the "liberal use of drugs and alcohol" end of the spectrum rather than "weekend trips to Ikea".

'I warned him enough times,' Rob states, 'but the little prick wouldn't listen. You know what he was like, advice for our Pete was something to be given to other people.'

He sighs and coughs and changes the subject. 'Anyway, how's things with you? Devon said you'd been off work.'

Not wanting to dump my issues on him the day of his brother's funeral, my answer is half musical reference, half wish fulfilment. 'I'm alright. 'Fit and Working Again'.'

'Good,' he nods. 'You look well. How's your Lee doing?'

Lee was my cousin and a schoolfriend of Rob. With no elder sibling, and in a house where the only music was my father's Springsteen tapes and my late mother's Motown – neither of which I appreciated until much later – it was Lee I'd go to for inspiration. What T-shirt was he wearing when I saw him at my gran's house on a Sunday? Whose lyrics tumbled out of his mouth? It was Lee's passion which ignited my own and he was kind enough to let me tag along when he went searching for more.

Lee emigrated to Canada five years ago. His wife had family there and after he'd been made redundant, they'd taken his pay off, sold their house, and decided to make a fresh start. We might live on different continents separated by thousands of miles, but we're still close. Closer than Rob and Pete had been, despite living only a few streets from each other.

'Lee's good,' I say. 'They've really settled in over there. He said to pass on his condolences.'

'Tell him thanks and give him my best next time you speak to him.'

It was through Lee and Rob that I met Pete. Despite being in the same year as me at Moorside High, I only knew him from a distance.

During lessons, my head would be kept low, obscured by textbooks and the arms of kids who'd the answers to everything. Whereas Pete's place in the classroom was generally outside of it. Exiled to the inhospitable wastes of the corridor. Cast out for some minor atrocity against the curriculum. An errant swear word or precisely-targeted paper missile.

At break times he'd stalk the periphery, paying the rest of us little attention, except to shake his head at our games of football, smirking as we charged about in a cloud of gravel. It would be outside school where we finally met, two fifteen-year-olds far beyond the gates and the bell, and not a teacher or stripy tie in sight.

It was 1990 and a Saturday which meant a journey into town with Cousin Lee to trawl our regular haunts of Manchester's many record shops. There was no Sunday trading back then, so in a week dominated by school this was our lone chance. We'd head in on the bus and do the chain stores, the independents, the market stalls selling second-hand. We might've had an idea what it was we were after but could never know for sure just what we'd bring home with us when the day was at an end.

Towards the middle of this particular Saturday, and with our pockets almost down to the lining, we agreed a final stop before heading off home. Piccadilly Records, then at its former home on Brown Street, for one last root through their wares: the fanzines on the counter, the LPs in racks and the row of T-shirts lining the walls like a headless, limbless chain of paper people, only made from one hundred percent cotton.

I'd been lost in all this, time having slipped away, when I felt Lee tug my jacket, and followed him outside. Our business seemingly done, we walked towards the Arndale, and the bus station, but as we neared the underground market two figures loomed up out of the depths. It was the brothers Moran riding the escalators.

I knew Rob as a friend of my cousin and after giving me a punch on the shoulder he and Lee fell into conversation. All thought of the bus and home was put aside, and I was left with Pete. We eyed one another, neither wishing to show any sign of weakness or even vague interest.

I'd never really seen him up close before. His mouth was small and pursed, his nose barely a bump just above it. With furrowed brow and two narrowed hazel eyes, he seemed to scrutinise all around him with an expression both curious and judgemental. Floating above all this was a bird's nest of light brown hair that refused to lie still on his head. It rose and crackled with energy, ideas, and a lack of care.

As I later found out, Pete's face could alter in a moment. Here, affecting the look of a choirboy, pious and innocent of your accusations. There, be the winking rogue, violating the sacramental wine and, with that wayward hair, seeming to have had a thousand volts fired up his cassock in return.

I didn't know it then but when I think back, there was something of the young Dylan about him. 1964 Dylan. *The Times They Are A-Changin'* Dylan. An era prior to Bob's own brush with the demon charge and bellowed claims of treachery at our city's Free Trade Hall.

It was Pete who broke the silence, gesturing to the carrier bag at my side and asking, 'What've you got there then, cock?' Proud of my choice and unperturbed by his easy use of "cock" as a verbal weapon, I pulled out a brand-new cassette of The Stone Roses self-titled debut. It'd been out for almost a year and my cousin owned it on vinyl and had made me a copy, but I wanted my own version, pristine and with the real artwork.

I was a collector, even in those early days, and this new addition would join the existing rotation of tapes – a Charlatans single, an Inspiral Carpets album, the *Madchester Rave On* ep – that went round and round in the tape machine I carried with me everywhere. The plastic block of a Walkman bulged in my coat pocket, waiting with a fresh set of batteries for the bus ride home.

Pete nodded with approval, as if he could hear the music contained on my cassette and was moving along with one of the snaking bass beats.

'What about you?' I asked.

By some miracle of facial muscles I would've thought impossible seconds earlier, his tiny mouth began to widen, lips parting into the grin I would see many times over the coming years. The bag in his hands contained the unmistakeable square of a twelve-inch and out came a dog-eared, oft-used album that might've been older than the pair of us combined. A ghostly circle lay imprinted Turin Shroud-style on the vinyl's outer sleeve.

I looked from the record to its new owner. Pete was still smiling and all he said was, '*Raw Power*.'

Partly through my own ignorance, but also down to the way Pete delivered these words, with a snarl and through the side of the mouth, I thought he was simply outlining his purchase's sonic virtues. Its cover held no clues as to who or what this music was. There was no title, no artist's name, just a waxy, bronzed someone or something before an expanse of darkness. This demon of the night would turn out to be Iggy Pop, but I didn't discover that until later.

Iggy would not have looked out of place as the figurehead on a galleon's prow, thrusting forward as the ship cut through foamy waves, striking fear and confusion into the hearts of enemies. Or as a creature designed for the big screen by Ray Harryhausen. Some weird being from *Clash of the Titans* or *The Golden Voyage of Sinbad*. A mythical harpy, perhaps. Half-human, half-bird and poised to unfurl its wings and attack our hero, sinking claws and fangs deep into his sword arm. I stared, transfixed. The artwork for my cassette, squashed down and sliced to fit a cramped rectangle, suddenly looked so very inadequate.

'It's a Canadian pressing,' Pete added. 'Me and our kid have gone halves on it.'

To "go halves" was a concept I was well aware of, but "Canadian Pressing", what did that mean? I wondered if it might be some slang term. Or was it like French Tickler? That was another phrase I'd heard lately but didn't quite understand. In search of enlightenment, I went back to examining the sleeve. Was this strange figure a Canadian? Back then, my knowledge of that country was limited to tall, lush firs and mounted police. I hadn't realised they could be such an odd-looking folk.

'Do you like The Stooges?' Pete asked.

It seemed odd he'd change the subject, but I felt relieved. I did indeed like the Three Stooges of whom there appeared to be at least four. I'd enjoyed many of their black and white antics on TV, but why should that matter? Or could this mysterious entity be a fifth member of their gang? Like the fifth Beatle? A lost Stooge for whom a life of slapstick had been too much or not enough?

I was confusing myself even more and decided it best not to say anything which might mark me out as some uninformed idiot. All I could think to do was replicate the nod Pete had just given me. This must've worked as he invited us back to theirs to listen to his bizarre record.

Several hours, and three or four spins of *Raw Power* later, their father Martin Moran had returned home, barking at his sons to 'turn that shite off', as he insisted on a respectful silence in which to check his pools coupon against the classified football results.

It was too late, though. In Pete I'd found a new friend, and soon we would be inseparable. A couple of teenage explorers embarking on a musical odyssey, determined to find out who, or what, made Iggy Pop.

Devon appears out of the crowd, his hand extended to Rob.

'My condolences again, man. I can't believe it. Forty-seven, that's no age at all.'

'Cheers, pal. And thanks for coming, it means a lot.'

'No worries, Rob. I wouldn't have missed it. There's a good turnout. Seen a few faces I've not seen in years and just been speaking to your old man. He's still a right rum sod.'

'Let me guess,' says Rob, adjusting his glasses. 'Was it about politics?'

Devon nods. 'Strikes and protests.'

'Why? Clyde's not still a postie, is he?'

I wasn't the only worker in dispute with my employer. The rail unions had been taking industrial action over the summer and Royal Mail staff were being balloted for strikes of their own. Discontent seemed everywhere.

'Nah, man. My dad's retired but he knows plenty who're still there. Sandra, though, reckons her lot'll be out before long.'

'The nurses, really?'

'Yeah, that's what I was telling your old man.'

'And what did the old fella have to tell you? I bet it was a long story.'

Devon smiles and Rob turns to me. 'The old fella doesn't have any short ones.'

'He told me about his days on the picket at Agecroft. Then some Poll Tax demo you all went on back in the day.'

Rob pauses, and almost grins. 'Fuck me, that's going back a bit. How many years is that now? I remember it, though. Pete, the gobby little shite was in his element. But it wasn't all of us. Our mam stayed home. She and the old fella had a row and our mam stayed home.' Rob pauses again, his eyes closing. 'Our mam. I keep saying our mam, except it's not our mam anymore, is it? Because it's just me.'

I share a glance with Devon, and he moves closer to Rob, resting a hand on his shoulder. 'If there's anything either of us can do, just give us a shout.'

'Cheers, lads,' Rob says, eyes open again, but with an added glassy sheen. 'What a fucking business, eh?'

'It's a shitter and no mistake, mate.'

We stand on sun-bleached grass and watch the first of the cars pull away down the drive. A woman I vaguely recognise gives the three of us a solemn nod from the back seat of a grey saloon. Some cousin of the Moran's, maybe, or a school friend from back in the day. Whoever she is, her appearance prompts Devon to ask a question that's been on my mind as well.

'Is Kelly here? I've not seen her about.'

'Nah,' says Rob. 'It's hit her hard.'

I feel myself relax at this news, the thought of one less difficult conversation scratched off my mental to-do list before I can escape homewards.

'Lauren's around somewhere, though,' Rob continues. 'She's a good kid. It's been a rough week for her, as you can imagine.'

'We'd like to say hello,' I say.

'Pay our respects,' Devon adds.

'That's good because she wants to speak to you two, an' all.'

Before Rob can tell us more, one of the funeral directors appears at his shoulder, although swoops might be a more accurate description. Dressed as he is, head to toe in black, with hands behind his back and bowing slightly this bloke seems more crow than human. Rob asks us to excuse him and the pair head back to the chapel before he can explain just what his niece might want with us.

I search the crowd, trying to pick out the young woman who might resemble her late father or absent mother, but without much progress. Devon appears to be doing the same only when he speaks again it isn't to point out Lauren Moran.

'Look at this lot, eh. Another grand day out for the Society of Professional Mancunians.' He means the music industry types, their sunglasses and studious attention to hair. 'Do you ever think that could've been us?'

I bypass our collective lack of follicles and reply, 'Nah, mate. Because we're from Salford.'

Devon snorts in amusement. 'That's the kind of shite Pete would come out with.'

Pete Moran wore the chip on his shoulder like a prize rosette. Attempts to pin him down or pigeon-hole him, tell him who he was or who he wasn't, would only bring out the rebel. Say he was from Manchester and Moran would correct it to Salford. Say Salford and he'd counter with Swinton. Say Swinton and he could refract it down almost indefinitely, to the street, to the house number, the bedroom, even the womb of his mother, Joan. Call him English and he'd bring up the fact his dad was born in Derry and so claim Irish heritage – though, how true this was only Martin Moran and his birth certificate could tell you.

Pete took great pleasure in baiting journalists and God help any who were privately educated or possessed a double-barrelled name. About the only categorisation he seemed to embrace rather than baulk at was being described as "difficult".

'You know what I mean, though, don't you?' Devon continues. 'All those albums Pete made, the tours he went on. Do you never wonder if we might've been there alongside him, rock 'n' roll stars?'

I take a second to think about this question. Do I sometimes ask myself if life may have held a different path for me that became lost for one reason or another? Yes, I do.

Do I daydream about how such a path might've turned out? Also, yes.

But do I want to get into that conversation today?

'I dunno,' I say, instead. 'I mean, it was a long time ago.'

'I know, man, but I reckon I could've got used to a life of sex and drugs.'

'I wouldn't let Sandra hear you say that, mate.'

Devon smiles and extracts a bag of tobacco from one suit pocket and a pack of Rizlas from the other.

'I see the quitting's going well.'

'Just be thankful you never started,' he says, beginning the task of assembling a roll-up.

'My asthma was good for something then.' Three muted cheers for a lifetime of wheezing. 'Wasn't switching to rollies supposed to help you give up, though?'

His logic had appeared sound, that taking the time to construct a cigarette whenever he had an urge to smoke rather than just pulling one from a pack would put him off.

'It was supposed to, yeah, but I enjoy making them. It's about the only creative act I get to indulge in these days.'

'It will be if you get the snip.'

'I am not getting the bloody snip, no matter what Sandra says.' His brows rise in annoyance, but his eyes are focused on the ingredients he juggles from hand to hand, the whole endeavour made more complex by his lack of a flat surface.

'If it's gonna be a sore point, mate, I won't mention it again.'

'Why don't you get it done?'

'I'm considering it, mate.'

'Really?'

'Yeah. I mean, the fewer unexpected life events me and Katie get the next couple of years the better. We could go in together, me and you. Have it done at the same time. For moral support and that. Wake up afterwards in matching gowns and adjacent beds.'

'Piss off, man. I'm trying to concentrate.'

Devon puts on an impressive display, it's like watching a magician at close quarters and trying to follow the movement of a playing card, some ball under a cup or a five-pound note I've offered freely from my wallet.

'I'll have you know,' he tells me, 'I only smoke these days during times of great stress or when I'm having a pint. And I've got today down for both.' His cigarette is almost complete. 'If we're still out at teatime, we could get a kebab.'

Come teatime I have no intention of being anywhere other than lay on my sofa. Not that I mention this.

Devon lights up and inhales before loosing a cloud of heavy grey smoke. As the fumes start to disperse, I notice his expression has changed, his forehead crinkling, his eyebrows becoming a single hairy entity. He points off into the distance with his cigarette hand.

'Who does that look like to you?'

I try to concentrate, but with my dodgy eyesight and the sheer number of recognisable mourners on display it's not immediately obvious who he thinks he's seen.

'Where?' I ask.

'Over there.'

'The woman off the radio?'

'Nah, to her right. The bloke yakking away on his mobile.'

I squint and move my head forward, zooming in like a camera as if the extra centimetre or two might make all the difference and bring this blur into focus. It's a performance Devon finds hilarious.

'Have you still not had your eyes tested?'

Behind the trees lining the cemetery's driveway, I make out a lone male shape pacing, an arm brought up to the side of his head. Each time I think he's taken on a settled form this fella disappears into more foliage and is lost from view. I try to piece together what I can.

The figure is tall and thin and ever so slightly stooped, as if at some point in his life a heavy item has weighed him forward. A heavy item like an electric guitar.

I rear back in shock as my mind takes this unexpected leap, shocked at the appearance of someone I never thought I'd see again. The fourth member of our teenage band and our very own Ghost of Christmas Past.

8

I don't read reviews. The only reason I know about the "pound shop Iggy Pop" thing is because some cunt decided to shove it in my face. Well now I'm gonna shove it in their face.

Pete Moran, 1998

Unless you're at a séance hoping to discover where the family treasure is buried, there's probably never a great time to be confronted by a ghost.

Not in the dead of night with an apparition looming at the foot of your bed, a gnarled finger accusing you of some long-forgotten misdeed.

Not in the kitchen as you tidy away your fine china or that branded pint glass you liberated from a bar in town all those years ago.

If you must endure a visitation from the afterlife, there are few places better suited to the experience than a cemetery.

Surrounded by the dead, adding another soul into the mix, it's at least in-keeping with the ambience of the place.

The problem with Steve Williamson, however, is not that he's a ghost. The problem is that he's very much alive and, for the first time since 1993, stood only a short distance away.

I've not seen him since the summer we both left Eccles College, haven't spoken to him since the Christmas beforehand. If our former guitarist *was* a phantasm from beyond the grave, I could happily ignore him as I don't believe in such things.

Had anyone asked who I was expecting to run into at Moran's funeral, I may have listed Kurt Cobain, Lord Lucan and Doctor Zaius from *Planet of the Apes* all ahead of Steve Williamson. In fact, it would've been less of a surprise had I spotted Moran himself, sitting quietly on the back row of the chapel. His face partially obscured by thick-rimmed comedy specs, fake nose and moustache attached beneath, as he took note of all those who did or didn't turn up for his send off.

Seeing Steve is one thing but approaching him is quite another and I'm all for watching from a distance, treating him like some animal in the wilds of a David Attenborough documentary, observing this lesser spotted mammal through a high-powered lens or the safety and camouflage of a hide while he grazes beyond the tree line and then bounds away without ever knowing we were here.

Devon, though, appears to be thinking of the other famous Attenborough, actor Richard, and more his murderous thug from *Brighton Rock* than the amiable Kris Kringle of *Miracle on 34th Street*. As such, he's already striding off in our former bandmate's direction.

I can't remember the last time we spoke about Steve, so what Devon intends to say to him is a mystery, but instinct tells me it's unlikely to be anything friendly.

'Steve!' Devon shouts, as I follow a couple of steps behind, warm temperatures rising higher, shirt collar and tie stiffening around my neck.

'Steve!' he hollers again. 'STEVE!'

Mourners are beginning to take notice, giving us curious glances and parting as we move through them. Steve Williamson turns toward us, mobile phone pressed to his ear. The look on his face is of someone caught in the act, and he fumbles to finish his call.

'Blimey!' he says. 'Alright, lads.'

His voice is far louder than it needs to be. I suspect this is not for our benefit, but for the watching crowd. A message that all is normal, that this is just an everyday reunion. There's nothing to see here, so please step away and resume your grieving.

Devon, cigarette in hand, stares at Steve for a beat or two. He takes a drag and exhales, then remarks, 'Nice suit, man.'

'Err, thank you,' Steve replies, smoothing the material down with a mixture of pride and nervous energy. It's a three-piece affair. Charcoal grey and fitted. Not cheap.

'Love the waistcoat.'

Whether this compliment is genuine or sarcasm, I can't tell but Steve seems under the impression it's the former and opens his jacket to give us a better view.

'To be honest,' Steve tells us, 'I was going to leave it at home. Manchester was never this warm when I lived up here.'

'The climate it is a-changin,' Devon states with an air of menace the Dylan track he's riffing on never quite possessed.

We make an awkward trio, conversation not exactly tripping off our tongues. I watch Devon while he glowers at Steve whose eyes are averted and fixed on the main road. Searching for help, maybe. A taxi or fast-approaching cavalry.

I turn my attention to Steve and notice a bead of sweat making its way down his forehead. Also, that his blonde hair, shaped and styled to perfection, shows little sign of ageing, none of the tell-tale grey at the temples and roots that I possess.

He mentioned home but where is that these days? I know he went down south for university but heard nothing of him after that. His accent, if he even has one anymore, gives no clue. He hasn't said much so far but the rougher edges of his speech sound like they've been smoothed away, leaving a voice altogether neutral.

We stand in silence, none of us particularly keen to speak. I wish Devon hadn't been so hasty in rushing over, that we'd been able to formulate a plan of sorts, but it's too late now. Here we all are for the first time in thirty years, watching the parade of mourners' cars creep down the drive.

Devon is the one to break the spell. After another drag on his cig, he asks Steve if he's seen any of the old gang about, if he's spoken to Rob.

'I caught sight of him after the service,' Steve replies with a cough. He seems aggravated, whether by the question or the cigarette smoke, and he clears his throat before continuing. 'But he was busy, so I haven't had the chance for a chat.'

From the way his eyes flick down to his shoes, highly polished black brogues, I get the impression he would be happy to avoid any kind of interaction with Rob today, just as I would've been overjoyed to miss out on this one.

'What about Kelly?' Devon says. 'Have you seen her?'

I forget about Steve for a moment and stare at Devon. He knows Kelly isn't here, Rob has only just told us.

'Not yet, no.' This is another line of enquiry Steve is uncomfortable with and he peers off into the distance again. I wonder if he does have a cab on its way and is willing it to arrive right about now.

Devon nods at Steve's reply and exhales more smoke in his direction. I don't think I've ever seen my friend like this before. Has he been waiting all these years for a chance to make Steve Williamson squirm? I'm surprised and impressed, but also a little horrified.

'This is a cosy little reunion, isn't it?' says Devon. 'And so unexpected, you know what I mean.'

'I wasn't actually planning on coming up,' Steve tells us, trying to regain his composure, 'but then I got a call.'

I swear I hear an alarm of some kind going off nearby. A car or an unfortunate incident with the crematorium's furnace. I soon realise that no-one else can hear this, that it's coming from inside my brain. An internal warning or peal of tinnitus.

'Call?' I ask, already knowing the answer.

That Lauren would invite me and Devon to her father's funeral makes sense. We were old friends of Moran's who still lived locally. We knew his family and they knew us. But that she would seek out whatever rock Steve has been hiding under would never have entered my mind. I begin to wonder how she even found him, but then stop. With the internet, you can find anyone or anything with a few clicks of a mouse. I wonder also why he came. Surely, he could've got out of it easily enough with any number of excuses: work, family, some urgent medical procedure.

Before any of this can be addressed, Steve seems drawn to something over my shoulder and his jaw starts to fall open. The gap between his lips becoming ever larger. His cheeks start to drain of colour, turning as white as his unstained teeth. The expression on his face causes me to look round and find out just what's had such an effect of him.

Two shapes approach us over the grass verge, nothing more than fuzzy blurs to my struggling eyes, but slowly they come into focus. One is male, the other female. My brain makes the same puzzling identification I assume Steve's has and I feel my pulse begin to quicken once more. The couple heading our way are Pete and Kelly Moran.

9

It's a lot to take in, you know. Double the sales of the first album and I'm about to head off on a tour of the U.S. though I still can't get a kind word out of the NME.
There was an incident the other year. A coming together in Kwok Man between an ex-grammar school boy and a portion of chow mein.

Pete Moran, 1999

I know this vision must be false so run a critical eye over the pair, rather than my two blurry ones. The man cannot possibly be who I think it is. The walk is similar, but the dimensions are off. He's too tall – not to mention, too alive – and as they get closer, I see that the male is Rob. But the woman still seems to be his sister-in-law. She's diminutive and curvy, with wavy dark hair. Exactly as I remember the Kelly Moran of our youth.

She was Kelly Lewis, back then. A year older than us in college and an object of desire for many. She was attractive and well-developed in all the ways a teenage boy could ask for and not just in physical appearance. She had a knowledge and appreciation of the finer things in life, which to our young minds meant music.

If I'd thought Pete was ahead of me in his musical education, then Kelly left the pair of us trailing in her wake. The house she grew up in was a treasure trove of vinyl – her father, Eric, was an obsessive collector. We'd often spend our days at the Lewis' home sampling his records while he and his wife, Ellen, were at work.

Kelly wasn't just knowledgeable; she was also opinionated. To her, *Fun House* was a better record than *Raw Power*, My Bloody Valentine surpassed The Jesus and Mary Chain, and Crass far superior to the Pistols. On this final point, she labelled the latter as "children's punk", a view we considered beyond the heretical.

She nearly managed to ruin Dylan's *Highway 61 Revisited* for us. We'd discovered it in her dad's collection and after she realised how much we'd taken to the album, she took great pleasure in pointing out not just the anonymous groin looming over Bob's shoulder on the cover, but also that of the singer songwriter himself. And like any great optical illusion, once our eyes had been drawn to these areas, they became about all we could see. In a nod to the title of the record's second track, Kelly rechristened the album, "Two-Crotch Blues".

Even now, whenever I see *Highway 61...* the first thing I notice is not Dylan's extravagantly coloured shirt, or his Triumph motorcycle Tee, nor his passing likeness to Moran, but the pair of gentlemen's nether regions.

Has Kelly made it to the funeral after all? Has she summoned, via medication or will alone, whatever strength is needed to make it through these next few hours? Only when the woman gets to within five or six paces do I wake up to the fact it's not her. The grieving widow will be in her late forties by now, the same as us and this is a version of her a good twenty years younger than that, transplanted straight from the early nineties by some curious lapse in the fabric of time. This is her daughter. This is Lauren.

Her dress is black, simple though striking. High-necked and low-hemmed with sleeves of short lace, it dances around her calves as she moves. Rob introduces us to his niece, and I express in person this time just how sorry I am about her father.

'Thanks,' she says, 'and thanks for coming today, all you guys. It means a lot, like.'

'It's the least we could do,' Devon offers.

'Yes,' Steve adds, 'he will be missed.'

From the look Rob gives our former guitarist, it's obvious he isn't best pleased about Lauren inviting him and I wonder if Steve's presence might go some way to explaining the absence of her mother.

'Where you having the wake?' I ask Rob.

'Just up the road,' he says. 'Chorlton Irish Club.'

I begin to relax. This venue is only a short walk from where I live. I can stick around for a while, share a few hours with these old faces, trade stories and catch up. Then, well before the afternoon becomes the evening and everyone has become far too lubricated to keep a lid on their simmering resentments, I can say my goodbyes and be home, shoes off and feet up, inside ten minutes.

Home, a place I was bound to for much of the summer but where, today, I cannot wait to return.

'However,' Rob begins, 'I believe our Lauren has something else in mind for you gents.'

I look from Rob to his niece. I find it difficult not to stare, she looks so familiar while being a total stranger.

'I was thinking,' Lauren says, her voice once again the nervous young woman on the phone, 'that we could go into town, like, the four of us. Do a bit of a crawl to some of the places my dad used to drink in.'

Had any of us thought this reunion was just a chance event, that we've been summoned here merely as a courtesy to the memory of our dead friend, that idea is now dissolving. Bringing us together for her dad's funeral, and now inviting us on some pub-based odyssey, Lauren obviously wants to know about one thing. The only thing that ties the three of us together and the thing we'd all rather not speak of, especially to Moran's daughter.

Incendiary Tract. A band that lasted barely more than twelve months, that only entered a recording studio once, that played just four gigs – the pedants out there might correct that to three.

A band that was such a small part of her father's life it didn't warrant a mention in his obituary.

A band that spontaneously combusted on stage at the Academy the week before Christmas of the year 1992.

I look at the daughter of Pete and Kelly Moran, and wonder how much she knows and how much more she wants to know? What, besides her looks, has her mother passed down?

Is this a request we can refuse? Lauren herself asked us here today to attend her father's funeral, and surely a couple of drinks afterwards in his honour had been assumed. A part of the social contract, so to speak. "The done thing", as Devon said, earlier. And just as he rushed over to confront Steve, Devon is now the first to step forward.

'Of course,' he says, 'we'd love to.'

I flash him a glance. We? Who's this "we" he's talking about? Since when did Devon begin referring to himself in the majestic fucking plural?

'What about your folks?' I ask Rob, clutching at a possible way out. 'I mean, won't they be expecting us at the wake?'

'Don't worry, pal. They know all about this and they're fine with it. They know it means a lot to Lauren and getting you three together again might not be possible. You can always nip over and have a word before you head off.'

I nod, in feigned agreement. At least, I assume that's what my head is doing. Inwardly, I'm trying to recalibrate my plan. A trip into town with a young woman I've never met before and a ghost from the past was not on my agenda for the day. From the look on Steve's face, I can see this isn't what he had in mind, either.

'To be honest,' he says, 'I'm on a bit of a tight schedule. I have to be on a train back to Euston and I'll need to pick up my case before that.'

'What time's your train?' Rob asks.

Steve's blue eyes are shifting, again. 'Five.'

'It's not even half-twelve, pal. You've got ages before then. Where you staying?'

'The Mal-mai-son,' Steve offers the four syllables up as if each one is being drawn from him with great pain.

'You're right by the station, then, aren't you? You can pick your stuff up as you pass. Plenty of time for a few drinks with my niece first.'

Rob Moran may not be happy to see Steve, but he's certainly keen for him to follow Lauren's wishes. Maybe so he can sit at his brother's send off and not have to stare across the room at a man he clearly doesn't care for.

'Fine,' Steve says, pulling back his sleeve to reveal a chunky, silver watch. 'Fine, but four o'clock is my cut off point. After that, I will have to get going.'

10

London? Why would I want to move to London? Bright lights? If I was after bright lights, there's a B&Q just up the road.

Pete Moran, 2000

A taxi arrives and we pull away from the crematorium, but once onto Princess Parkway our progress is halted by heavy traffic. A main artery toward town restricted by some unseen blockage and we crawl along at the speed of a hearse with an atmosphere to match.

It takes an eternity to put the cemetery behind us and even as we replace the endless rows of gravestones with playing fields and a park, the mood inside the car fails to improve. Since Lauren gave our destination, no one's spoken. Even the driver is quiet, sensing his four travellers, all dressed in funereal black, would prefer it to remain that way.

The radio plays low in the background. A hubbub of chat and chart beats, so faint it might be coming from the vehicle in the next lane. Combined with the hum of the engine it creates a white noise to mask our lack of communication.

Steve is in the passenger seat, focused straight ahead and no doubt looking forward to his afternoon escape on the train back to wherever he now calls home. Devon is behind him, eyes boring a hole through the headrest and deep into the skull of our onetime bandmate.

Lauren sits to the rear of the cabbie, staring at a tote bag on her knees. The bag mysteriously appeared at much the same time as the taxi, just after I'd passed on my commiserations to Joan and Martin, her paternal grandparents. A metal tin is visible at the bag's open end and a strange shape bulges the fabric at its side. Lauren's hands are clasped together over the tote, either guarding against some unexpected foot to the brakes sending its contents sprawling or a simple act of prayer.

In the middle of all this, sits me. I'm unsure where to look and whether to speak. Conversation might come as a relief, might put a stop to the thought in my head that we've made this journey before or one like it, at least.

I consider striking up an exchange with the cabdriver, the usual about how busy his shift has been so far or the gridlocked road or even our long hot summer. If I was on my own, I may've asked him about his job, that of ferrying strangers around all day. How does he find it? Would he recommend this sort of thing to someone who might find themselves unemployed in the coming months, someone who normally spends his days stuck inside a warehouse, someone who doesn't possess a driving licence? Today, though, isn't the time for such thinking and I park my future work worries to concentrate strictly on the problems of the present and the past.

After skirting Moss Side and Hulme, we approach and join the Mancunian Way and I view the city from a different angle than I'm used to, one that isn't through the window of a tram. Eras swim together in my vision. The grimy off-white of the older buildings, the redbrick of so many recent blocks, and now the thin glass digits grasping at the heavens.

Surrounding them all are cranes that promise more and more new developments as Manchester's skyline is reimagined. It's a process that shows no signs of stopping, unlike the half-finished exit ramp we pass on our left where the tarmac curls away to mid-air nothingness. A path towards some endeavour which never played out, the beginnings of an incomplete thought.

Crash barriers and the lip of a kerb keep the unsuspecting from this wrong turn, but I begin to project an alternate reality down that phantom slip road. One where Moran remains alive, and where my back is not a problem. I'd be in work right now, halfway through a ten-hour shift, and what would be on my mind, massive life change or just my dinner?

Our driver brakes, blasting his horn at a transit switching lanes. He apologises and shares a moment of irritation with the drivers among us. Even at the slow speed we were going, it was quite a jolt and Lauren only just managed to hold onto her bag.

Now in front of us, this cursed vehicle seems familiar. It's colours, flashes of orange and white, trigger a memory. A December day long ago, travelling on a similar stretch to the one we are now. The four of us, me, Devon, Steve, and Pete rattling along in an almost identical van on our way to the Academy.

And here we are again, only this time our singer is no longer with us, his earthly form consigned to the furnace just an hour ago, his presence heavy inside the cab, his only child sitting to my right.

In thinking of that bygone Christmas, I can't help but recall the film *Scrooged* and Bill Murray's cynical TV executive stepping into a taxi to be tormented by his own Ghost of Christmas Past, in the shape of the New York Dolls' frontman David Johansen. Murray had been taken back in time by the crazed, cigar-smoking Johansen in one of the Big Apple's iconic yellow cabs, the sight of which so disturbed his former bandmate, bassist Arthur Kane, that after watching it on television he apparently felt the urge to throw himself out a window.

As I sit in a beige Ford Mondeo moving along the ring road, I reflect it's just as well I'm not in easy reach of either door handle.

11

Friday 18th December 1992

Our journey from Swinton to Oxford Road's university district was not a pleasurable one. In the front of our Salford Van Hire transit, the Moran brothers shared a cigarette, filling the vehicle with an acrid stink, and neither Pete nor Rob thinking to crack a window and allow some less polluted, albeit colder, air to circulate. For those of us in the back, there was a secondary level of unpleasantness to deal with: the absence of any actual seating.

Devon hugged the largest of his drums as a form of ballast, hoping to weigh himself to the van's floor and minimise turbulence. In a corner, Steve cradled his Gibson Les Paul, the expensive guitar bought for him by his old man, the local building supplies magnate. Which left me, one hand gripping my amplifier and the other wedged deep into a hole near the wheel arch, fingers slick with grease as I struggled to find purchase.

As much as I desired stability, I had to be careful not to tear any skin from the digits that would later be running up and down the fretboard of my bass, the instrument which, at that moment, was clamped tightly between my thighs.

This was not the glamorous Rock 'n' Roll lifestyle I had read about in the music press. I felt like a stowaway undertaking passage to the new world. Human cargo buffeted by the swaying of our vessel and gradually succumbing to motion sickness.

My mind kept showing me the image of a tit-helmeted constable pulling us over, demanding to search the van and coming upon a trio of queasy, vomit-splattered urchins in the hold. Had I a hand to spare, its fingers would have been crossed for luck in our evading discovery.

As we barrelled down the East Lancs Road in silence, Rob Moran turned to check on the three of us in the rear. 'You fuckers are quiet,' he remarked. 'Nervous, are you? I know I'd be.'

'Eyes on the road, cock,' said Pete. 'We don't pay you to state the obvious.'

'You don't pay me at all, you little prick.'

With that the extent of conversation on offer, Rob stuck a cassette in the deck and after a fleeting intro of tape hiss on came The Jesus and Mary Chain's 'Never Understand.' Ten to fifteen seconds of feedback and fuzzed guitar later, Pete reached over and cut the track short.

'What the fuck do you think you're doing?' Rob asked.

'This is shite.'

'Is it bollocks.' Rob's hand came off the steering wheel, pushed the cassette back in and restarted the song.

Once again, Pete leant over and brought the music to a halt. 'Shite, I tell you.'

Had a window been open, I would not have put it past him to eject the tape all the way out of the transit and onto the tarmac, to be crushed under the tires of late afternoon traffic. Instead, with his feet resting up on the dashboard, Pete stared calmly through the windscreen, while his brother's head swivelled back and forth, incredulous at such blasphemy.

'You fucking little heathen. Carry on with this attitude and I'll dump you right in the middle of the dual carriageway.'

'Rob, it sounds like pigs squealing as one of their mates sizzles in a frying pan.'

'That's very poetic, pal. Maybe, if you put some of that effort into your songs, they might be one level above a turd.'

This attack on Pete's art spurred him to react. 'You cheeky bastard.'

I knew Pete loved the Mary Chain. Rob knew this as well, but then that was the Morans. Winding each other up over something both were aware had no basis in fact.

'Anyhow,' Rob said, 'what's all this crap about pigs and bacon? You're not going all Morrissey on us, are you?'

'Cunt.' Pete replied.

'Is that me or Moz you're talking about?'

'The pair of you.'

With that settled, Pete pushed the cassette back in and filled the van with heavy distortion.

It was almost a clear run towards town, passing the rows of static cars coming in the opposite direction, inching their way home, working weeks at an end. Our progress only slowed on the Mancunian Way, but we crept off at the next junction and were soon zig zagging the final leg, backstreet to backstreet. The constant left, right, lefts throwing the three of us in the back from side to side, each turn punctuated with an accidental crash from Devon's cymbals. Finally, the van stopped, and its doors opened.

We were at the Academy because of the Ramones. A year earlier they had played the venue and the four of us, plus Rob and my cousin Lee, had stood in the crowd, watching them hurtle through their set with barely a pause for breath in between. Each song had blurred into the next, a line of graffiti-riddled subway carriages speeding along in front of your eyes and merging into a single whole, the combined physical energy forcing you back a step.

Twelve months on and New York's finest were back. It might not have been *the* Ramones, not the classic line up, only two of whom remained suited up in their trademark leather jackets, but we did not care.

Tommy had long since vacated his place behind the drums, but Marky was in the seat again having been ousted for a spell in the mid-eighties. Dee Dee had recently left the group, so bass duties were handled by the newly christened C.J. Ramone. Joey and Johnny though were still around, singer and guitarist locked in eternal rivalry.

It did not matter to us because we were not there to watch them. We were there to *support* them.

Incendiary Tract were not high on the bill – technically, Incendiary Tract were not even *on* the bill, our name being absent from the posters around town and flyers left in record shops – but due to dogged persistence from Pete, harassing promoters into submission, we had been handed a thirty-minute slot when the doors opened at half-past seven. Any Ramones fan wishing to stake their claim down at the front in readiness for the main attraction would be forced to endure us as they waited.

It would not be our first time on the Academy stage, having performed a similar function the week before for Sonic Youth and been well received. The writer of a local music fanzine had even begun to warm to us.

Mark E Moon was the name he wrote under, in reference to an album by Television. This choice of moniker had apparently irked another Manchester-based Mark E, this one a Smith who just happened to be the leader of The Fall. Adding further to their feud was Moon's decision to title his irregularly released collection of reviews, news and musings *Mere Pseud Magazine* in a nod to one of Smith's songs.

Moon had not been kind in reporting our first couple of gigs – scathing would be more accurate – but at least he was paying attention. After our last performance, just our third in public, his views had softened.

The previous weekend he had interviewed Pete and I in the Koffee Pot in town, although the piece was yet to appear in print. He may still have been poring over his recording, trying to find something of use among the noise of a busy café and the ramblings of two over-excited eighteen-year-olds.

We waited in what was described to us as our dressing room, but felt more like a hastily cleared storage space, and I watched my bandmates, if mates we still were.
Devon practised with his sticks, tapping out rhythms on an aged wooden table. Steve sat on a fold-out chair, moving through scales on his Les Paul. Pete seemed agitated and paced an area barely that of a phone booth, muttering lyrics under his breath, repeating them as calming mantras.

At dead on seven-thirty, came a knock at the door and seconds later we were onstage. The lights already down, the crowd mostly in darkness. Only the first handful of rows were visible, and I made out faces we knew, friends and family we had persuaded to sacrifice their Friday evening and nine pounds fifty in advance to come and watch us play.

Little had passed between us backstage, there were more nods than words. Pete outlined a planned setlist that no one was about to disagree with. We would start with the best song we had, hoping to tempt in any of the stragglers who hung about outside the main room.

It was a track our singer and I had crafted over the last month or so, sitting on the floor of his bedroom with a battered old acoustic and fitting the pieces together like a jigsaw. We presented it to Devon and Steve and then fleshed it out, adding drums and lead guitar. After playing it live at our last gig, we had pooled our spare cash and paid for half a day in a studio to commit it to tape. The first of many recordings we hoped our group would make.

At the end of that fast and tight four minutes, I was already sweating, but the exertion had been worth it. Those at the front had swelled in number, there were shouts of approval and scattered applause. As exciting as this was, I was more distracted by Pete and Steve.

All through our opening track they had taken turns in leaning towards each other, exchanging words no one else could hear and were doubtful part of the lyrics. At one point, I was sure I had seen our singer hawk up a lump of phlegm and deposit it at our guitarist's feet, landing just shy of his new suede trainers.

I looked behind me at Devon, the lights around him flashing in a random pattern and glinting off his shaven skull. From his expression I realised he shared my concern, but there was little we could do other than raise our eyebrows and see how things played out.

We took a breath and went into the next song; one we had only recently come up with. A slow building affair with a long introduction before Pete's vocals would start a minute in. I played a throbbing circular bass riff which Devon punctuated with percussive blasts and then Steve's jagged guitar began, his notes dampened at first but growing louder as the time past. The minute mark came and went without a word from our singer, who should have been centre stage at the microphone, but instead was stalking the area to its left close to Steve.

Pete moved like a wild animal circling and cornering its prey. A hungry lion padding around this grazing giraffe, cutting off any possible escape route. Steve concentrated on the strings of his Les Paul, either unaware of the threat or ignoring this nearby predator. Pete continued to aim growls at our guitarist rather than into the microphone.

We were stuck in a loop, the same repetitive intro awaiting vocals. Faces in the crowd were turning and drifting away, slipping back into the darkness. I glanced again to Devon, unsure what was happening and what to do about it, and at that moment, a stage light flared in my direction, and I was blinded.

Disoriented, I planted my feet and shook my head, trying to disperse this void while fingers carried on, muscle memory pushing through the crisis. Then, I remembered the helicopter.

The sound of its blades, the intensity of its single pale beam and the dread I had felt outside. I blinked in the hope of resetting my vision, but with no success. I took long slow breaths in and out, was beginning to approach a level of calm and that was when I heard it.

The amplified crunch. An electric clang. Blunt force meets alternating current.

As my sight returned, I saw only shapes. Shadows grappling that I would come to identify as Pete and Steve. They were in too close to land effective blows and threw their arms too wide to properly connect. There were no real punches, only forearm slaps. Each attempted hook brought another discordant groan from the guitar trapped between them. It was a clown fight replete with diverse sound effects. If they had been strangers, I would have found the whole thing hilarious.

As I recovered, I saw Devon begin to climb out from his kit to intervene and I tried to lift my instrument away from me but found I couldn't. The lead and strap had become entangled, and

I twisted and turned to find a way out but was stuck under this cumbersome plank of wood. All I could do was watch in horror. When the pair finally hit the floor, Steve's guitar howled.

Still bound to my bass, I looked offstage, hoping for the sight of onrushing help or a responsible adult, but all I saw were two familiar heads peering out into the chaos. Joey and Johnny Ramone.

The tall, gangly Joey, hidden behind sunglasses and his curtain of hair, above the pudding-cut of Johnny. Da Brudders were no strangers to acrimony, by all accounts they barely spoke, but even they seemed shocked at what was taking place before them.

By the time Devon and the security staff managed to drag Pete and Steve apart, the two were bloodied and the Les Paul a mess, its neck hanging limply by its side. The guitar seemed beyond repair, as did our band.

Still tangled up with a weight I could not find my way out from under, I stared helplessly into the crowd, searching for a friendly face, someone from college or even my cousin. The only one I noticed was that of Mark E Moon who, notebook in hand, was frantically scribbling down all he had witnessed and penning an epitaph for Incendiary Tract.

12

Five people I'd invite to my dream dinner party? "Dream dinner party"? Who've you prepared these questions for, Princess Anne?
I dunno, any fucker. Just make sure the Albert Finney Poirot's there cos some cunt's bound to get slaughtered.

Pete Moran, 2001

We step out of our taxi in the Northern Quarter, the hub of bars and restaurants only a short distance from the workplace I've escaped for a day. With the area now such a popular one, it's easy to forget that back when I started at the warehouse there'd been no Northern Quarter. There'd not been much of anything round here.

I remember the day I first noticed things beginning to change. My bus journey would end at the Arndale and I'd wander through the quiet, mainly derelict district over to what was then still Cartwright and Sons. If I was in a hurry, I'd take a shortcut via an open-air car park, and one day I did just that, heading along this route with the start of my shift fast approaching, only to find my way blocked. A partition had been erected, the space off limits. In time, building work started and an apartment complex appeared. Later came a hotel.

This has been happening to me a lot, recently. After my spell off work, I returned to town to find more and more of the places I'd pass daily reduced to nothing more than piles of brickwork and dust behind wire fences.

Rather than take us into one of the newer establishments, Lauren leads us down a side street away from the present and very much into the past, to a pub whose threshold I've yet to cross despite over thirty-years boozing in this city, the Three Jolly Bargemen.

I pass the Bargemen's foreboding doorway and iron-barred windows often enough, hurrying either toward or away from another ten-hour shift, and ignoring the siren call of dawn to dusk karaoke. And when I say "siren" I mean that in both senses of the word.

To some the constant off-key wailing is an indication to steer well clear; to others, a trick to entice you inside. From the mild disgust on Steve's face, I can tell he isn't in the latter. The Bargemen is not the kind of venue he dressed for when slipping on his waistcoat this morning.

'My dad always brought me in here,' Lauren explains, leading us into the bar area where we're greeted by a high-eared dog. 'Whenever we came to town, this was where we'd start off. He was very attached to the place.'

We move nervously past the hound and after a quick scan of the pub's interior I identify the source of Moran's attachment. It wasn't a case of sentimentality or geography but sheer adhesiveness.

The walls are the colour and texture of cheap rice pudding, freshly layered and still moist. The carpet has soaked up so many spilt pints that every time you lift your shoe it feels as if a suction cup is attached to the sole. Close your eyes and imagine a low gravity walk on some desolate moonscape, accompanied by the damp smell of an Alsatian and ringing fruit machine.

As for the tables, whatever liquid is pooling and staining their finish might as easily burn the skin from your elbow should you lean on it too long. I picture Pete in here, sitting down and then being unable to tear himself away. A more-than-willing fly caught in the landlady's web.

We choose a spot in the main room and Lauren takes out her purse. 'What are you all drinking?'

'Put your money away,' Steve says. 'I'll get these.'

'Nah, it's alright.' Lauren holds up several crisp twenties. 'Uncle Rob gave me some cash for the first few rounds.'

'"First few rounds"?' Steve asks, when Lauren is out of earshot. 'How long is this going to take?'

'Relax, mate,' I tell him. 'I mean, it's not even one, yet.'

I feel a hypocrite advising Steve to be calm when my heart has been in my mouth for most of the last hour.

Devon's attention has moved to the bag leaning against Lauren's empty stool. The metal tin inside is a large rectangle, its decorative Christmas scene partly visible along with years of scratches and dents. Once home to an assortment of biscuits, what does it contain today?

Hopefully a fresh selection and nothing more. We could have a few drinks in Moran's favourite boozer, share anecdotes of the "good old days" while we munch on a chocolate bourbon or two. Then, when Steve makes an exit for his train, we can all go our separate ways, back to our separate lives.

'That's not him, is it?' Devon asks, still studying Lauren's tote.

'What's not him?' I reply.

'In there.' Devon points at the tin, careful not to get too close in case his belief is correct. 'She's not thinking of scattering him today, is she?'

'I don't think so,' Steve says, 'they'll still be sweeping him up out of the furnace. You know what Pete was like for finding his way into *crevices*.'

Steve takes great pleasure in putting an unwholesome emphasis on this word, distracting Devon from the contents of the bag. The two glare at each other and I feel the need to step in.

'Not today,' I tell them. 'Not in front of his daughter.'

'I'm sure she's fully aware of her father's lax attitude to monogamy.'

'She might well be, Steve, but I hardly think she needs reminding of it.'

'Yeah, and people in glass houses, you know what I mean?'

Steve ignores Devon and leans forward, his elbows resting only briefly on the wet table. 'Do you think he was worth much at the end, financially?'

'Not everything comes down to money, man. I'd have been perfectly happy to have spent my life behind a drumkit for no more than I'm earning now.'

They lock eyes again, each daring the other to take it further. If this is what they're like before a drink, I dread to think how they'll be after three or four.

'I doubt the crem' would've put him in a biscuit tin, mate,' I offer, hoping to defuse the tension.

'You say that, but maybe it was part of his wishes. Wouldn't be the most unpredictable thing he'd ever done, would it? Remember the letter?'

'What letter?' I ask.

'You must remember the letter.'

I shake my head and Devon continues. 'We were all out one day, on Deansgate or wherever, and this guy comes running down the street holding an envelope. He gets near us, and Pete rips it out of his hand and starts off up the road.'

'That rings a bell, actually,' says Steve.

It starts to come back to me.

A warm nineties afternoon, pavements full of people and this bloke with his urgent message rushing to get through, trying to make the last post and then having to chase our singer off into the distance. Moran had returned soon after with a big grin on his face.

'What was it he said when he came back?' Steve asks.

'That he didn't know what the hurry was,' Devon replies, 'there was only a second-class stamp on it.'

Steve laughs. 'Yes, that was it. Good stuff.'

Lauren signals from the bar with a couple of pint pots and Devon moves to stand up. 'You might think it was funny, Steve,' he says, 'but I thought it was pretty snide.'

He heads over to help Lauren, and Steve gives me a shrug before his jacket begins to buzz. Out comes his mobile and after checking the screen, he ignores the call and puts the device back where it came from.

'Work,' Steve says, and I give a nod. The pair of us sit alone. I don't know what to say to him. I don't *know* him. Even back then, I didn't. Not really.

We came from different schools and though both of us went to Eccles College we didn't share any classes; his being more business oriented while mine were art related. Had it not been for the band, we might never have met and once it was all over there was nothing to keep us in the same orbit. After he left for university, I hadn't seen him again until this morning.

Lauren and Devon return with the drinks. Four pints of some dark ale.

'We should have a toast,' I suggest, and lift my drink.

'Yeah,' Lauren says. 'To my dad.'

'To Pete,' the three surviving members of Incendiary Tract say as one, clinking our drinks and taking a mouthful. With our glasses back on the table, there's silence.

Whatever Lauren intends for this reunion, she's in no hurry to share, and the obvious question for us to ask would be about Kelly, but no one appears ready to broach that subject. I settle for small talk and ask Lauren if she still lives in the town where we all grew up.

'Nah, I left Swinton a while back. I've been in Levenshulme for a few years now, sharing a house with some friends. It's nice. There's plenty of people I know round there, and Piccadilly is literally one stop on the train. Where do you live, Jim? Or do you prefer James?'

'Jim's fine,' I tell her. 'I've not been James for a long time. I'm in Chorlton.'

'I'd love to live in Chorlton, like,' she says, 'but the rents are so expensive.'

'I know. We were lucky when we bought ours.'

I say luck, but that doesn't really cover it. I'd met Katie in the mid-nineties, and we were renting for a long while. Then her mum died and when grief and legalities had calmed, we used what she'd been left to buy a place in Chorlton. It was in our price range because it needed a ton of work. We don't owe much on the mortgage now as when my dad passed and his house was sold, we paid most of it off. So, like I say, luck is probably a bit strong.

'What about you, Devon?' Lauren asks. 'Are you still in Swinton?'

'Nah, but I've not strayed far, we're up Clifton way.'

'I haven't been to Clifton in ages,' she says.

'Jim hasn't, either.'

'It's a bugger to get to from mine, as you well know, mate.' My being reliant on public transport means that the two of us would always split the difference and meet up in town. Learning to drive was on a list that included sorting out my eyesight. It was a list that seemed to constantly be getting mislaid, possibly because of my eyesight.

I try and deflect the conversation away from me and on to Steve. 'You're heading back to Euston? Are you down south, then?'

'Yeah, man,' Devon adds. 'We haven't seen you round these parts in forever.'

Steve lifts his glass to take a drink, only to put it down again. 'Yes, well, by the time I graduated my father had got rid of the business and he and my mother moved to Spain.'

A larger company had bought Williamson Building Supplies and then closed the premises some years later. The land had been sold on for a tidy profit and was now home to half a dozen detached houses.

'There was no reason for me to come back up to be honest, so I took a job in London and ended up settling down there. We've been in Twickenham for a while now.'

'And are they still in Spain, your folks?' I ask.

Steve considers his pint. 'No. they live just down the road from us, now.'

He doesn't appear best pleased with this, and Lauren seems about to speak when Devon is hit with sudden inspiration.

'What was it your dad said in an interview once?' he asks her. 'About why he never moved to London?'

I don't recall the interview he means, so I'm not sure where he's going with this, but suspect it'll end in a dig at Steve.

Lauren pauses to remember, her previous thought lost. 'It was something about how he was suspicious of those who disappeared off to The Smoke at the first sign of success. Like they were fleeing the scene of a horrific crime.'

'That's it,' Devon says, clearly aware all along. 'He said they should have their back gardens dug up in search of missing persons.'

As Devon relays this, his attention is fixed on Steve's face. Again, I redirect the subject. 'What line of work are you in then, Steve?'

'Finance.'

I give this another nod. 'I don't really understand finance.'

'Few people do,' he says, 'which is probably just as well.'

'What do you do, Devon?' Lauren asks.

'Plumbing. Went straight from school into an apprenticeship. This was long before it became the next big thing and every man and his dog decided to take a punt on it, you know what I mean.'

'I'm sure there's more than enough U-bends to go round, mate,' I say.

Devon smiles 'That's pretty good, man. We actually have a saying in the business, "U-bends, they're like arseholes. Everyone's got one."'

'I think you'll find that's opinions,' Steve points out.

'And I think *you'll* find it works for both.'

Lauren glances at me, perhaps worried at what she's got herself into and I shrug comically, trying to make light of the situation. Before the pair can continue their argument, she asks me what I do for a living.

'I work in a warehouse. Not far from here, actually.'

'What sort of stuff is it?' she adds.

I pause and wonder how best to account for over half my life. 'Shifting things about, mainly. Point A to Point B. I mean, box them up, slap a label on and fill out a form. Get them ready to be shipped off wherever.' The next morning, of course, it would be as if the whole operation had been magically reset to its original position ready to begin all over again. It was like that tale about the Greek fella pushing a boulder up a hill, only with less mythic undertones and more Personal Protective Equipment. Not that I do much of the shifting about these days, what with my back.

'You should be running that place by now,' Devon says.

Maybe he's right, maybe I should. My quarter of a century mark is only months away and yet when I started, I never thought I'd be there for even a tenth of that. But before I realised it, I'd been there so long the thought of doing something else never occurred to me. Until, last week, that is. I ask Lauren what she does.

'Photography. I'm lucky because I don't really think of it as work, like.' The curious second shape in her bag now becomes recognisable as a camera. 'It's mostly music related. Though, sometimes I'll do other assignments, weddings and that, for the extra cash. But I prefer gigs, promos, album artwork, that kind of thing. I've done bits for local bands and others passing through on tour.'

'Anyone we'd have heard of?'

'Brown Brogues, Girls Names, Protomartyr, PINS.'

It's a list which sounds more like random words thrown together in some form of abstract stream of consciousness poetry. A breathless Patti Smith Greenwich Village café ramble.

'Are you making those up?' I reply, only half-jokingly and cause Devon to laugh.

'Jim, man,' he says. 'You're so out of touch, aren't you?'

It's true. My finger is hardly on the pulse when it comes to new music. If anything, I live a couple of doors down from the pulse and yet my single reason to knock on would be to ask them to keep the noise down. It might be easier than ever to keep up with the latest releases, but I always find myself slipping backwards into the comfort of the same dozen or so albums.

Lauren and Devon continue to discuss her photography. 'Have you done any of your dad?' he asks.

'Yeah, last year I took a few of him round town. They ended up in the paper.'

'I saw them,' Devon says. 'They were really good.'

'The ones in the *Evening News*?' I ask.

It'd been a double-page spread on Moran's two-plus decades in the business. An interview to coincide with what would turn out to be his final album alongside moody black and white shots of him around Manchester:

Moran sitting on the wall of a building site on Great Ancoats Street. Hands deep in his pockets, collar turned up against the elements, huddling into a vintage army jacket.

Moran on a bench next to the Alan Turing statue in Sackville Park, asking the mathematician for a bite of his apple.

Moran in Piccadilly Gardens, balancing on Queen Victoria's knee, his left arm trapping the doughy monarch in a headlock.

'It was a really fun day.' Lauren smiles and I finally see something of Moran in her, his infectious grin. 'Just me and him, like, mooching around with a camera and him telling stories, pointing things out to me. Places he'd been to when he was my age that were no longer there. We literally kept bumping into people he knew and people he didn't, who just wanted to say hello. It was one of the better times.'

The smile fades and her eyes move to the bag at her feet. I know how hard it can be to lose a parent unexpectedly. My old man hung on for six grim months after his cancer diagnosis, but my mum's passing was a complete shock. I was in my early teens at the time and mortality wasn't a concept I'd thought much about. I look over at Lauren and find myself conflicted. As much sympathy as I have for this young woman, I can't help but be suspicious of what this day holds for the rest of us.

13

*You know what, I actually quite like London.
No, really, I do. I just think it's a shame the universe saw fit to waste it on all them bloody southerners.*

Pete Moran, 2001

During our short time in the Three Jolly Bargemen, customers and staff have offered condolences for Lauren's late father. A hand on the shoulder and comforting words from the women, a nod and raising of glasses from the gents, and each caring soul casting a suspicious glance at the trio of middle-aged blokes sitting with her. The landlady's dog, roving between furniture, seems particularly distrustful. If any of us had thought it might feel awkward for a young woman to be drinking with men she doesn't know, the situation has been well and truly reversed.

Moran was clearly much loved here, and I can imagine him getting up on the karaoke to bang out his own version of anything from Iggy to Ziggy, from Screamin' Jay Hawkins to Screaming Lord Sutch.

Today the machine is silent. As a mark of respect, its microphone rests at half-mast. Though, judging by the amount of brown tape holding the thing together, there might just be a problem with the stand.

Lauren excuses herself to go and speak with a few of the regulars and Steve waits until she's a safe distance away to lean in close. 'I take it you've both seen *An American Werewolf in London?*'

'It's not that bad,' I tell him, and it isn't. The Bargeman is not The Slaughtered Lamb, an inn on the Yorkshire Moors the unsuspecting backpackers stumble into. We may have drawn a few curious stares from the locals, but at least all life and chatter didn't grind to a halt the moment we entered. Nor have we received veiled threats about what awaits us when we leave.

'Oh, isn't it?' Steve asks. 'Have you seen their dog?' The German Shepherd has made several laps of the area around us, taking a close interest in Steve. 'That thing looks as if it hasn't had a decent meal since Adam was a lad. If it starts sniffing anywhere it shouldn't, I'm out of here.'

'Nah,' Devon says. 'It's alright this place. There's even an old geezer over there with the same waistcoat on as you.'

Our former guitarist doesn't even bother to turn and check whether this is true, choosing instead to limit his movement to an adjustment of his cuffs.

'To be honest, I doubt very much anyone in here shops at Armani.'

Devon isn't impressed with Steve's choice of designer outlet. 'I bet you've got one of those waxed jackets that all the twats wear, you know what I mean?'

'The urban farmer look?' I suggest.

'Urban wanker, more like.'

Before this argument can escalate, Lauren is back and the table quiet, once again. Steve checks his sizeable timepiece, watching the seconds slowly tick by before Devon finally takes the plunge.

'Pass on our respects to your mum, won't you,' he tells Lauren. 'How's she doing, by the way?'

This isn't a question Lauren seems ready to answer and she takes a mouthful of ale before she starts.

'I dunno, really. I stayed over at hers the other night, but she barely came out of her room. I heard her talking on the phone, like, telling some friend of hers how glad she was my dad was finally out of her life. But then five minutes later, she was in tears. I tried to speak to her, but she wouldn't let me in.'

'They weren't still together, then?' Devon asks.

'Nah, they'd not lived under the same roof for years. Not properly, anyway. My mam and dad had a strange relationship.' Lauren's attention moves to her half-empty glass. 'I got out literally the first chance that came along and went to study up in Edinburgh. They kept telling me I was the first Moran or Lewis to go to university. They were so proud, the pair of them.'

Her focus leaves the pint pot for a moment, to look around the room, whether hoping to see her father somewhere or just giving herself time to say what she needs. If her smile is

Moran's, then her eyes are pure Kelly. So dark it's a struggle to identify where the iris ends, and her pupil begins.

'I dunno if they expected me to move back in when I graduated, but I couldn't. I dreaded the end of every term. I'd stay with friends or my grandparents, my mam's folks. When they realised I wasn't coming home after my course was finished, that's when they started living apart. Dad moved out and bought a house a few streets away. I always thought they'd get divorced, like, that seemed the next step, but they never did. Every so often they'd find their way back to one another, but it'd never last. They'd wind up at each other's throats and split again. That just made it all the worse.'

Our attention is distracted by a throaty laugh from the far corner, the sort of sound effect right at home in an '80s horror, but which soon subsides allowing Lauren to continue.

'Me and my dad got close again in the last few years. He'd come to see gigs with me and gave me a key to his house, told me that I was always welcome, but to make sure I called beforehand. I knew what that meant. To give any "guests" time to be long gone when I arrived. I dunno why he bothered, like, it wasn't as if I was a kid, anymore. I'd no illusions we'd all live happily ever after.'

For a second or two she stops and takes a heavy breath, as if the air around her has become thick and she's having to swallow it down.

'I'd arranged to head over to his in Swinton, then I was gonna see my mam when she'd finished work. I called his landline to let him know I was on my way, but it just kept going to the answer phone. I thought it was a bit odd, but nothing more.

Maybe he'd had a late one and was still asleep. He didn't have that many reasons to get up early, he was always more of a night person. He might've stayed over somewhere else or just nipped out to the shops and got waylaid in conversation, he'd talk to anyone.

'He never had a mobile I could call him on, always refused to have one. Said they blunted his creative flow, like, and infringed on his right to peace and quiet. Anyway, I had these prints he wanted to see, another load of pictures I'd taken of him. One of them I'd had framed, as a surprise for him. I phoned, again, but there was no answer, so I just went over.'

The sounds from the rest of the pub carry on in the background but have faded to almost nothing as we listen to her speak.

'I tried the doorbell, heard it ringing, but that was it. There was no sound from inside. Except Bowie, his cat, meowing. I shouted through the letterbox, but still heard nothing, so let myself in.'

As Lauren talks, she stares at the drink on the table as if the scene she's describing is playing out inside the glass and she's re-watching the whole thing through the numbing prism of alcohol.

'I went into the front room and his record player was still on, just spinning and spinning, but with no music playing. I turned it off and followed the sound of Bowie into the kitchen. I...'

Her voice breaks and so does whatever dam has been holding her emotions back. As the words had poured out once she finally began to talk, so now do the tears. Steve, the closest to her, puts his arm around Lauren and she sobs onto his shoulder.

*

It's a while before she's ready to talk again and in the meantime, Devon nips out for a smoke and then goes to the bar. Soon there's a fresh round in front of us and we pick up where Lauren left off.

'I didn't know what to do,' she says. 'I couldn't get through to my mam at work, like, so I called Uncle Rob. He came round and took care of everything. I just literally sat on the floor with Bowie, crying.'

For as long as I'd known Moran, he'd always had a cat called Bowie. Surely, this couldn't be the same one. Back in our teens it'd been a ginger tomcat, hair the colour of Thomas Jerome Newton's in *The Man Who Fell to Earth.* Over the years it must've reinvented itself, like the singer it was named for.

Was it now a black and white feline working its way through a Thin White Duke phase? Maybe a blonde beast with a spiky mullet, inspired by Jareth the Goblin King from *Labyrinth* or an incident involving a plug socket and its paw.

'The next day,' Lauren continues, 'I went back to Swinton to get some things, cat food and the like, I'd taken Bowie with me to Levy. I was packing up some bits and that's when I saw this next to the record player.'

She leans down to her bag and extracts the biscuit tin, placing it on the table as we move our drinks aside to make room.

'There was an empty sleeve on top of it, so I took the record off the turntable and there was my dad's handwriting.'

The tin opens with a metallic 'pop' and she lifts out a plain paper sleeve, musty with age. Inside is a seven-inch record, at its centre is a white label and, in red biro, Moran's familiar spidery scrawl noting four words and a date:

Incendiary Tract, Spirit Studios. 11/12/92

A long-ago December day and our lone visit to a professional recording environment. As far as I knew the only thing that morning had produced, apart from a good deal of animosity, was a demo tape. But, here in Lauren's hands, is an actual record under our name.

She passes it to me, and I carefully remove this strange artefact from its sleeve. I turn the vinyl over and notice the other side is untouched. A smooth, shiny black abyss, a pool of water under a night sky and my own reflection gazing up at me. Except, it's the youthful me, James Edwards, staring back: healthier hairline, but spottier chin.

I flip the image away, returning to the A-side and the grooves which hold a song I've not heard in thirty years. A song we'd not even been able to agree on a title for and one I've no wish to hear again anytime soon. If I could cross my fingers at this moment, I would do, in the hope Lauren hasn't had time to convert it to mp3 and stored the track on her phone, waiting to be played.

With the record held up to the light, I tilt it in my hands, searching for some other mark or inscription, a clue as to its provenance. Matrix number. Engineer's initials. Cryptic words carved around the middle. I find nothing. It's as empty as the B-side. There's no indication when or why Moran had our demo pressed onto a 45.

I pass it to Devon and then try to imagine Moran sat in his armchair listening, tapping on the armrests, his feet pumping on the floor. Maybe even singing over the top of his teenage self. Then, rising from his seat to start it up once more, and walking into the kitchen to get a can from the fridge or bowl of food for Bowie, only to suffer a fatal heart attack. The turntable continuing to spin, but his song at an end. Dust accumulating behind the needle with each revolution, accentuating the dull thud of its endless cycle in the run-out groove.

'I never thought about it for a couple of days,' Lauren says. 'Then I literally couldn't sleep one night so I decided to listen to it. I'd brought the tin home with me, like. I dunno why, it just seemed something I should do, that's all. I sat in front of my record player with my headphones and heard my dad again.'

She swallows and I think she might break down once more, but she takes a second and continues.

'I went online and Googled Incendiary Tract but couldn't find a single thing. There was nothing about any band with that name. No information linked with my dad. So, I asked my mam. She told me to forget all about it and took to her bed. I asked my Uncle Rob, and he said I should speak to you three.'

I glance over at my former bandmates to find Devon hiding behind his pint pot and Steve a little too focused on the 45 in his hands. It appears I've been put forward as our group's official spokesperson.

'And your dad never mentioned it?' I ask.

'Not a word, like. A week ago, I never knew the tin, or the record, existed.'

I clear my throat. 'And what is it you want to know?'

Lauren fixes me with her mother's coal-black eyes and answers, 'Everything.'

14

Wednesday 21st August 1991

I snapped awake and stared up at the ceiling, sensing immediately something was wrong. It was the cracks. Those on my ceiling I could trace like familiar streets on a local map, but these were different. These were someone else's cracks. This was not my room. I hoped the sensations in my body were also not mine.

There was an aching in my brain and a burning in my throat. I wanted to take liquid on board while also feeling the urge to expel it. My bladder was full and my stomach empty, and the movements required to remedy either were far beyond my current capabilities. All I could do was lie still, as would the victim of a horrendous accident, fearful of the slightest activity and the irrevocable damage which might ensue.

It took a while before I felt safe enough to twist my head and survey my surroundings. I was on a single bed with a matching twin pushed against the opposing wall. In between was a no-man's land of clothes and records, discarded trainers and tapes.

Enlightenment hit me; this room belonged to the Moran brothers.

I had been to their home, a two-up, two-down semi just off the East Lancs Road, on many occasions, but this was the first time I had stayed over. Rob was at his girlfriend's while her parents were away on holiday, leaving his bed free for me to crash in. Pete was nowhere to be seen but from the banging of utensils and burning smell wafting up the stairs, I knew he could not be far away. In his absence, I attempted to piece together the previous evening.

We had had tickets to a gig – my first, The Fall at the Ritz – only my dad was none too keen on me venturing into town at night. As the lone parent of a young lad, he worried. I was just sixteen and the regular bouts of gang violence that made the news – causing the Haçienda to close its doors earlier in the year – had been enough to mark the city as off limits after dark.

Determined to defy my old man, I had been forced to engage in teenage subterfuge and told him I would be round at the Moran's and might end up staying overnight. With my alibi squared, Pete and I journeyed into town.

The hours prior to the gig had been spent perched on a lock at the rear of Whitworth Street, along the tow path of the Rochdale Canal, the unseen snake which follows you through Manchester like a threat. Slithering in the shadows behind buildings, mostly out of sight though never far away.

We passed a fat bottle of cheap cider between us. Still some years away from becoming a seasoned drinker, I was largely sceptical of alcohol. I welcomed the strange feeling it gave me but winced at the cloying taste. Not that this had stopped me from drinking enough that by the time we had queued up and made our way inside the venue I was forced to veer off hastily in the direction of the gents.

Tuesdays at the Ritz were known to many as "grab a granny" night, but the only thing I could recall getting my hands on were the porcelain curves of a lavatory bowl. My inaugural experience of live music and I did not witness The Fall play even a single song. I had already had more than my share of 'White Lightning' and the only 'A Lot of Wind' I heard had come from the neighbouring traps. How Pete and I had made it home to Swinton afterwards was a blank.

It was mid-morning when I woke and Mr and Mrs Moran were both out: the former at work, the latter at the laundrette. Only Pete's cat was present. Bowie inclined his ginger head in the doorway, taking a long look at me, and weighing whether I was edible or willing to indulge him in some other way. Upon deciding I was neither, he turned tail and stalked off.

The clatter from the kitchen subsided and was replaced by footsteps on the stairs. Pete entered the bedroom with a cup of tea and a bacon butty, or an approximation of one, at least. The bread was badly scorched, the meat inside overdone beyond reason. It looked less like breakfast and more an attempt to destroy incriminating evidence. The snack may not have looked all that appetising but given my current state I thought it a kind gesture nonetheless, until I realised neither it nor the hot beverage were intended for me.

Pete left them on a table just inside the room and disappeared again. I considered dragging myself across the carpet in their direction, but given the debris and obstacles on the floor, I stayed under the sheets. From the bathroom next door, I could hear Pete singing.

'Here comes the…' his voice was then lost in a stream of piss ripping through water, the sound of paper being slowly torn.

A flush of the toilet and blast from the taps was followed by Pete walking back into the room wiping his hands on his jeans. Without a word, he lifted up a corner of the mattress I was sprawled atop and pulled out a handful of his elder brother's "specialist publications". Pete returned to his cup and plate and sat cross legged on the floor. He was barefoot and wore a white Happy Mondays T-shirt and scruffy blue jeans.

Leaning to his right, he pressed play on a nearby cassette deck and the music was on us in a flash, as if flicking a switch and filling the room suddenly with light. The air was charged with a driving, insistent rhythm, a train rattling right past the house. Any chance of further sleep was beyond me.

Pete hummed along with the track, 'Run Run Run', between mouthfuls while ogling pages of the magazine in his lap. He paused only to join in with the chorus, '…take a jacket too.'

As my brain was not yet at full capacity, it took an extra moment to process his words. My first thought being, deep as I was in the fog of a hangover, I had simply misheard him. Only when he repeated the line again did I realise something was amiss.

Earlier in the year, over in Walkden at the Unit Four Cinema, a rundown establishment known locally as "the flea pit" we had been introduced to 'Heroin'. Not the drug, but the Velvet Underground song.

Pete and I had gone to watch Oliver Stone's *The Doors* – it was rated 18, but Pete had managed to charm our way in – and at the point Jim Morrison first encountered Andy Warhol, a scene which played out to the strains of John Cale's incessant, frenzied viola and Lou Reed's anguished vocals, we were hooked.

Yet sourcing such contraband was not easy. Beyond the knowledge of Pete's brother and my cousin, there was no one locally to supply us with these things. We had to find them ourselves, following breadcrumb trails left for the curious.

From The Doors to Aldous Huxley, from Huxley to William Blake. From sneaking in to catch another film, *The Silence of the Lambs,* to *Manhunter* on VHS to the novel *Red Dragon* to Blake, once more. We would uncover such secrets then trade them with the like-minded.

For 'Heroin' it was a case of waiting in our seats after everyone else had left until the credits finally rolled around to the soundtrack information. The usher had given us dirty looks, clearly this was a habit he did not look kindly upon.

The following week, we had spent our Saturday marching up to a succession of music shop counters enquiring loudly as to whether they had 'Heroin' to sell or where we might find the Velvet Underground. While some staff had been mildly amused by us, others marked us down as a pair of timewasters and told us to bugger off. Eventually, we returned to Swinton with the band's iconic banana covered debut album and it had become a staple in our musical rotation. So, I knew the number Pete was singing along with and was sure his interpretation was wrong.

'Those aren't the lyrics,' I said in a voice low and rough. My vision was still on the cracks in the ceiling as I lay flat on his brother's bed. Upright being a position I was unwilling to consider at that point.

'What's that, cock?'

'I said, those aren't the right words.'

'Well, it's what I hear, you know.'

As defences went, it was a strong one. I could hardly prove otherwise but felt compelled to try. 'No fucking way,' being the gist of my argument.

'We'll have to agree to disagree, cock,' Pete said, as the riff chugged away in the background.

'Bollocks,' was my learned reply. 'I refuse to believe the man who asked the world to 'Walk on the Wild Side' would also remind it to bring a fucking anorak.'

'It's a completely different song.'

'I know it's a completely different song, mate, but this is Lou Reed we're talking about, not your mum.'

That Pete was winding me up, there was no doubt. It was a chance to get his own back on me after the state I had ended up in the previous night. Somehow, he had got us back to Swinton, although I still could not recall any of it.

'Just shut the fuck up, and eat your butty,' I told him. 'Let me sleep.'

Pete turned the music off and all was quiet. I leant back on the pillow and closed my eyes in silence. Glorious silence. Then, CRUNCH. CRUNCH, CRUNCH, CRUNCH.

It sounded like footsteps on a gravel path. Only, the Morans had no gravel path and neither did their near neighbours. I looked towards Pete and saw that each violent interruption matched a bite of his charred breakfast, soon to be joined by an exaggerated slurping of tea and rustling of glossy pages. Sleep was, once more, out of reach.

I searched around for distraction and, with any luck, sustenance. A couple of recent issues of the *New Musical Express* and *Melody Maker* stuck out from Rob's bedside table, but I had already read both and saved myself the money it would have cost to buy them into the bargain.

I had a part-time job making deliveries for the local newsagent who was always highly impressed by my work ethic. I would turn up early every morning and be out of the shop before the other kids had even arrived. Most days those on my route would receive their papers well in advance of other streets. Most days, that is, apart from the ones when I would park myself and my BMX up in a quiet spot and leaf through someone else's copies of the music weeklies.

Pete had a similar perk at the pub where he was a pot collector, a pub where his dad was a semi-permanent fixture. Pete hoovered up any dregs left in the glasses before he took them back to the bar, always finishing his shift in a better mood and with a redder face than he had begun it.

Having briefly drifted off into my own world, it took me a while to notice the complete absence of sound in the room. The chorus of crunching, slurping and rustling had come to a halt. I glanced over to Pete and saw him staring back at me.

'Can I ask you a question?' he said.

I toyed with the idea of taking his request seriously for maybe half a second. 'Isn't that a question in itself?'

'The General strikes again.'

Pete had recently christened me General Smart Arse, for obvious reasons, and on our mental scoreboard, I chalked up my opening point of the day.

'Ok,' I said, 'but this question has to make more sense than the conversation we've just had.

He agreed and moved forward with his enquiry.

'What do you think Crystal here wanted to be when she was our age?'

Crystal, it transpired once Pete held up the porno he had been leafing through, was that month's centrefold. Not being the sort of query I was braced for, I thought this might be another joke at my expense. If Pete was ever taking the piss, he could never look you in the eye as he did so. All through our previous exchange his focus had been glued to the magazine, but now he and Crystal watched me awaiting a reply.

I gazed at the redhead and the eroticised medical outfit struggling to contain her. It was skin-tight and rubber and ill-advised for anyone employed in the cardiology department.

'A nurse?' was the best I could croak. I needed water and something stodgy, not a curious line of interrogation.

'Nice one, cock. Nice one.'

We had been friends for a while, so I was accustomed to Pete's use of "cock" as an extreme form of punctuation, yet I was not sure whether he added a point to his own cerebral total every time he said the word without being pulled up on it. If he did, I was trailing woefully behind, and it was not even dinnertime.

He put the dirty mag down on the floor but was not finished talking. 'Do you think this is what she imagined for herself, though?'

'Crystal?'

'Yeah, Crystal.'

'Being wanked over by teenagers?'

'Yeah.'

'I really couldn't say, mate.' The conversation was becoming more philosophical than my booze-addled mind could deal with.

'I look at our old man, you see.'

'What?' I interrupted, 'when you're having a wank?' It was another cheap score for me, but they all count.

'I look at our old man and when he finishes work, he comes home and has a can. Every night, a can. He walks in the door and our mam will go to talk to him, "not before I've had a can, love", he'll tell her. Me or our kid will try to ask him something, "not before I've had a can, son". He'll sit in his chair, and stare at the TV set, which might not even be switched on and he'll drink a can.'

While Pete was talking, I moved back up onto my elbows to listen. I recognised his tale or the basic theme of it. My dad would do something similar. After my mum passed away it was just the two of us at home, and when he finished his shift, if he knew I may not be in, that I might be round at a friend's or elsewhere, he would stop off for a pint or two at a pub in Salford. I put this down to him not wanting to come home to an empty house.

When it came to work, our fathers were in similar positions. My dad had neither career nor vocation. He had left school without qualifications and come of age in an era when you could walk out of a job in the morning and into another by the afternoon. He had done a bit of everything.

Pete's dad though had been a miner up at Agecroft Colliery for most of his life until the place closed last year. After six months with no work, he was with a firm on the other side of the city. A new starter in his mid-forties. But with unemployment on the rise, and him the last in, he would also be first out when the axe came down. Both our fathers had spent time on the dole, and neither found it the leisure-filled utopia many made it out to be.

Pete held up the porno, again. 'Do you think she has a can after work?'

Looking at the model in her nurse's outfit I shrugged and went for the lazy comic answer. 'I hope she doesn't have one before, that'd be malpractice.'

'Nice one. Tell me, General, have you ever thought of a career in comedy? Because I wouldn't bother If I were you.' He paused to devour a further bite of his butty and then went on. 'What have you thought of?'

'What do you mean?' I asked.

'You know, as a job?'

We were done with school and had picked up our GCSE results only a few weeks earlier. The next step of our education was ahead of us. Two years at Eccles College. But what did I want to do after that? I had no clue.

I was sixteen and had never left mainland Britain, had rarely even left Greater Manchester. I knew nothing about pretty much everything. Though here I was, at a crossroads being asked to make a choice that would define the rest of my life. My paper round was enjoyable, but I could hardly do that until I retired. The only other taste of employment I had had was a two-week slice of work experience at a factory during our final year at Moorside High and the main thing I took from that was how much I loved a subsidised canteen.

I was not old enough to drink – legally that is. I was not old enough to vote or be in charge of a motor vehicle. But I was deemed qualified to make such a momentous decision about my future.

'I haven't really thought about it,' I told Pete.

'But what've you picked for A-Levels?'

'Art, English and Design Communication.'

'And would you want to be one of those? An artist? A writer? Do you wish to communicate with people?'

'I'd like to communicate with Crystal.' I had lost track of the score between us, but surely, I must have been back level by now.

Pete stared at me, an expression of mild boredom on his face as he waited for a sensible answer. In the little over a year we had known each other, I had never seen him be this serious for quite so long.

'I honestly dunno, mate,' I said, leaning back to look once again at the cracked ceiling above. I thought of those I admired and would want to emulate. The posters on my walls at home, the singers and bands, the sports stars and, at one stage, even the Pope. Why he was up there, I could not tell you. Maybe it was the Beatles-like adulation he could inspire or, more likely, his big hat.

None of my relatives were writers or artists. Nor were any of the parents at our school or anyone living in the terraced houses down our street. I could not recall a careers officer mentioning opportunities to write novels, paint idyllic scenes and portraits or even fill the post of God's envoy on earth. Never for a minute did I think I might one day be Supreme Pontiff or the next Charles Dickens.

Maybe I lacked imagination.

Maybe I lacked faith.

I had no belief in either myself or some all-knowing, all-powerful other.

'Do you think you'd enjoy being an artist or a writer?' Pete said.

'Are you supposed to enjoy work?' I replied, and thought of our parents, those living and passed on. Did their jobs fulfil them, or simply pay the bills?

'Maybe not, but wouldn't you like to do something you *did* enjoy?'

'Like what?'

'Like music.'

'What do you mean, music?'

I raised myself to lean against the wall and stare at Pete. The dirty magazine was shut and under the empty plate and mug by his side.

'Just that,' he said. 'I think we should start a band.'

'But we can't play.'

'How do you know? Have you ever tried?'

He had me there. I had never even touched a guitar let alone attempted to play one. 'But we haven't got any instruments.'

'We'll get some. We've got birthdays coming up and Christmas isn't that far away. Plus, we can pool your paper round money and mine from the pub.'

Laid out in simple terms, it began to sound possible. I loved music, why would I not want to create my own?

'What would you play?' I asked Pete.

'I wouldn't, I'll be the singer.'

I guffawed at this and ended up in a coughing fit which hurt my parched throat with each hacking bark. 'You can't sing,' I managed, eventually.

'How do you know I can't sing?'

'Because I've heard you, that's how.'

'When?'

'When you were having a slash.'

Some folk sing in the shower, others while driving a car. Pete liked to sing while he urinated. His songs of choice always contained passing references to water, such as The Stone Roses' 'Waterfall', or in the case of Patti Smith's 'Pissing in a River', references to passing water. The lyrics to all of them he would twist to his own lowbrow ends so that at times they would be impossible to recognise.

'I've no idea what you're talking about, cock.' His attention flicked away, his small mouth doing its best to contain a grin.

'You do it all the time,' I said.

'Are you taking the piss?'

'No, *you* were taking the piss.'

'I've warned you about that, General. Stop trying to be funny, it doesn't suit you. Anyhow, you don't need to be able to sing to be in a band, you know. Does anyone we listen to sound like fucking Sinatra?'

'I think it's pronounced Frank.' I replied before narrowly avoiding the training shoe which bounced off the wall behind me.

Pete was right. None of the vocalists we liked had what you might describe as traditional voices. I thought about this idea. Could it work? Was it really as simple as he made it out to be?

'But there's only two of us,' I said. 'We can't be a duo.'

A smile began to spread across Pete's face, and he sat back, hands behind his head. 'Don't you worry, cock, there'll be others.'

15

*I only really got into Dylan when I discovered his needlework.
The protest stuff I could take or leave. The Travelling
Wilburys, no ta. It was his needlework I liked.
His needlework.
You're unfamiliar with his needlework?
Do I need to explain just what it is, Mr Jones?
Whatever, cock. It's the works... Bob Dylan... used... to needle
people... with.*

Pete Moran, 2002

I relay the story of Incendiary Tract's beginnings to Moran's daughter without mentioning nurse Crystal's aspirations or my own immature point-scoring.

'Did you never want to be the frontman?' Lauren asks me.

'No chance. I don't want to be in the spotlight. Give me the shadows, any day. I mean, writing was my thing, the lyrics and that. I'd no interest in singing them. Your dad, though, loved the attention. He was a natural performer.'

'Well, I'm not,' she says. 'I'm really camera shy. I like being on the other side of the lens, capturing a moment, like. The fraction of a second that might be otherwise lost. How come you chose the bass, why not guitar?'

'We knew finding a bassist and drummer would be more difficult and a bass was a lot cheaper than a full kit, so I went with that. Guitarists are ten a penny. Plus, you have to be a show-off. Don't you, Steve?'

'Blame Hendrix and Van Halen,' he says looking almost relaxed now, upper body curving forward over his nearly empty glass having finally discovered a taste for the ale.

'So, how did you two come to join? Did you all know each other already?' Lauren asks, glancing to Devon and Steve.

I think back to the time when Incendiary Tract had been a duo searching for our missing counterparts and trying to get the idea to take flight. While just between the two of us, it'd still felt like a daydream as opposed to reality. We put up notices wherever we could, a card in the window of the newsagents where I worked – a prime spot secured at favourable discount – and having begun our studies at Eccles College, hand-written posters were pinned up around the corridors, sheets of A4 which might survive a day or two before they were torn down.

There'd be occasions when Moran should've been in class but spent his time following the caretaker instead, watching him rip away our advertisements and then walk off, leaving Pete to put up another in the exact same place.

Devon takes up the story. 'I heard a whisper that a couple of lads were putting a band together. I never knew your dad or Jim before that. We were the same age but went to different schools. They'd gone to Moorside, I went to Ambrose Barlow. Anyhow, we had a friend in common who passed along my number. I'd not had my drums all that long, really, bought them with money I'd earned over the summer. I wanted something I could make a bit of noise with in the garage.'

'And your parents didn't mind?' Lauren asks.

'As long as the only headache I gave them was from my playing, they were fine with it. Though I think they'd liked me to have played a different kind of music. Our house was full of Motown and reggae, and my sister was into her pop. I could knock out that sort of stuff, a bit of the Funk Brothers for my mum or give my dad a version of 'I Shot the Sheriff' to keep them sweet, but I prefer my music loud and fast.'

We'd called Devon up to discuss the various bands and albums we were into and what kind of style we were going for, had even played the Stooges to him over the phone and asked if he could play like that. He said he'd give it a try and we arranged to head over and hear him play.

The Bradshaws lived not far from Swinton precinct on a cul-de-sac where his mum Kath had opened the door and then directed us to their garage toward the sound of an energetic beat. Our first glimpse of Devon was him sat behind his drumkit, still in overalls. A kid our age but straight from work, and, with his shaven copper brown head, one of the few Swinton residents who wasn't white.

That day we'd watched Devon go at his drums with enough verve and intensity to impress us, not that it'd taken much to do that back then. Moran was not exactly a singer and I certainly wasn't a virtuoso. It was more about Devon as a person and how he fitted in with our plans. He was easy-going, liked a laugh and, much like me, had no interest in usurping Moran's role as self-appointed leader. Devon loved music and just wanted to play. He didn't seem too arsed about anything else and so we'd found our drummer.

'What about you, Steve?' Lauren asks.

'I'm afraid, that was more complicated,' Steve begins to explain while Devon hides a growing smirk behind his pint. 'There was a poster on the board at college that said, "guitarist wanted", so I copied down the details. But when I rang later, this gruff gentleman on the other end informed me it was all part of some hoax, and I wasn't to call again.'

'That was your grandad Martin,' I tell Lauren.

'It certainly sounds like him,' she says. 'I don't think he ever saw music as a real job for my dad, even after he'd been on *Top of the Pops*. So, what happened?'

'Pete managed to get the receiver away from him and I was told to report to a house just off the East Lancs Road. I turned up there with my guitar and amp the next afternoon, but your father refused to let me in the door.'

'Why?'

'His shoes,' Devon butts in. His smirk now a fully-fledged grin.

'Because they were muddy?' Lauren's face is crinkled in confusion and understandably so.

'No,' Steve sighs. 'It was because they were slip-ons.'

Devon tries to justify Moran's reasoning to a bewildered Lauren. 'Your dad was deeply suspicious of any footwear that wasn't a trainer, a Doc Marten or didn't look like a Greggs' pasty, you know what I mean.'

Steve nods along to Devon's words. 'Pete was adamant I wouldn't be allowed across the threshold. That if I still wanted to audition, I would have to do it on the path. He said he would run an extension cord out of the kitchen window for me to plug into.'

She begins to laugh. 'And did you?'

'Fuck no. To be honest, I was about to turn around and go home when Jim made him see sense.'

'Sense, of a sort,' I say, recalling the day in question. Cold, late October and with heavens that looked as if they would open any minute. 'I just asked your dad what was worse, letting Steve in the house or having Mr and Mrs Moran come home to find an electrocuted teenager on their driveway.'

'In the end Pete let me in, but he did make me leave my shoes on the step.'

'Steve was a bloody good guitar player,' I tell Lauren. 'So, we had our band.'

'And *he* had a Les Paul,' Devon adds.

While I saw the fact our guitarist owned an actual Gibson as a bonus, Lauren's dad had taken it a different way. Added to Steve's alien choice of footwear, this was enough in Moran's eyes to denounce him as a member of the landed gentry and thus an enemy of the people to be targeted with revolutionary activity. Which for Pete meant covering Steve's guitar case in **PAY NO POLL TAX** stickers he must've got off his dad.

Steve had been less than impressed and that two teenage lads would start out in such a way it was hardly a surprise they'd end up knocking lumps out of each other fourteen months later on the Academy stage.

It wasn't as if Steve was even posh. His dad had started out at the bottom of the building trade, working on sites after he'd left school. In time, he'd noticed an opportunity and gone for it, growing his business from almost nothing. When I told my old man that I was in a band with Mr Williamson's son, he remembered him from drinking around Swinton way back, and used a single word to describe him, and that word was "rough".

Mrs Williamson, with a better head for figures than her husband, had kept the firm's books and, keen to keep it in the family, Steve had been groomed as heir to the throne. They lived in a nice three-bedroom place bordering Worsley or, depending on where you could convince yourself the border actually lay, deep within it. We'd go round there to pick Steve up in the van before a gig and his mum would always invite us in while we waited, asking us about our songs and future plans. His dad was usually still at work, overseeing some part of his firm late into the evening.

With a couple of drinks inside him, Steve feels the call of nature and disappears through a doorway with a crude sign for the gents on it. Seconds later, he returns, looking disturbed and shaking his head.

'Bloody hell, man, that was quick,' says Devon. 'Did you even wash your hands?'

'I daren't even unzip. I think I contracted something just walking in there.'

'How about we head over to the Castle?' Lauren suggests with our pots almost empty. 'That was another place my dad liked.'

We make the short walk to Oldham Street and the tile-fronted Castle Hotel, settling ourselves around a small table next to the jukebox, an arm's length from the cramped serving area that belies the size of the place. It being an early weekday afternoon, the pub is quiet.

Two gents prop up the bar. They're not much older than us but are dressed far more casually. At the table next to us sits a man almost entirely obscured by a broadsheet newspaper. A young woman takes a break from polishing glasses to serve me while Steve excuses himself, and Devon and Lauren pick out some tunes. Within minutes we're all back round a table almost identical to the one we've just left.

'They've got nothing of Pete's on there,' says Devon. 'So, we put this on, instead.'

A familiar yelp tears out of the speaker, that of another deceased figure from the city's music scene, swiftly followed by the chiming guitar intro to The Fall's 'Prole Art Threat,' a suitable enough tribute to Pete Moran.

'I think that might be why my dad would come in here,' Lauren says. 'That there was literally no danger of any of his stuff coming on. He never liked to listen to his own voice, was really critical of himself. Always picking apart his vocals and finding fault with them. That's what made it so surprising he'd been listening to your song, like.'

What I find surprising is that self-criticism on Moran's part. After we'd recorded our track at Spirit Studios, he'd played it over and over for the next day or so, revelling in it, feeling validated. The existence of that song proved to everyone that our band was real, and Pete was a singer. Our next step to success had felt just around the corner.

Lauren brings out the biscuit tin and we delve under that lone piece of vinyl into a mass of paper in all colours, shapes, and sizes. Gig tickets, some with stubs still attached, others long since torn off. Some in perfect condition, pristine and flat. Others having been folded up and stored inside wallets or pockets. Some from gigs we played at, others from those we'd attended. There's even the one that led us to form our own band, The Fall at the Ritz in August of '91.

There are flyers from countless venues, more than a few of which exist now in name only. The posters are a mixture of the unused and those peeled away from walls, still bearing remnants of plaster. Most interestingly of all, waiting for us at the bottom of the tin, are three issues of *Mere Pseud Magazine*.

16

Saturday 3rd October 1992
Incendiary Tract (in support of Babes in Toyland)
Manchester University Students Union

A last-minute inclusion on the TOYLAND bill, INCENDIARY TRACT seemed little more than BABES themselves. This teenage Swinton four-piece slotted in at SHORT notice after another local act were REGRETTABLY, and there are those who will say SUSPICIOUSLY, forced to vacate their place on stage and take up residence in the nearby LAVS with a bout of food POISONING. But were these late stand-ins a welcome PANACEA or mere PLACEBO.

Their rangy guitarist played with FURIOUS abandon, his posing that of a foppish beanstalk libertine scratching at CRAB-ridden genitals. Their drummer, obscured by bandmates and kit alike, appeared to SWAT haphazardly as if chasing an infestation of nuisance FLIES. Their bass sound was SO distorted, SO stomach quivering that I almost had to RUSH off to evacuate my OWN bowels.

And then there were the vocals. Or, perhaps, there were NOT. Whether any of these extended JAMS have been afforded a title is as open to question as whether they contain any KNOWN words, so bewildering is that which EMANATES from the mouth of their singer.

His STYLE is that of early man attempting to communicate whilst feasting on a white-hot chip shop PIE. An unintelligible mumble LACED with the threat of being showered in pastry and LUMPS of half-cooked potato.

Their brief set – one might say, NOT BRIEF ENOUGH – was brought to its close with a cover of The Stooges' 'Death Trip' which might more accurately be labelled a SMOTHER version.

That said, as they were eleventh-hour replacements making their DEBUT, I feel inclined to give them the benefit of the DOUBT. Next time, however, I may not be so KIND. One to keep a TV EYE on, if only to make sure they don't SPIKE your sandwich.

Mark E Moon
Chairman of the Bored
Editor, Mere Pseud Magazine

17

I've been lucky enough for this life to take me all over the world, you know, but I always end up back here, and I think I always will. Call it Manchester, call it Salford, call it Swinton. I call it home.

Pete Moran, 2004

The fanzines are standard construction, each a cluster of A4 white sheets folded in half, nestling inside one another, and held together by staples. At the time they would've been stacked with the rest of the homemade efforts on the counters of Piccadilly Records and other like-minded shops.

Now on the table before me, two are in perfect condition with not a squashed corner or blemish in sight, so well-kept you might almost believe they were made yesterday as part of a resurgence in DIY culture. The third hasn't been treated with such care, its cover is stamped with a long-dried muddy footprint.

Inside each there's news, drawings and reviews. The handwritten is alongside the typed and lower case mixed in with bellowing capitals. Every page is numbered in a small circle along its lower edge.

Together with the articles are vintage advertisements, addresses of now defunct independent labels offering mail order releases, and blocks put aside for local businesses. Taxi firms, record stores, even the builders' merchants owned by Steve's father is there.

'I never knew your old man was into the music scene?' I ask and show him the tiny square of text.

'To be honest, he wasn't, but he did appreciate a competitively priced advertising opportunity when he saw one.'

As cheap as it may've been, I can't imagine Mr Williamson seeing much of a return on this investment. Who, upon reading one of these fanzines would spend their cash on a couple of lengths of copper piping when they could have bought the album *Copper Blue*, by Sugar, instead?

'Do we know what happened to Mark E Moon?' I wonder aloud.

'Don't know and don't much care,' is Steve's reply. 'He was a bit of a pompous prick, if you ask me.'

'Takes one to know one, you know what I mean.'

'Very witty, Devon.'

Unlike Steve, I admired Moon. The love and passion for music he needed to create these issues on a regular basis might have exceeded the commitment of those he wrote about, and he did it all for scant reward and, in many cases, the outright disdain of the groups he covered. Mostly, though, I admired him because he was the only person I knew of who could be described as a writer.

At some point, long ago, I became afflicted with the creative urge and even before Incendiary Tract came along, I'd already tried several remedies for it.

At school, I put a comic together with a friend, we were only twelve or so and it was before music really took hold of me. I invented characters and worked on storylines, then painstakingly drew the whole thing out. Without access to a photocopier, each issue would have to be done by hand and when they were finished, we'd pass them around class. It ate up great chunks of my time, but I loved it, and time was something I had a lot of in those days. Though as we got older and homework increased, the enterprise fell by the wayside.

In college, I wrote short stories, mainly for coursework, but also for the simple pleasure of taking an idea that was tiny and making it large, letting my imagination have free rein and seeing just where it could take me.

Then when I was in the band all my effort had been directed into that. Me and Pete would sit and work out the songs, again taking something small – just a single line or prospective title – and adding to it until it was fully-formed. We probably wrote six or seven tracks before it all ended. Afterwards life seemed to take me down another path entirely, and any thoughts of a creative existence became lost.

'Do you think Mark E Moon still writes about music?' Lauren asks. 'Maybe we could Google him, he's bound to be online somewhere.'

'I don't even know his real name,' I tell her. 'We only met him a handful of times.'

Apart from the pseudonym he published the fanzine under twenty years ago, I know nothing about Mark E Moon. I couldn't speculate as to what he looks like these days or, if I'm honest, even what he looked like back then. Is the memory I have of him real or has it been mixed and twisted with a lifetime of other faces? All I have in my mind now is a vague blur. For all I know, I may've sat next to him on the tram or stood behind him in a queue at the Post Office.

He could work for a local paper or website, reporting on cultural matters. Or he might just as easily have got out of the business altogether and be doing something else. The truth may be somewhere in between. By day, a mild-mannered accountant. By night, tossing his opinions off on an internet message site like the rest of the world.

He might even be in this very pub at this very moment. Standing at the bar or somewhere in the parlour. Maybe at that nearby table, hidden behind the newspaper and listening to all our talk, chuckling away to himself. I wonder if he's still as passionate about his craft or did life side-track him along the way, as it did me?

As I flick through one of the 'zines, I discover him in a picture, a black and white photocopy of a polaroid. He's standing between the four members of Sonic Youth, one of whom is holding up two fingers behind his head and giving him a pair of rabbit ears. Moon is much as my memory recalled him to be, early or mid-twenties with styled dark hair and spectacles that could almost have been added later in pen to grant him an air of learnedness.

In the rear of the shot floats a familiar shape that attracts my attention. An unmistakeable head, photobombing long before the act had been given a name. Our shaven-skulled drummer, Devon Bradshaw.

'Look at you, mate,' I say, pointing him out, 'gegging in with the rock stars.'

'Fucking hell, man, that's me!' he shouts, as if he's just won the lottery. 'That's me and Sonic Youth!'

Lauren leans in to take a look. 'Wow, that's brilliant.'

'We opened the bill for them one night,' Devon tells her. 'I don't remember the picture, though.'

'If it was afterwards,' I suggest, 'you were probably shitfaced like the rest of us.'

Devon laughs, continuing to admire his younger self.

'I can do you a copy if you like.' Lauren says.

'Please, that'd be great.'

'Yes, you should hold on to that,' Steve remarks. 'It'll be the closest you'll ever get to mixing with the stars.'

Devon looks up from the fanzine in his hands, his demeanour switching from joy to irritation in a flash. 'Well, that's bollocks for a start.'

'Oh, really and why's that then?'

'Because I once unblocked Mark E Smith's toilet.'

'Really?' Lauren says and Devon nods with pride. 'What happened?'

'He asked if I wanted a brew, and we had a bit of a chat about plumbing.'

This brings a scoff from Steve. 'You met Mark E Smith and all you talked about was plumbing?'

'No, we talked about football an' all. But he mainly wanted to talk about plumbing. His dad was a plumber, his grandad was a plumber.'

'And what of his father's father's father?'

'I dunno, Steve. It wasn't a dinner party. I was there to graft.'

'What was Mark like?' Lauren wants to know. 'He and my dad knew each other but I never met him.'

'He was good as gold with me,' says Devon. 'If he'd given me any mither, I'd have packed up my tools and he would've had nowhere to take a dump.'

'Bullshit!' The loudness of Steve's outburst sends a ripple through the Castle's patrons, ruffling the paper of the figure at the next table, forcing the gents' eyebrows at the bar skywards and almost causing the young woman behind the pair to drop a glass.

Devon is ready to fire off a reply, but I distract him. 'How come it was blocked?'

'What?'

'The toilet?'

'That's not for me to say. A good plumber knows when to keep his mouth shut, you know what I mean.'

'I'm impressed,' Lauren offers.

'Well, I'm not,' Steve says.' It all sounds a bit far-fetched if you ask me.'

'But no one did ask you, did they?' Devon is furious. I don't think I've ever seeing see him so wound up.

Steve stands from his stool, extending to his full height then bending down as if talking to a child. 'I'm off for a slash.'

'Another one,' Devon shouts after him. 'Fucking arsehole,' he mumbles under his breath.

I shift on my seat. I could do with getting up myself. I've got a dull ache in my hip from sitting down too long. I should stand and have a wander, possibly straight out the door. That Steve and Devon have already succeeded in winding each other up, does not bode well for the rest of the afternoon. Hopefully Steve will be on his way back to London before things go too far.

Sat taking all this in between sips of her drink is Lauren, the architect of whatever this day is set to be – an enforced reunion of people who'd happily gone about life for thirty years with zero contact. Is she searching for significance in the last record her father played before he died? As much as that 45 might hold some deeper meaning, it may just as easily have been an unfortunate coincidence.

Was it a regular ritual of Moran's, to sit alone and listen to his teenage voice or had he stumbled upon the tin while having a clear out? Lauren has been left a puzzle and she's determined to solve it, but what if the puzzle is best left unsolved? What if its pieces were scattered for a reason?

How much could she already know of this whole affair? She had three or four days before making those phone calls to comb the internet for word of Incendiary Tract. She told us she found nothing, and I know I never did on the odd occasions it occurred to me to search. Usually, late evenings and drunk from a session with Devon, typing our band name into my laptop and then falling asleep on the sofa.

Apart from one side of a seven-inch and a handful of live reviews in these fanzines, there's little to suggest we ever existed. Our legacy is contained solely in the contents of an old biscuit tin and the pasts of the men Lauren has brought together.

The *Mere Pseud Magazine* pieces cover our first three performances but there doesn't appear to be an edition about the last. The only mention of that Ramones gig is a brief remark at the end of the Sonic Youth write-up and nothing more.

There's no crumpled ticket stub for that fateful night. No carefully rolled poster or half-folded flyer. A thorough investigation online might bring up facsimiles of such ephemera, but not one word about what took place at the Academy. At most there may be a lone unanswered question on a forum appealing for information about the onstage scuffle between a group whose name has long been forgotten.

And how many people were even at the Academy early enough to witness our demise? Thirty or forty, and how many of those would even remember it? I doubt any of the photographers had bothered to waste their film on us, four spotty teens from Swinton, when the Ramones would be on a few hours later. Would you, with only a set number of exposures before a new roll would have to be loaded into your camera?

We were on stage about ten minutes and the local journos were probably still in the bar having another pint by the time our set and our band had come to an end. The spectacle would've gone unrecorded.

In this new era of the smartphone, such a thing could never happen. We would've been all over the web in seconds with posts on social media and videos of Moran and Steve brawling uploaded to YouTube for everyone with an internet connection to watch. Desperate tabloids might turn us into a curiosity. We would've become notorious. Some chancer may even have signed us up to rush out a Christmas single, capitalising on our fifteen minutes of infamy. Then the next viral sensation would arrive, and we'd fade into the background, returning to insignificance.

But Mark E Moon was present that evening and I watched him scribbling into his notebook. What happened to those words? There must be other issues of *Mere Pseud Magazine* still in existence. Moon's last, withering thoughts as he watched us implode, hidden in a cardboard box in a dusty attic, collecting bird droppings at the bottom of a budgerigar's cage, or waiting in Lauren's bag to be brought out when the time is right.

With only dregs in our glasses, we decide to move on for the next round, but not before I feel the need to stand before the jukebox, Devon's five choices for a quid having just finished.

'I wouldn't bother, Jim,' he says. 'We're off soon.'

'I'm putting a tribute to Pete on.'

'They've got none of his stuff. We've already looked.'

'That's not what I'm after,' I tell him.

'What then?'

I ignore his question and imagine the confused glances being exchanged behind me while I click through CD covers. Iggy's *Lust for Life*, a Pixies best of, New Order, Stevie Wonder, Joy Division, CAN. None of which suit my purpose.

'Hang on a minute,' Steve says. 'I know what he's up to.'

'What, man?'

'If I said the words Swinton Poolhall to you,' he explains to Devon, 'what springs to mind?'

There's a pause before our drummer makes the connection.

'Nah, Jim, man. Don't do it. They'll know it was us.'

Along with the alcohol, all this talk of the past has awoken my inner teenager. 'It'll be fine. We're going after these. They won't realise til we're halfway down the road. Is it on here, Devon?'

'Is what on there?' Lauren asks.

'Your dad got us barred from Swinton Poolhall,' Devon tells her.

'The one under the precinct?'

'The very same.'

'What did he do?'

In the larger history of Rock 'n' Roll misbehaviour, it was harmless. There was no brawl, we didn't abuse the staff, either physically or verbally, no pint was spilt on the baize, nor errant cue ripped through the felt. Far worse things took place around there and yet we were exiled.

'They barred us,' I say over my shoulder, still searching, 'because your dad put 'The End' by The Doors on the jukebox.'

'Is that all?' I hear the puzzlement in Lauren's question. 'They literally kicked you out because of that?'

'Not quite. We got kicked out because every time we went in there, just as we were about to leave, Pete would stick a pound in the jukebox and choose six songs.'

Inflation being what it is, you got more music for your money in those days, but the problem with her father's behaviour was that his six songs were always the same half-dozen and comprised only a single choice. The full-length album version of 'The End'.

'When was the last time you did it?' Lauren sounds amused, and I can't help but smile, my reflection grinning back at me in the machine's glass.

'Not since the '90s,' I say.

'Is that because you're an adult now?' Steve enquires. 'Or supposed to be, at least.'

'Lighten up,' I tell him. 'It's just a bit of fun and it happens to be a great tune. I mean, I could sit and listen to it all day.'

'Well, some poor sod is going to have to, aren't they? For the next sixty-odd minutes or so, anyway.'

I think about the guy sat reading his paper near us, catching up on current affairs and enjoying a relaxing pint, suddenly having to listen to Jim Morrison relay his oedipal complex again and again and again and again, like the worst kind of pub bore. I wonder if the guy is a Doors fan. He may not be in an hours' time.

'They've got it,' I say, more to myself than anyone else. I put my coin in the slot and tap out the same sequence of numbers five times then sit down to disapproving looks. 'Come on, Steve. Have you never heard a song and thought to yourself, I need to listen to this over and over again?'

'Not one that's twelve minutes long, I haven't.'

From a speaker in the corner, shimmering notes and a quivering cymbal drift out, the lead guitar lick winding and rising like a snake from a basket. 'The End' has begun.

'I always think of *Apocalypse Now* whenever I hear this.'

'Well, Devon, perhaps we could get the barmaid to light up a few sambucas to really set the scene for you.'

'War's no laughing matter, Steve.'

'I'm not suggesting we napalm a village of women and children.'

'Just sambucas?'

'Yes, just sambucas.'

'Fuck it, why not.'

'Count me out,' I tell them.

'You're a conscientious objector?' Steve says.

'It's more my constitution objecting at the thought of it.'

'At what point do you think they'll realise, like?' Lauren asks.

'Exactly. When will they realise and what will they do about it?' I lean forward, believing I've found a kindred spirit in childish hijinks. 'Ideally, you'd want the place to be teeming, people chatting away, not paying much attention to the music in the background. Then slowly it begins to dawn on them, "didn't we just hear this?" And what do they do, let it carry on and hope the next song will be different or reset the whole thing?'

'You've put a lot of thought into this haven't you, Jim?' Steve says.

'Possibly too much, if anything.'

'And what did they do at the poolhall?' Moran's daughter asks.

We never did stick around long enough to find out. We'd stay for most of the first play through, finishing a last game and our pints and crisps, while Pete offered up his own alternative lyrics:

'No HP or meat pies, the end.'

Also:

'Aired spleens outside the coal mine.'

Then it was time to leave before 'The End' started again. But one week we went in, and they refused to let us have a table and our time in there was done.

'Some twat grassed us up, I bet,' Devon suggests.

'I don't think I've ever been inside the poolhall,' Lauren says.

'Well, you've not missed a great deal.'

She smiles. 'Were you in there a lot?'

'After practice, yeah.'

Steve, the only one of us with a licence and car, would pick me and Moran up and we would head to Devon's house and squeeze into the Bradshaw's garage for a few hours, running through our growing repertoire of songs. Then before it got late, we would go over to the precinct and the poolhall.

'And you'd stick 'The End' on six times and leave?'

'Pretty much,' I say and shrug. 'It was a simpler time.'

Swinton and its precinct dominated my early life, offering me enough that I rarely felt the need to venture beyond the town's borders. I could lose hours rooting through the music-filled shelves at Woolworths and the racks of CDs and cassettes at the nearby Play Inn. Even longer was spent in the local library, hidden away though it was behind the beige brutalism of the

Lancastrian Hall – its design appearing to be based on cereal boxes stacked and slotted into one another, giving no hint at the magic that lay within.

The children's section was where I made my way through the works of Roald Dahl or Judy Blume before I graduated to the floor above and the large and intimidating collection for adults. There the cryptic titles of espionage thrillers whispered to me. *The Odessa File. The Matarese Circle. The Secret Pilgrim.* Code words granting me access to a new world. I'd head home with a plastic bag of freshly stamped books and newly released album or single.

I knew Swinton like the back of my hand. The playing fields and the parks, spaces to enjoy a kickabout or loosely umpired game of cricket. The short cuts and ginnels, which areas to avoid in my school uniform, streets where the colour of a tie might set off a chase ending in some tedious act of low-level brutality. I knew the off-licences, had identified those more gullible and less scrupulous than the rest when it came to underage drinking. I even knew where you could find the remains of a rogue Sex Pistols/Happy Mondays graffiti mashup:

NO HOLIDAYS IN THE SUN FOR THE LIVING DEAD

The blood red capitals still visible on the shutters of a travel agent, sprayed either by some local wit or disgruntled former employee.

There was a time when I'd found the place huge, when it was my entire universe, but then it began to shrink. The short walk to the precinct no longer seemed worth it compared with a bus ride into Manchester for all town had in store. I never saw Swinton as a bad area to grow up, though. There were positives and negatives, much like any other place on earth. And it had the Lions, a once successful rugby league team and the focal point of our weekend for much of the year.

Their Station Road ground was in walking distance for my dad to take me whenever he could. The place became a second home where the two of us would stand on its open terraces and watch hulking warriors battle each other and the elements – back then, league was not the summer sport it is today.

The game not being my mum's cup of tea she could get her men out of the house for an afternoon giving her some peace and quiet and when we returned afterwards, she'd happily listen while I recalled the action we'd just witnessed as she tried to get me warm.

Further sources of entertainment included the local free paper's letters page for the weekly airing of grievances. It was the day's version of Twitter, albeit better moderated and with at least seven days wait for a reply. One popular topic was to which city did Swinton truly belong. Was it Manchester, who provided the "M" of its M27 postcode, or was it Salford, whose base of civic operations lay across the road from the precinct?

The thought of being part of either had never entered my mind. Swinton was just Swinton. Manchester meant the Arndale and all that was beyond the River Irwell while Salford only really began for me where my gran lived on the Height, by the roundabout and the church where my mum's ashes would be scattered. The Salford rugby team were our rivals and the idea that one might hold dominion over the other from anything more than a weekend's sporting result felt absurd.

In time I graduated once more, to the pubs around the precinct and the poolhall buried underneath like a dirty secret – low lit and low ceilinged, its air was a haze of cigarette smoke and casually loosed expletives.

It's been years since I set foot in Swinton. Even before my father passed away and we cleared and sold my childhood home, I'd long since stopped returning to the old places.

Back in the present and the Castle, 'The End' is gathering speed, pushing hard towards its climax.

'Right,' I say to the others and reach for my glass. 'Drink up. We've less than three minutes before it comes on again.'

18

I find William Blake endlessly fascinating. And it's not just the art or the words, it's everything. The being derided by his so-called betters. The facing utter indifference and ploughing on regardless. The sedition, obviously.
"I must create a system or be enslaved by another man's".
That's pretty much the dream right there, you know.

Pete Moran, 2006

We exit into the warm August afternoon to be hit by the curious disconnect daytime drinking brings. From leaving a pub's gloomy confines, hours seemingly passed, expectant of night to have fallen, only to find the sky outside light and bright, and time having barely moved.

There's a detachment from the world as well. Those around us rush about as we float down the street on a very different wavelength. I'm glad to be up and moving, the ache in my hip has subsided, though that could also be down to the booze. We've only had three, but I feel as if I could lie down and doze on the sun-baked pavement.

Steve and Devon also seem sluggish. Only Lauren, who made the wise decision to switch to halves after the first round, looks energised, and I enquire where she wishes to head next.

'Spirit Studios,' she replies.

'It's still going?' Steve asks, a step or two behind us.

'No, not for ages. It's a bar now, Northern Monk refectory, but I thought we could get a drink in there anyway, like.'

'Sounds like a plan, man.' The ingredients for another handmade cigarette have appeared between Devon's fingers.

We're halfway up Oldham Street when Lauren turns to me with a question. 'Why Incendiary Tract?'

'For the name?'

'Yeah.'

'Well, that was from your dad. He nicked it from a line in the paper.'

It wasn't so much a line as a short phrase. Just four words. I can't remember where we were when he found it, only that we were bored and had access to a newspaper. It might've been the college canteen or the back seat of a bus, the engine's warmth heating our skinny arses. With a lack of anything better to do, Pete had rustled his way through page after page, passing comment on various stories until he came across an article that took his fancy. He'd thrust the paper at me, his finger tapping the newsprint, bringing a quote to my attention, and readying it as set-up for a gag: *Writer Rushdie's incendiary tract.*

'This fella should see a doctor,' Pete had said.

My better judgement lost out to growing tedium and I took the bait. 'Why?'

'You know, his incendiary tract. Our mam had one of them last year, cock. Turns out it was a water infection.'

Attracted first by the opportunity for comedy, the phrase became lodged in his brain to be repeated at irregular intervals.

Writer Rushdie's incendiary tract.

Writer Rushdie's incendiary tract.

Pete had a reasonable idea of what 'incendiary' meant but, as a word he'd only ever seen in written form, was unsure of its pronunciation. Rather than let this be a problem, though, he saw the benefit in that he could stretch it as he wished, from three to five syllables, tapping it out on a chair or turning the thing to beats in his mouth.

Dum dum, dum dum, dum a dum, dum.

Dum dum, dum dum, dum a dum a, dum.

With no one to teach him about music he was teaching himself, searching for a way to deliver vocals in his own way. Over time writer Rushdie disappeared from the news and then from the phrase itself, leaving us with our band name.

'He was like that when I was a kid, as well,' Lauren tells me. 'Always messing around with words. The pair of them were, really, him and my mam. They had a bit of a secret language going on. Our own special code. Pigtown Latin, they named it, you know, because of how some people would call Swinton 'Swinetown'. There were literally no rules. Only that if they liked how something sounded, it would be absorbed into the vocabulary. The birthday cards we'd send each other would be unreadable to anyone outside the three of us.'

'He was always up to stuff like that in college,' I say. 'Sneaking weirdness into his essays. Inappropriate quotes from films or long runs of alliteration.' Somehow, I pluck a line from the distant past, '"Hitler's henchman Heinrich had a hirsute horse".'

We turn left onto Hilton Street. 'There's a mural of him round here, isn't there?' Devon asks.

'Who?' I reply, feeling giddy. 'Himmler's hairy horse?'

Devon takes a drag and fixes me with a stare. 'You know who I mean, Jim.' The rebuke leaves his mouth in a nicotine speech bubble.

Dotted about the city are a collection of works by artists depicting Manchester icons. Moran's had appeared earlier in the year, a black piece on a white background, a shadow version of Pete. Left hand rooted in a jacket pocket, right holding a cig to his mouth, sunglasses high up in his hair and eyes peering right at you. It's a good likeness, almost scarily so.

The mural, though, had been up barely twenty-four hours before it became the target for graffiti. A cock and balls drawn across his face – expertly rendered, if anatomically inaccurate in their placement. Not that this was the first example of street art being defaced in these parts.

Years ago, workers stripping greenery off a power station at the intersection of Thomas and Tib Street had made an unexpected discovery. In the modern equivalent of finding Cro-Magnon era cave drawings or a Cezanne in your attic, they unearthed an alleged early Banksy hidden underneath some shrubbery. A poodle with the head of a bulldog.

The decision was made to preserve this work for posterity, and several strips of timber and a rectangle of plexiglass were sourced and knocked up into a protective cabinet. But within days the see-thru material was see-thru no more, covered as it was in a variety of stickers and tags. The piece was once more lost to the public eye, though the small station has since become a canvas for local creatives. One side was briefly home to a sizeable, and there are those who might say proportionally correct, portrait of Tony Wilson.

With glasses perched on the end of his nose and eyes that followed you up and down Tib Street, he could so easily have been looking out through a '90s television screen. Though, for a man so apparently fond of the quote, 'if it's a choice between truth and legend, print the legend,' the late Anthony H might've preferred the painter to have omitted his double-chin.

The sullying of Moran's mural could've been done by anyone. A bored student. Some rival artist with a spray can. Or an individual who didn't much like Pete Moran, his music, or his face. Then again, you couldn't rule out the possibility that this extra set of sex organs had been added by the subject himself.

It wasn't simply words Moran liked to play around with. He possessed a vulgar streak you could steer a narrowboat down and I doubt he ever met a surface he didn't believe greatly improved by the addition of cartoon male genitalia. GCSE textbooks. Lifestyle magazines in dentist's waiting rooms. The guestbook on a school trip to the Royal Shakespeare Theatre – *As You Like It* and then some.

I can picture Moran stumbling upon his image, a few drinks under the influence and staring as if into a mirror before deciding to add a certain special something, then returning from the nearby art supplies shop with the tools required to apply the offending article and chortling to himself as he did so. Moran would've reasoned this act might add to his aura. Not only had an artist been inspired to create the piece, but "someone else" had then gone to the trouble of defacing it.

I know exactly where this mural is, having passed it often enough, but not knowing if Lauren has seen it in its current X-rated form, I don't wish to say. She leads us there, regardless.

At the centre of Stevenson Square, flanked by bus shelters and Eastern Bloc Records, lies a disused underground toilet. Its entrance padlocked, and the surrounding brickwork now decorated with art, the air of the place improved by plants and flowers. On the side of a nearby outbuilding is where we find Moran, cock and balls now obscured by football stickers from visiting European sides. Partially torn off they give our former singer just enough space to peek out from under.

Lauren is already reaching into her bag. 'Can I get a shot of you all next to it, like?'

We assemble around the reproduction of her father like a police line-up. I stand on one side with Devon, while Steve is alone on the other. As she clicks away, passers-by shoot us curious glances. This scene of three middle-aged men in suits being photographed by a young woman, not interesting enough for anyone to demand explanation, but not so commonplace as to be completely ignored.

Lauren takes her time to find what she's after, moving from portrait to landscape and back again, capturing several pictures in both. Finally satisfied, she passes the camera to us.

I stare into the viewfinder, an ex-bandmate peering over each shoulder. I feel something catch in my throat. The funeral never got to me, nor the service or eulogy, but the contents of this tiny glass screen does. The four of us back together again after so long, even if one of our number is spray-painted onto a brick wall.

This was the Moran I knew, standing at our centre, infecting us with his spirit and drive. I zoom in, closer to the face. His eyes, narrowed and inquisitive, rendered in black and staring directly into mine. I feel a shiver. Tony Wilson's eyes might just have followed you up the road, but Moran's will stalk me until this day is done.

Out of the square we follow the road's curve, headed for the site of our sole recording, but after turning right onto Tariff Street it's obvious something is amiss.

Northern Monk Refectory, our destination, is in darkness. I look through the window and make out the shapes of chairs upside down on tabletops, but no sign of life. Taped to the door is a sign:

CLOSED DUE TO ACT OF GOD

Devon and Steve seem keen to debate this. 'What kind of act of God closes a bar?'

'Maybe their card reader has gone down?'

'That or something unspeakable has risen up from a toilet.'

Lauren stands on the street, open mouthed and close to tears.

'It doesn't matter,' I tell her. 'We can find somewhere else.' But as the words leave my mouth, I know them to be a lie. Whatever Moran's daughter had prepared for inside that closed bar is lost. She's planned this day to follow the strands of an unknown part of her father's life, but those strands are now coming apart and any link to the past fading, if not broken entirely. The premises might be back open tomorrow, but by then it'll be too late.

19

Why did I call my last album Northern Bastard? *Let's just say there was an argument with someone at the record company and I know that phrase was bandied about a bit afterwards, only, you know, they never used the word bastard. They weren't quite so restrained.*
Unsurprisingly, we've since parted ways.

Pete Moran, 2008

With Northern Monk Refectory off limits, we find ourselves at Port Street Beer House and step inside as Black Sabbath's 'Black Sabbath' creeps from the speakers. It's a song that's always been a favourite of mine but hardly one to improve the atmosphere of our day. Not with the ominous gestures of its "figure in black". There are echoes of the mural we've just passed, the shadow Moran and those watching eyes, and I wonder if they can still see me, if they've tracked us here.

Steve goes to the bar, then joins us in the beer garden, far from the haunting imagery and Ozzy's wailing. Seated on wooden benches around a wooden table, on a wooden floor surrounded by wooden fence, it might be easy to imagine ourselves in some alpine lodge atop a snowy mountain but for the disused building next door.

Plastered in graffiti, windows boarded up and the zig zag of an old fire escape clinging on in desperation, the whole thing held in place by little more than rust and misplaced hope.

Lauren is quiet, her plans in disarray. Slow, awkward moments pass as the rest of us gulp our pints. I wonder how best to distract this young woman who's a stranger to me and clutch at one of the few facts I know about her.

'Are you gonna show us some of these pictures you take?'

She doesn't immediately register my question, but then reaches into her tote bag and brings out a mobile with a screen almost twice the size of my own. After a few taps she passes it across the table.

'That's my new site, I've got most of my stuff on it.'

There are plenty of shots of bands and singers in poses and live settings, but as I scroll and search, I see nothing so far of her dad.

'It's very professional,' I say, 'must've cost you a fair bit.'

'A guy I went to uni with is a web designer, so we did a skill-swap type of thing, you know.'

I don't know and tell her this, which makes her smile.

'It's literally what it sounds like. He did my website for me, and I took his wedding photos. No money changed hands.'

'And was that a good swap?' I ask, continuing to scroll.

'Not for him, like. They're about to get divorced.'

I find one of Moran from the same set as those in the *Evening News,* stood at the old Free Trade Hall, leaning back against an archway and exhaling a cloud of cigarette smoke into the air. I click on it for a larger image, to focus in on the face, but his eyes are obscured behind shades. Whatever I'm looking for, maybe a Moran less daunting than his mural, I don't find and return to the site's homepage.

Devon is next to me looking at the phone. 'Lauren M?' he points out.

I'd bypassed the words, but there it is at the top of the page in minimalist font, the majority of her surname lopped off.

She looks away, embarrassed. 'I'm still not sure about that, I thought it would make me stand out a bit more.'

'Wouldn't your dad's name have done that?'

'Yeah, but not how I'd want it to.' She sits forward to explain. 'When we'd go somewhere and meet people, he'd introduce me and be all like, "this is my daughter, she's a photographer. If you need any pictures doing, she's your girl". And it was nice an' all, but it made me uncomfortable. I never wanted to feel that I was making it off who he was.'

'That's a very independent attitude,' Steve says.

Lauren shrugs. 'I've got friends who think I should make more of it, but I dunno, that's just not me.'

It wasn't Moran, either. He took a special kind of umbrage at the thought of someone getting on in life simply because of who their parents were or who they knew rather than through talent or hard graft. I wonder what he would've said If you'd told him back then that he'd end up doing the same for his own child.

'Most of the bands I shoot literally don't know I'm Pete Moran's daughter, that's if they even know who he is, like. The younger ones don't, and I prefer it that way.' Lauren pauses for a second, biting her lip before continuing. 'There was this gig I did over in Liverpool, some American band on tour, and an older guy who was hanging about had been staring at me. Afterwards he came up and asked if my dad was Pete Moran. I told him no.'

She seems uncomfortable and avoids our eyes. 'The guy apologised, and said he'd known Pete from way back, that he knew his daughter did band photos and that I was the image of his wife Kelly. So, then I apologised and admitted I was Pete's daughter and he laughed and said his own kids probably did the same thing to him. It turned out he'd done a song with my dad years ago, after you lot, and then gone into production. His kids were there, and he introduced me. It was funny in the end, but I still felt snide about trying to deny who I was.'

I debate telling Lauren that embarrassment about parents is just a part of growing up. Those tricky years when you believe nobody over the age of twenty-five could possibly understand a thing you're going through, that they themselves were never young.

My mum was dead before I reached that hormone-addled stage, but there were times I'd felt embarrassed by my dad and times I felt equally snide for having those feelings. His lack of employment embarrassed me, as did the state of our house. Did I wish he was something more or someone else?

I'd allowed a story about him to circulate, one he'd told me himself, one more exciting than him simply being a man on the dole. He'd signed on for the army in the late sixties and been deployed first in Germany; learning to ski, picking up a bit of the language, he enjoyed it.

Then in '71, he'd been sent to Northern Ireland where he understood the locals all too well and found little enjoyment patrolling their streets with a gun. From Belfast he'd gone AWOL, somehow getting all the way back to Manchester where he was later discovered hiding out at my nan's.

Me being a kid and wanting to impress others at school, I'd told a few of them. It was a good story, especially for someone like me who enjoyed spy fiction. At that point we'd had no phone at home and one lad had taken this as an extension of the tale, that my dad was still, twenty years later, absent without leave and hiding from the military police in an ageing Swinton terrace.

The truth was we didn't have a phone at home because it'd been disconnected through non-payment of the bill.

Lauren is keen to change the subject and while Devon gathers the tools needed to craft another cigarette before him, she finally asks what we recall about Spirit Studios.

As unofficial band spokesman, my former bandmates again look to me to continue a tale none of us particularly wants to rehash. I begin with the song resting in the biscuit tin. How we'd put it together, played it live and then decided to make a recording.

'We all chipped in and booked the place,' I say. 'Just for a couple of hours. We hoped to get a few tunes down, a proper demo tape, something to send out to labels. We thought a morning was all we'd need. I mean, it was naïve, but we couldn't really afford any longer. And if things had gone to plan, we might've been alright, but, well...'

'I don't think the engineer had much patience with us,' Steve offers.

Devon pauses in construction of his cig. 'I don't think he had much patience, full stop.'

Countless bands from the area had used Spirit Studios. The Smiths, New Order, Happy Mondays, Stone Roses. Our visit was unlikely to be as fondly remembered as any of theirs. It certainly wasn't as productive.

The only thing that grew from our session was the animosity between Pete and Steve and we left with pride dented, tempers frayed and a cassette containing a solitary three-and-a-half-minute effort.

'It should've been straightforward.' I tell Lauren. 'They only had a four-track operation, and our sound wasn't exactly complicated, but it didn't help that none of us had ever been in a studio before. We didn't know what we were doing. You could see the guy in the control room muttering to himself and every time one of us tried to go in there he would dock us five minutes off our time. We probably ended up with less than an hour.'

'The problem,' Devon says, still assembling his roll-up on the table, 'was that your dad wanted to rerecord his vocals and this twat here kept mithering to redo his guitar part.'

My mate is already well on his way to being drunk. I watch as his fingers struggle to perform the delicate movements needed to align tobacco and Rizla.

'Is everyone a *twat* to you, Devon?'

I hear the alcohol in Steve's tone, raising volume while his cultivated accent begins to slip.

'No, *Ste-ven*, they're not. Some people...' Devon leans over, gesticulating with his semi-constructed cigarette for emphasis and sprinkling its contents out the open end, '...some people are cunts.'

He sits back in satisfaction, then remembers the presence of the young lady next to him. 'Sorry about the language, Lauren, my filter must be on the blink.'

'That's alright,' she says, 'some people *are* cunts.'

'Too fucking right, girl.' Devon laughs, under the mistaken impression she too is referring to Steve.

'My dad certainly could be, and my mam, well, she isn't a whole lot better.' Lauren looks down at her glass. 'There were times I almost felt like I hated the pair of them.'

Devon's grin disappears and he ditches his attempt at a cigarette. 'I know the feeling,' he says. 'Parents, eh, who'd have them?'

'Do you not get on with yours then?' Lauren asks.

Devon sighs before he answers, the smell of beer wafting over the table. 'I've only great memories of my mum, God rest her soul, but when it comes to my dad, things weren't good for a long while.'

He takes a mouthful of his pint, then continues. 'We rubbed each other up the wrong way. He had his idea of how things should be done, and they never quite matched up with mine. But he paid the bills, so it was put up or shut up, know what I mean. My mum was kind of in the middle, always having to smooth things over. I think she was the main reason he didn't kick off about us practising at ours.' Devon puts the glass to his lips and downs the contents in a single, flashing gulp.

As well as evenings in the Bradshaw's garage, we'd also be there on weekends, especially early in the summer of '92 leading up to our run of gigs.

Devon's mum, Kath, would bring cups of tea out to us and listen to the noise we made with a smile, whereas his sister, Louise, preferred to shout down from her bedroom window and issue threats about calling the police. Clyde Bradshaw, after a week at the sorting office, was usually in front of his TV set and the cricket.

There never seemed that much tension about, so I was unaware Devon and his dad had a strained relationship. If our practising never resulted in complaints from his neighbours, Clyde didn't seem to mind us being there. His own preferred entertainment was sitting in the comfort of his living room and watching fast bowlers terrorise English batsmen. The West Indies might not have been touring that year, but Pakistan were and there'd been days when we'd arrive at their house and sit with him watching England struggle.

I remember the first time a wicket fell, Moran had clenched his fist and given a snarl of joy which surprised and confused Mr Bradshaw.

'What's this? You don't like England, Peter?' Clyde called us all by our full names. Moran was Peter, Steve was Steven, I was James, Devon was son.

'Nah, I'm Irish.'

'I-rish?' Clyde prolonged the two syllables, as if testing their veracity. 'You're I-rish?'

On the screen a heavyset moustachioed batsmen trudged back to the pavilion passing a moustachioed heavyset teammate on his way out. Mr Bradshaw turned to me.

'Did you know this, James? Did you know your friend here was an I-rish-man?'

To this I'd replied along the lines of, 'I didn't know he was yet a man,' leaving my mate to mutter about General Smart Arse being on the march again.

I'd been learning about Pete's heritage over the summer as Martin Moran's links to Ireland were first brought up. The Euro '92 football tournament was being played and for anyone hoping to inspire a little patriotic fervour in our frontman he had a standard reply: 'I'm Irish, me, cock.'

Over those months, Moran and Clyde went on to form something of a bond and while his wife carried brews out to us, and his daughter peered in the side window flicking the Vs at her brother, Mr Bradshaw would bring news of Pakistani pacemen tearing through the English middle order. It was probably telling, thinking back, that whenever Clyde did come out to the garage, it was to speak to Moran rather than Devon.

For me, though, they'd been fun times in a busy household, with all that entailed. It reminded me of a time before my mum had passed and how it'd been at home, how lucky I was. My parents had no shortage of affection and kindness, about the only thing they lacked was a healthy bank balance.

In the present, Lauren is thinking of her relationship with her father. 'I resented my dad being who he was, not that he was a big star or anything. It wasn't like everyone knew him, but literally wherever we'd go there'd always be that one person who did know him and would come up to us and my dad either couldn't or wouldn't say no to them. I resented him for being famous and I think my mam did, too, like. I never wanted to share him with fans, I just wanted us to be normal and, really, we were normal. We'd go the same places and do the same things as other kids at school. We'd go to Alton Towers, stuff like that.

'There was this time I remember when we were there, queueing up for the rides, I must've only been twelve or so. Some guy had come up to us and my dad had been all pally with him. I could see my mam getting worked up. They had this blazing row and he disappeared off to the toilets to do a line. I didn't know that's what he was doing at the time, I only put it together years later. When we got home that night she went out and came back leathered, so then there was another argument.'

As Lauren talks, she looks at the three of us in turn.

'Whatever my dad did, my mam would always have to do something in return to get back at him. They were like children. I wasn't even a teenager, but it felt like I was the responsible one. That I was the adult.' She stops to take a drink. 'For the last five or six years I've literally been walking a tightrope between the two, not wanting to come down on either side.'

She looks away from us all, moving a finger to her eye to wipe something away. 'I think it might've been better if I hadn't come along until later, like. They weren't that much more than kids themselves when they had me.'

It's a brutally honest appraisal and one she probably couldn't give at her dad's wake surrounded by family and well-wishers, looking to share happy stories of the late Peter Moran. It's the kind of thing you could only really unload on three total strangers or a therapist.

'Do you guys all have children?' she asks.

'One of each,' Devon says.

'Same here,' I tell her.

'We've got three girls,' Steve adds.

Devon's eyebrows rise. 'Jussst three?' he enquires with a noticeable slur.

Steve's eyes focus in on him, 'I should think I'd remember how many children I've got.'

'Did your mum and dad never think of having more?' I ask Lauren, before these two can wind each other up any further.

'No, the closest I've got is a couple of cousins. Uncle Rob has two lads. They're both a bit younger than me.'

'Are they big into their music?'

'They're big into anything they can smoke to,' she says with a wry smile.

'Really?'

'Yeah, and I don't think my uncle exactly approves, like. It's something he and my dad never saw eye to eye on.'

'Oh dear,' Devon says, a sentence or two behind us in the conversation. 'More young men fallen under the spell of Mary Jane.'

'I'm pretty sure no one has called it "Mary Jane" since Woodstock,' Steve offers.

Devon looks as though he's something to add, but his mouth just hangs open. He seems to have lost his train of thought and they glare at one another until interrupted by a buzzing sound from Steve's jacket.

His mobile comes out and he scans the screen ready to return it to his pocket and ignore the call when something must click in his brain, changing his face from disinterest to alarm.

'Fuck!' he exclaims.

'What's up?' I ask.

'Look at the time!' he shouts, holding his phone out for me to see.

17:08.

I look at my own mobile for confirmation and see that we've somehow been out for over four hours already, drinking and talking and needling each other.

Steve is up and panicking, not that it'll do him any good. His five o'clock train to Euston is probably somewhere around Stockport by now, minus at least one passenger.

'Why didn't someone tell me?' he shouts.

'We're not your mum, Steve,' Devon replies, unable to keep the amusement off his face. 'How've you managed to lose track of time with Big fucking Ben on your wrist?'

'Fuck, I need to call the hotel. Fuck, fuck.'

'Don't worry about it,' I say and try to settle him down. 'It's a Tuesday night, it's mid-August, they're hardly likely to be booked up. There's no big gig or a match on.'

Steve paces his side of the table, fumbling with his phone for a number to ring, someone to help him, to get him out of this beer garden and onto that train.

'All my stuff is there.'

'I don't think it'll be a problem,' Devon says. 'They'll have called the bomb squad by now and had it safely destroyed, you know what I mean. A nice, controlled explosion. There was that big bang before, wasn't there?'

'I just thought that was your guts,' I reply to add some levity to the situation, which Steve ignores.

'They better fucking not have. I left a suit with my case that cost me a grand.'

'You didn't wear your best suit to Pete's funeral?' Devon asks. 'How disrespectful.'

'Oh, but I did.'

Devon glances over at me and in the spaces where his eyeballs should be, all I see are two large, shiny brown marbles.

'I'm sure it'll be fine,' I tell Steve.

'Oh, will it, Jim?' he says, hands pulling at his box-dyed hair. 'I've missed my fucking train, and I've got nowhere to sleep.'

Almost as quickly as it began, Steve's panic subsides. A short call to his hotel is enough to secure him an extra night's accommodation and the knowledge his belongings are safe and sound. We agree on another drink before moving on and Lauren stands up.

'I'll get these. Well, Uncle Rob will.'

She takes the purse from her bag and heads inside. As the door clicks shut behind her, Steve explodes.

'Just what is your fucking problem?' he growls at Devon.

Our former drummer appears shocked at this outburst. Puzzled that his constant badgering has resulted in this moment.

'Come on, lads,' I say, with one eye on the door. 'Let's just calm down.'

'Not until this prick gets off my back. He's been chirping away at me all fucking day with his snide little comments.'

'What's my problem?' Devon replies, his shock turning to counterattack. 'I'll tell you what my problem is, shall I? YOU, that's what. YOU are my problem, Steve fucking Williamson. YOU, turning up here after all these years like nothing ever happened. YOU, fucking up our band.'

Before the next line comes out of my friend's mouth, I know what he's about to say. I feel like I've known for thirty years or since this morning, at the very least.

'YOU!' Devon spits, his teeth bared in anger, 'fucking that poor girl's mum.'

20

You say I'm difficult, but how do you define difficult?
Recalcitrant? OK, define recalcitrant.
Define, please, wilfully uncooperative.

Pete Moran, 2009

Well, here it is. The moment I've dreaded since Devon first pointed Steve out to me back at the crematorium. I'd been braced for talk of the band and reminiscing with old friends, I was ready for that. But this? I didn't leave the house this morning expecting this. If I'd known the day would take this turn, I doubt I would've made it out of bed let alone all the way into town. I would've said my back had locked up and stayed home.

The way Devon charged over to stand before Steve, as if to confront him and demand some form of justice, I thought he'd planned to do it there and then, on the grass verge. This was why I'd hoped Steve would get on his train and return to wherever he's been hiding. I wanted to avoid this. A kangaroo court in a wood-lined beer garden. In hindsight, it might've been better if Devon had done this earlier in the day rather than with Moran's grieving daughter on hand.

I've not thought about that night at the Academy in years. I'd consigned it to the dustbin of life. It was a memory that no longer served a purpose. It was the past and that was where it belonged. Revisiting it would help no one. But seeing Steve again has raked up so much I thought I was done with. The sight of my bandmates rolling around on the floor, the guitar trapped between them emitting the death rattle of Incendiary Tract. I hear those awful sounds again in the barbed words traded across the table in front of me.

It'd been a struggle to pull Pete and Steve apart that night, but when the deed was done, they flew off in different directions, like particles too alike to coexist.

Steve had called his father who came and took him and his fractured Les Paul home while Pete walked out of the venue and into the night with not a word to anyone. It was left to me, Devon and Rob Moran to pack up our equipment and vacate the premises under threats from the promoter. The drive back up the East Lancs Road was even quieter than the opposing journey we'd made that afternoon.

What led to the fracas, only the protagonists knew, but neither were anywhere to be seen in the days that followed. My cousin Lee asked what'd happened, but there was nothing I could tell him. I was as much in the dark as he was.

Back at college on the Monday for the final week of term, there was no sign of Pete or Steve leaving me to face curious looks from those who'd been at the gig or heard tell of it, second hand.

Christmas came and went, as did New Year. When I returned to my studies in January, I did so without my best friend. According to what his older brother told my cousin, Pete had quit and taken a job in the local garden centre.

Steve Williamson was around, as were a great many fragments of gossip, pulled together over the Xmas break. Oddly shaped pieces to fit together in search of the full picture.

One rumour went that, on the weekend before our final, fateful gig there'd been an incident at a club in town. A party from Swinton had gone into Manchester on the Saturday evening. A party that didn't include Pete's girlfriend, Kelly. Although, she'd turned up later, to Discotheque Royale, and discovered her boyfriend in the even stranger surroundings of the women's toilets. His trousers around his ankles alongside a young woman in a similar state of undress.

This tale brought only questions rather than answers:

What was Pete doing in Royales, a place I'd never known him to go?

Whose trousers had he worn to comply with their door policy? He had not, to my knowledge owned any since school.

And lastly, just how reliable a marker for good intentions is access to a pair of slacks, anyway?

Pete and Kelly had been together for over a year, since our opening weeks at Eccles College, though the path of their romance had never been smooth. They were an exhausting couple to be around, could break up and make up multiple times in the space of a single day. That the two would later get married felt both highly unlikely but also a foregone conclusion.

As well as rumours of Pete's infidelity and the brawl at the Academy, another story began to spread. Somewhere between those two events, Kelly was said to have indulged in an act of sexual revenge with none other than our own guitarist.

Details were sketchy about this supposed romp, not that that could stop it drifting through the corridors of secondary education like a stink bomb and wrinkling many a nose. It gave a tidy explanation for Pete and Steve's onstage tussle.

Kelly had left Eccles College the previous summer and was studying at Manchester Met, while working part-time in a clothes shop in the Arndale. With Pete gone, too, this had left only Steve and, in the last six months before we finished our A-Levels, we never exchanged a word, passing like strangers as we headed to our respective lessons.

Steve did have a reputation when it came to the opposite sex or liked to think he did. He was never shy about broadcasting his escapades, but would he go so far as to shag our singer's girlfriend? Did I believe it? I didn't *want* to believe it.

Then, just as things appeared to be calming down, it emerged that Kelly was pregnant. The local rumour mills went into overdrive with speculation of just who the father might be. This gossip only really slowed when I heard that Kelly had given birth to a baby girl six months later.

Pete and I had lost touch, no mean feat in a town the size of Swinton. The band was over, and our lives diverged. I stayed in contact with Devon and occasionally we'd try to make sense of what had happened, though never with much success. As time passed, the matter seemed put to rest.

In the here and now, the matter has been resurrected.

'Fuck off, Devon,' Steve roars. 'You don't have a clue what you're talking about.'

'Why? Because I never went to *u-ni-ver-si-ty*?'

I've one eye on these two and the other on the door, hoping Lauren won't walk through it anytime soon.

'Don't do this,' I tell them. 'Not today.' My firmest parenting voice has no effect. It usually works on the kids, but then they've never been as pissed as this pair.

Any attempt at mediation is ignored as Devon and Steve continue to argue, insults and spittle flying back and forth. They're caught up in their own private arena and I may as well not be sitting here. Thankfully, no one else is either. For the time being, there's only the three of us in the beer garden.

I try and add a gesture to my words, moving hands to make a point, but as I do I catch my half-full pint and swat it clean off the table. The glass hits the fence next to us, and smashes on the floor. Devon and Steve fall silent. They stare at me, open mouthed. The sharp clatter having severed their quarrel mid flow.

Did I mean to do that? Subconsciously, maybe? I've never considered myself one for angry displays of emotion. And never mind these two, how drunk am I? A minute ago, I'd have said not very, but now? Regardless, it seems to have worked. Rather than concentrating on each other they're now fixed on me.

'For fuck's sake, Jim,' Steve says.

I feel something in me rise. 'Don't "for fuck's sake", me. I've had about enough of both of you. I mean, there's a time and a place for this bullshit and it isn't *here* and it isn't *now*.' I accentuate "here" and "now" with a finger to the table that stings the tip of my digit. 'And it *definitely* isn't in front of Pete's daughter.

'If you two want to knock the shite out of each other, be my guest, but save it until later, alright? In the meantime, pull yourselves together. This isn't about you today, OK, either of you,' I point to the door behind me that is still closed, 'this is about *her*.'

I sit back and wish I had a nice relaxing pint in front of me to drain triumphantly.

'Sorry, man,' Devon looks suitably chastened.

'Don't,' I say. 'I don't want your fucking apologies. I want you to behave until this is done, until that young girl has gone home. After that, you can do whatever the fuck you like.'

While my words sink in, I hear the light hum of traffic from a nearby street and the blood thumping in my ears. I am, I now admit, quite drunk.

'Jim Edwards,' Steve offers slowly. 'Ever the peacemaker.'

'Well, someone had to be, didn't they? What with you and Pete squabbling like children every five fucking minutes.'

Back then, there was always something. Whether it was negotiating our guitarist's entry into the Morans' semi-detached or calming Pete at the pool hall because Steve liked to take an age in picking his shot, an act he persisted with simply because he knew how much it wound Pete up. At the time, I thought their behaviour was just two bored teenagers taking the piss, but later I realised there was genuine dislike bubbling away under the surface.

The door to the bar opens and Lauren steps out carefully balancing four drinks on a tray. With all the commotion, none of us had thought to go inside and help her.

'I'm afraid we've had a bit of an accident with a glass,' I say.

A member of staff comes out to brush up the debris and we make our most apologetic faces, offering to pay for the damage. When everything is cleared away and we're all settled with fresh glasses, Lauren has a suggestion.

'Seeing as though Steve doesn't have to head back to London, maybe we could stay out a bit longer and visit some of the venues you played, like. If none of you mind, that is.'

Considering how keen I was to get this day over with and rush home, I now see the benefit of the day lasting, of delaying future unpleasantness. Over these hours I've barely thought about the warehouse, and medical retirement, and I've no wish to start now. Instead, I feel determined to drag this Moran business out for as long as I can, hoping the others might see how bad an idea excavating our past really is.

'That's fine with me,' I tell her. I turn and fix my former bandmates with strong stares. 'What do you lads say?'

'Why not,' Steve replies. 'I've got nowhere else to be.'

'Yeah, sure,' Devon agrees. 'Where do you want to go first?'

'How about the Boardwalk?' Lauren says. 'I know it's not there anymore, but I could at least get a few photos of you all outside the building.'

'That's a great idea,' I say.

'Shall we get a taxi?' Devon asks.

I ponder the idea of us squeezed together in the close proximity of a black cab, even for a short drive. It might not be for the best with the current state of things. Plus, I've been sat down far too much today and though the soreness in my back and hip has been dulled by the booze, I decide a stroll is in order.

21

I don't ask for much in life, you know. I like books and records, a nice pint. I am partial to the occasional spliff, purely for medicinal purposes. Maybe a line or two every now and then, just to keep my hand in, and a warm body to cuddle up to at night.
Other than that, I wouldn't say I have many vices.

Pete Moran, 2010

It's a nice day for a walk and we leave the Beer House and head through Piccadilly Gardens, the magnetic core to which people and transport are drawn, often to collide. Workers and shoppers gather on the grass, a rare expanse of green in the bustling centre. Rough sleepers camp outside doorways and commuters rush for trams that criss-cross the area and buses which skirt around it.

On Portland Street we pass the tiny Circus Tavern and the sci-fi anomaly Fab Café, remnants of the old Manchester amid its newer, shinier face. The four of us move in a stagger with Devon leading our way and Steve lagging behind, leaving me in the middle with Lauren.

She has her tote bag over her shoulder and is quiet. We walk in silence until I feel ready to break it.

'I saw your granny Ellen at the service,' I say, 'but not Eric.' Lauren's attention is fixed ahead, on what lies down the road.

'My grandad has problems with his legs, so he literally doesn't get out all that much.'

'I'm sorry to hear that. You'll have to tell him hello from me when you see him next. We were always round his and your grans back in the day. Does he still have all that vinyl?'

'Yeah, their back room is full of his records. He stopped adding to it a while ago, like. Otherwise, I think my gran would've left him.'

Eric Lewis was about forty when we were teenagers and open to any music he could get his hands on, much of which was not a hit with his wife. I remember Lauren's gran christening her husband's collection his "Japanese knotweed," after the plant known for its rapacious growth.

At the time it occupied an entire room of their house and you had to wonder, and I'm sure Ellen Lewis did, just how long it would be before the vinyl took root in other parts of their home, as well.

'His system was legendary,' Steve offers from our rear.

'*The* System,' I turn and correct him. 'Eric was very particular about that.'

The System was not Eric's Hi-Fi, but the name he assigned to his accumulated records. Me and Pete had even composed an ode to The System. Though, composed was probably a bit strong, as, in fact, was the term ode.

It was more a layman's attempt at a John Cooper Clarke style poem, cobbled together from the names of artists and titles that lined the shelves:

> *The Velvets and The Stooges.*
> *Let It Bleed and Let it Be.*
> *Paranoid. LA Woman.*
> *Master of Reality.*
>
> *Electric Warrior.*
> *Hunky Dory.*
> *The Wailers, Burnin'.*
> *Patti Smith's Horses.*
>
> *Coney Island Baby.*
> *Station to Station.*
> *The Residents. Ramones.*
> *Rastaman Vibration.*
>
> *Leave Home, Low, The Idiot.*
> *Sex Pistols. Cut by The Slits.*
> *Gang of Four, Entertainment!*
> *Second album from Skids.*

The Pop Group. John Cooper Clarke.
Joy Division. Remain in Light.
The Birthday Party to the Bad Seeds.
Bad Brains, I Against I.

Warehouse: Songs and Stories.
Strangeways, Here We Come.
George Best. Daydream Nation.
Happy Mondays, Bummed.

New Order. Disintegration.
Extricate, The Fall.
Public Enemy. The Breeders.
Honey's Dead. Faith No More.

It was awful, of course, but it was a start. Our first tentative steps on the road to becoming songwriters. We spent countless mornings and afternoons hiding out at the Lewis' place and avoiding college. Some kids would go round to a friend's house to root about in their parent's drinks cabinet, we went to Kelly's to rummage through her dad's vinyl.

I remember an occasion in the August of '92, with college on hold for the summer. Our band had been going for a while, but the gigs and troubles were still to come. Any idea of performing live on stage in front of an audience was no more than a dream to us.

We'd not been long in the Lewis household when Pete and Kelly disappeared upstairs. We heard their laughter and the bump of hastily removed footwear bouncing on the floor above. Then, came the creaking of a bed, which encouraged us to play something loud. As I'd sat myself an arms-length from Eric's record player the duties of resident disc jockey were mine and I chose the New York Dolls' self-titled album.

Steve and the girl he was seeing that week, a Sarah of no last name, were on the sofa. In an armchair opposite me was a friend of Kelly's, Deborah Moore.

I had quite the thing for Deborah Moore. She was to Kelly as I was to Pete, an acerbic sidekick with little interest in being the main attraction. Her look was heavy eyeliner and dirty blonde hair, a style cultivated in less than five minutes or the better part of three hours. She was the introspective type. As was I. She could even be described as sullen. As, on occasion, could I.

A month or so earlier, we'd shared a moment in a club in town, passing each other on the way to the bar or the dancefloor, not exchanging a word but tumbling into some dark corner for a good fifteen minutes. My hands on her arse, her nails digging into my upper back, our tongues writhing like eels in a bucket. We'd returned to our friends where she barely acknowledged my presence the rest of the night.

I was confused and intrigued in equal measure. Even more so when, a few weeks later, it happened again. The same scene playing out in a different dark corner of a different club. The same tongues, the same hands on the same arse, the same nails dug into the same upper back followed by the same indifference.

Together again in the Lewis' semi-detached, I was hoping it might be third time lucky.

A new track, 'Jet Boy', had just begun to fire up and me and Steve both knew the song well, right down to how many times the razor riff would repeat before the handclaps began, when the lead guitar would cut in and how many single drum hits and cymbal crashes would precede the voice of singer David Johansen.

But just before the vocals did kick in, there seemed to be an extra drum hit. A rogue dull thud. I looked at Steve who was staring at me, equally puzzled. We both glanced at the Hi-Fi, where the record played with no further strange occurrences, and then towards the window.

Steve stood up, ambling over to the lace curtains and parting them with a single finger to peer out. Within less than a second, he'd jumped back in fright, pausing only to shout, 'it's him, it's him,' before tearing out of the room.

I went over to see for myself and sure enough, there was Eric Lewis' van and Eric Lewis himself, at the bottom of the path trying to locate his house keys by rhythmically patting his pockets, chest to thigh and back again, like some dancer at an Oktoberfest celebration, only clad in greasy overalls rather than the usual leather shorts.

Steve was at the foot of the stairs, clawing the banister. 'Pete!' he bellowed. 'Pete, her dad's home.'

We began a hasty clear up, while the sounds of similar frenzied activity came from Kelly's bedroom. Steve and Sarah got rid of any cigarette butts from the ashtrays, while Deborah Moore collected the empty beer bottles. Another peek outside was enough to discover that Kelly's dad had found his keys and was moving towards the house. Someone needed to stall him.

The track was still playing and, as I glanced over at the record player, I knew what was required. I picked up the sleeve and went into the hall, positioning myself ready for action. As I saw the door begin to open, I turned and walked away.

If I timed this correctly Eric's first sight upon entering his home would be me striding into his vinyl room with the gatefold of a record still spinning away in the other. I even made sure to turn my wrist so that the black and white cover with pink lipstick scrawl would be clearly visible.

It worked like a charm, and he came bounding straight after me. Any thought of just where his daughter might be, what she was doing and with whom was far from his mind.

'Woah, now, young fellow me lad,' he'd said. 'Where'd you think you're going with that?'

As with many a great enterprise, there were rules when it came to The System. Strict rules to be adhered to all times. Gatherings must not descend into parties. No alcohol or cigarettes were permitted in or around the collection. It was to be treated with the utmost care and respect. I was in flagrant contravention of one of the most basic guidelines, that the distance between vinyl and sleeve be kept to an absolute minimum lest albums find themselves switched.

As he followed me into the back room, Mr Lewis' eyes went straight to the recent copy of *Melody Maker* I'd wedged in between Lou Reed's *Berlin* and Stevie Wonder's *Innervisions*, so we could put the Dolls away when we'd finished playing with them.

Kurt Cobain peered out at the pair of us from the music weekly's cover. A blue hooded top pulled so tight around his face it looked as though his bandmates had tied him into his sleeping bag while on tour.

Eric grimaced at this sight, either from the ill treatment of his collection or a painful flashback to a similar fate on some youthful camping holiday. The System was his pride and joy. A mighty oak grown from the tiny seed of his first musical purchase way back in 1965, Bob Dylan's *Highway 61 Revisited*.

'The integrity of The System must be maintained at all times,' Mr Lewis said, carefully taking the gatefold from my hands and placing it on a desk behind the door. His next step was to remove the paper we had used as makeshift bookmark and slide a blank 12-inch sleeve in its place.

"The System" was how he managed the vinyl that lined the room around us. On each wall were shelves and on each shelf maybe a hundred or so records. All catalogued in strict chronological order, from the album Kelly had christened "Two-Crotch Blues" all the way through to Mr Lewis' most recent addition, Sonic Youth's *Dirty*. The latter had been out only a matter of weeks and we'd played it through twice that morning – much to the annoyance of Sarah who we never did see again, but to the great pleasure of Deborah Moore, giving me high hopes for a future courtship or further dark-cornered fumbles.

With The System back in order, Eric's thoughts finally turned to his daughter. 'Now, where's that young lady got to?'
Pete and Kelly were still nowhere in sight, I'd need to delay her old man further. He made a shooing gesture, hoping I would exit his precious sanctuary, but I didn't move and so neither did he.

My recent actions had given him pause for thought about leaving me in there unsupervised.

'Actually,' I said, inserting a lengthy pause to eat up as many seconds as possible, 'I'd like to learn a bit more about The System, if that's alright with you, Mr Lewis?'

'Oh, right, I see.' A surprised but proud smile broke out across his face. 'Please, call me Eric. Where to start, where to start? Well, The System assumes at least a working knowledge of music history on the part of the interloper.'

I loved how he spoke about his collection as a thing. This living, breathing organism that grew and grew, much to the consternation of his long-suffering wife. I was also amused by his use of the term, "interloper". The whole charade was worth it just for that. I wondered how he might use the word in relation to Pete whose grubby paws had just been all over his daughter, "I returned home, your honour, to discover the interloper defiling my only child."

'Pick somewhere at random,' Eric told me.

I studied the shelves for a while, wasting more time before pointing to a small white tab off to my right. On closer inspection, there was a year written on it, 1980. Rather than start with the first record of the eighties, Mr Lewis' hand had moved back towards the final one of the preceding twelve months.

'Ah, December '79. *London Calling* – double album, of course – my last buy of the seventies. *20 Jazz Greats*, prior to that.'

I followed his finger as it rewound across the spines through a distant era. *Metal Box* in its distinctive silver canister. *Machine Gun Etiquette*. A Raincoats album. *Dragnet* by The Fall.

Cabaret Voltaire's debut, *Mix-Up*. Gang of Four. The Slits. Buzzcocks. Wire's *154. Stations of the Crass*.

'And that's just the back end of the year,' he said.

Further along the shelf I recognised *Unknown Pleasures* and about halfway between that and the tab where 1979 began was a copy of Iggy's *New Values*.

As I think back now, it was a kind of primitive version of the internet, one you could reach out and touch. Pick a record off the shelf and see where it was recorded, who contributed, who the producer was. It was all there in the sleeve notes. Even cryptic messages etched onto the run-outs waiting to be deciphered. With the way it was catalogued you could grab a handful of vinyl and take the temperature of the music scene at any one time. See what was being unleashed upon listeners ears in any given month of any given year all the way back to the sixties.

You had to commend Mr Lewis, he was at an age when someone like us would've considered him in his middle years and so lost to anything up to date, but his love for music allowed him to be open to everything. There was nothing he wouldn't listen to, even rap. While he found some of the lyrics, "a little blue", the opportunity to match the samples used to the original songs in his collection kept him interested.

I nodded my head, truly impressed at The System while trying not to look towards the doorway where I could see a grinning Pete giving me the thumbs up with one hand while trying to fasten his jeans with the other. Seconds later, Kelly walked into the room with not even the slightest flush to her cheeks. She might as well have been sat alone on her bed doing a spot of needlework or reading the Old Testament.

With her arms wrapped around her dad in a hug, she mouthed the words, 'thank you,' over his shoulder.

We turn off Oxford Road and there's the Ritz, site of my debut gig shame, among the ghosts of the Cornerhouse and Haçienda, institutions which once bookended this stretch of Whitworth Street West. The former now settled up the road at Home, opposite the red-brick apartments that replaced the latter. The newly christened Tony Wilson Place established just across from his old one.

I entertain Lauren with the story of The System as we walk and when I'm through she has a question. 'How come Devon wasn't there?'

He's still walking in front and turns to emit a cloud of cig smoke and his answer. 'Gainfully employed, you know what I mean. Busy learning my trade while these twats had all the fun.'

'We worked as well,' Steve counters.

'A couple of days, here and there, in your old man's warehouse,' Devon fires back. 'Would he have sacked you if you weren't up to the job?'

'No, he'd probably have increased my hours.'

Steve had held a part-time position at his dad's builders' merchants between terms. The first step in Mr Williamson's plan for his lad to take over the business. Steve, of course, had ideas of his own.

'Your parents must have been proud that you went to uni,' Lauren tells him.

Steve lets out a noise that is half cough and half laugh. 'My mother definitely was, but not my father. Proud is not how I would describe him. To be honest, he wasn't all that keen on me going.'

'How come?' Lauren asks.

'I was his one chance for him to pass on his *grand empire*. Words were exchanged on the subject. It was my mother who managed to talk him round. She was very supportive of me and always has been. She's a lot cleverer than she's ever had the chance to show. I think she should have gone herself. To university, that is.'

I was always fond of Joanne Williamson, though not in a schoolboy crush type of way. If Pete had found a kindred spirit in Clyde Bradshaw, then I found the same in her and while we'd wait for Steve to perfect his hair or choose whatever he was planning to wear for our gigs or nights out, I would talk to Mrs Williamson.

Where Eric Lewis had his records, she had rows and rows of books. Most were similar to those my mum would get from the library but there would be other works mixed in, Charles Dickens and Salford's own Shelagh Delaney, William Blake or the odd prowling Virginia Woolf. Mrs Williamson was kind enough to let me take one or two with me and kinder still not to grill me afterwards, asking only if I enjoyed them.

One day, however, as I was scanning her shelves, Joanne surprised me with an unexpected topic. While I looked at the books, she was looking at me.

'You remind me of your mum,' she'd said.

I wasn't aware Mrs Williamson had known my mother, but she explained they'd gone to the same school on the Height and showed me a class photo with the two of them in it. They weren't close friends but knew each other in passing. At that stage, talking about my mum wasn't something I was comfortable with and so I'd redirected our chat back to the shelves.

Given how enthusiastic Mrs Williamson was about the band, it's easy to imagine she would've pushed for her son to have a chance to better himself. But when it comes to her husband, Phil Williamson, the man is a fleeting presence in my memories of that time. I'm not sure I could even pick him out of a line-up. He was very hands on at his firm, so we rarely saw him. Whereas Pete's old man and mine were troubled by their lack of work, Steve's dad seemed to struggle with having too much of it.

'I've always been closer to her than I am to my father,' Steve continues. 'Maybe bringing me into the business was his plan for us to connect. If he was proud of anything, it was that place. And I was proud of what he'd achieved but it just wasn't for me. I did two summers there and, to be honest, that was quite enough. I did not want to work in a warehouse for the rest of my life'. There's a pause, before I hear him add, 'no offence, Jim.'

'Oh, none taken, mate,' I reply without turning around.

Cartwright and Sons was still far in the future for me that summer, but I'd moved on from my paper round and was doing a few evenings a week at the cinema in Walkden. The same place where I'd watched *The Doors* with Pete. I served popcorn and soft drinks, dispensed tickets to anyone who looked even remotely old enough and regularly left my post to sneak in and watch as many films as I could get away with.

There'd even been a brief workplace romance, though little of it took place in work and it was not all that romantic. Vicky was her name and if my shift finished too late to catch the last bus home, she would give me a lift back to Swinton in her clapped-out Renault. Along the way she would stop the car somewhere quiet and badly lit before proceeding to mistake my penis for the handbrake.

We cross Whitworth Street near Deansgate Locks and The City Road Inn – a turreted relic that'll probably outlast us all. Soon the four of us turn onto Little Peter Street in search of the Boardwalk and another memory from long ago.

22

Thursday 22nd October 1992
Incendiary Tract (in support of The Jesus Lizard)
Boardwalk

Ah, tea! Such a gratifying beverage, yes? And YET susceptible to the degradations of time as are we all. Now, surely you recall that mug from, when was it, THREE? WEEKS? AGO? You know, the one you distractedly placed on the windowsill of your bedroom so as not to douse your dissertation in stains and splashes. The MUG you then promptly FORGOT all ABOUT.

Do you remember how refreshing it was at the TIME? I mean, sure, you had to make IT using one of those CHEAP bags you found at the back of the cupboard because SOMEONE (I mention no names, MRS GRIST) hadn't been to the shops and it may have been a good month or so out of DATE, but it hit the spot. DID. IT. NOT?

Well, this bright and early Autumn hour, you've just thrown the curtains wide to say GUTEN MORGEN to the glorious day and discovered said mug right where you left it. Only, science BEING science, nature doing its STUFF, it's no longer a half-drunk lovely cup of char, it has mutated into something SOLID and GREEN and thoroughly NASTY.

Oh, and it STINKS. I mean, really HONKS. Christ on a Raleigh 3 speed, the SMELL! You've been wondering what that STENCH was for the past fortnight but had assumed it to be merely a stray SOCK, in witness protection from the laundry. Well, now you know otherwise. Don't bother attempting to wash the thing out, bin it. BIN! IT!

Mark E Moon
Chairman of the Bored
Editor, Mere Pseud Magazine

23

I love 'Dirty Old Town' but it annoys me the way it's become easy shorthand for Salford, like that line of Blake's about Dark Satanic Mills getting trotted out to reinforce a very limiting idea of the North, you know. Have you seen those articles about the BBC staff?

The level of glee this shite's reported with you'd think these innocents had been snatched from some crimeless, poverty-free utopia and dumped in 1980s Beirut. London's got it's armpits like everywhere else. Just because you choose not to look doesn't mean they're not there.

There's more to Salford than crime and filth but if that's the profile they want to push, what precisely are you saying about the people? It's very convenient to forget this city gave the world A Taste of Honey, Love on the Dole, *produced not just the best Scrooge, but the best Poirot and the best Gandhi.*

Pete Moran, 2012

As we walk Little Peter Street, there's little of it I recognise, but then I've not been down this way in years. Even when I was a frequent visitor to these parts, it'd always be under cover of night and influence of alcohol and any memories of those times are sparse and unreliable.

The first few hundred yards are comprised of nothing but a car park to our left and identical, redbrick and grey apartment blocks to our right, one of which occupies the geographical space that was TJ Davidson's, a recording studio and rehearsal rooms where Joy Division filmed the 'Love Will Tear Us Apart' video. Someone lives there now. Not with the same floor or the walls or graffiti riddled door, though I like to think something remains. The ghost of Ian Curtis, perhaps, with his guitar shaped like some lost Dali design for a revamped twenty pence piece, while five yards away the renter/owner watches this same scene on a tiny mobile rectangle.

When we reach Bugle Street, something definitely remains. The pointed roof of a corner structure giving the impression of a place of worship, which for many people it had been. The Boardwalk, former cotton mill and Sunday school turned nightclub and gig venue, now lost to office space.

We stand opposite and watch the staff leave for the night. In our formal attire we might easily pass for a bunch of their colleagues, having a post work chat before heading home.

'I never could remember where this place was,' Steve says.

'Me neither,' I agree, 'In the dark was the only time I could ever find it.'

'In the dark and a bit pissed?'

'That does sum up my teenage years, mate.'

*

The centre of Manchester back then was a world away from the place I visit five days a week as an adult. In my youth, I never felt able to draw a stable map of it in my mind, one that matched the city I saw on Saturday record hunting trips with what emerged when the sun went down. A place fully made up and illuminated by unnatural light.

Aspects of it moved and shifted. Nothing was settled. Nothing pinned down. There was a fluidity, as if the old canals could bear anyone to anywhere. Pieces were slotted together to find their best fit. Anything seemed possible.

My brain was following a similar course. It was a work in progress, rewiring impulses and stabilising connections. Neural pathways were being created and my thoughts had begun to move beyond college.

Like Steve, I'd had ideas of university. But where would I go? What would I take? Which courses gelled with imminent rock stardom? English seemed a natural progression if I was to carry on writing before going on to a career covering music or rugby league or wherever my mind and imagination might take me. I was still discovering who I was and who I might become. What did the future hold for me? Where would I be thirty years down the line?

The city was searching as well, trying out new roles and finding its way in the modern world. Who back then could have foreseen Manchester's glass skyline or a national establishment like the good ship BBC dropping anchor in Salford docks? Or that Ancoats, the area I've worked in for so long, the supposed birthplace of the Industrial Revolution, and a district all but forgotten until recently, might now be flourishing?

In the late nineties when I started at Cartwright and Sons there'd been little to tempt anyone out that way, but now scaffolding clings to former mills as they're transformed into luxury living, a far cry from the history of a place once infamous for deprivation and toil.

Barring the small blue plaque with a yellow smiley face fixed to the outer wall there's little left of the Boardwalk's previous existence, the fans who passed through its doors, and the countless bands who played and practised.

'Can I get a picture of you all in front of it?' Lauren asks.

We stand beneath the blue circle. Three middle-aged men under a cold, dead sun. I position myself in the middle, a buffer between Devon and Steve. The truce is holding, for now.

Lauren clicks away, then passes me her camera and I can't help but grin at the resulting pictures.

'Jesus,' I say, handing it on to the others, 'the Ramones are looking rough.'

The backdrop of plaster and brickwork, coupled with a black and white filter Lauren has applied, brings to mind the cover of the New York punks' debut. Joey, Johnny, Tommy and Dee Dee backed up against a wall. An air of menace clinging to them, along with their drainpipe jeans.

'You mean, the Ramones had they just left Crown Court,' Steve suggests.

'Nah,' Devon says, 'we look more like three twats from an office.'

'Do you mind?' Steve replies, a forced smile showing his too-white teeth. 'I'm a twat from an office.'

'So, you are, man. So, you are.'

I watch the pair, knowing their armistice isn't likely to last and am hardly shocked when it fails to hold.

'What's this over here?' says Steve. 'The light appears to be catching something near Devon. Oh yes, silly me, it's his slap head.'

'Well, at least I've learned to embrace my age. Unlike some folk.'

'And what's that supposed to mean?' Steve enquires.

'Nothing, Mr Just for Men.'

Steve raises a finger, about to fire back an insult, when I interrupt. 'I'm sure Lauren hasn't brought us all together to listen to you two argue about the state of your thatches. I mean, you're more interested in the gig, aren't you?'

She has a grin on her face, amused by the vain bickering of men having trouble accepting the passage of years. 'Yeah, what was it like? I can't imagine getting up in front of a load of people.'

'There weren't all that many people there when we went on,' I say. 'Other bands were after us and before The Jesus Lizard. No one you'd know, though…'

'Powers That Be,' Devon says.

'What?'

'One of the other bands were called Powers That Be.'

'How the fuck do you remember that?' I ask. 'It was a lifetime ago.'

'Oh, I remember it all, know what I mean.' Devon glances over at Steve, so quickly that, if I hadn't had my eye on them, I may well have missed it. 'I might be losing my hair, man, but my memory still works.'

'Did you enjoy it?' Lauren asks, bringing the conversation back to the gig.

'What? Being up on stage?'

'Yeah.'

'God, no,' I tell her. 'I found it terrifying. Dreaded it for days beforehand.'

'Well, I loved it,' Steve remarks. 'All that adrenaline and sweat flying around.'

'You make it sound so appealing, like,' Lauren says with a laugh.

'I have a slightly less rose-tinted view of those times than Steve,' Devon tells her.

'Is that because your view was mainly of our arses?' I joke.

'That's about the size of it, yeah.'

'And who had the best?' Steve asks him.

'The best what?'

'The best arse.'

Devon smirks, 'I dunno how to break it to you lads, but it was Pete. He knew how to shake it an' all, even if sometimes he did look like his legs were on fire.'

'The first gig,' I tell Lauren, 'The Student Union one, was probably more of a happy accident. Your dad had been mithering these promoters for weeks to give us a chance and then one day this spot on a bill appeared and we were in. We hadn't expected it to happen, so we never had time to get nervous. But the second one…'

I trail off recalling the struggles we'd had to stay both in tune and in time with each other. I was still getting to grips with my instrument. We all were, really. Rather than properly embrace the idea of being an actual band, we were still playing with the idea of it. The reality of how much hard work we'd need to put in had yet to hit home.

'We knew it hadn't gone well,' Steve says, moving discarded cigarette butts along the pavement with his brogue. 'To be honest, we were just off. Timing, playing, everything. And then when we read the review in the fanzine, we were gutted.'

There it'd been. Our failure staring back at us in short, sharp printed sentences.

'Your dad was livid,' Devon adds. 'He was ready to go round to Moon's house and confront him.'

'And did he?'

'No,' I say, 'we never knew where the guy lived. Pete was all for tearing a strip off him if we saw him about town, at a gig or in Rockworld, but we never did and as the weeks passed your dad calmed down.'

Whereas Pete had become angry, I'd taken the review differently. It rattled my confidence and there was a part of me that even considered quitting, but it was my friend that pushed me on. Pete was the one with all the belief, the urge to stick two fingers up to any critics and when he did finally make it in the industry, a part of me wasn't all that surprised.

24

I'm forever getting told I don't respond well to being criticised and yet people keep doing it. So, you know, who's really at fault here?

Pete Moran, 2013

After finishing up at the Boardwalk, we re-join Oxford Road for the next and final stop on Lauren's list, the Academy. It's pretty much a straight run down to the venue where everything went so wrong all those years ago and I fear what awaits us there today. Lauren and Devon walk ahead, keen to press on. Her for answers about her father and him for his confrontation with the past. I trail behind with Steve.

In the distance looms the Mancunian Way, grey and ominous, and the thought of passing under it gives me an uneasy feeling. This flyover represents our last real chance to avoid whatever lies beyond and once out the other side, there'll be no turning back.

Between a brain still boozy and the bright sky and heat haze, it appears as a shadowy gateway, a concrete manifestation of a Fall lyric about unnoticed signs or entrances suddenly revealing themselves. And what if we do enter and pass through it? Can we be sure where or when we'll emerge and just what will be uncovered?

Steve comes to a halt. 'Shall we nip in there for something to eat?' he asks and gestures across the street to a Tesco Express.

He must feel as anxious as I do, his urge to delay all this for a while, to preserve the "before" for a little longer, knowing the "after" will go on forever. The mention of food brings on a sensation of intense hunger. Had I not been trapped in my own thoughts, I might've been the one to suggest we stop. How long has it been since I had something to eat? How long since we were up on the Mancunian Way in that taxi passing the exit ramp to nowhere? I look up expecting to see this benign growth jutting out, wondering if the only place it may have led us would've been right here, if some things are just unavoidable. But I realise I've got the streets mixed up, and it's on one adjacent to this.

My geography is muddled. Time is muddled. I'm muddled. It's like I've been awake for days. Did I really only leave for the funeral this morning, see my wife and kids at breakfast? I should send Katie a text and let her know I might be late, but also to have some form of contact with the present. The past has been clawing at us all day, attempting to haul us back into its embrace, whereas I feel keen to haul us all into that Tesco.

'Yeah,' I say, 'let's go in and grab a sandwich.'

'I wouldn't mind some stodge, like,' Lauren agrees.

Devon is unconvinced. 'We can get food up the road.'

'Well, I'm starving,' Steve replies. 'We missed lunch.'

'You mean dinner.'

'If I had meant *dinner*, Devon, I would have said *dinner*.' Steve waits for a lull in the traffic, then makes his way over. Lauren turns to me and raises her eyebrows at their antics before following him. It's the same look I gave her hours ago, in a pub, but which pub?

'Fucking lightweight,' Devon says. 'We could just as easily have got something down near the Academy.'

I wonder if he's just going to wait on this very spot until we return. His mind intent on confrontation. I try to persuade him to join us and appeal to his sense of nostalgia, reminding him the store had at one time been a bar.

He looks at me, puzzled. 'Did it?'

'Yeah, it was Kro2. I mean, everywhere used to be somewhere, mate.'

Devon shakes his head in denial. 'I don't remember that.'

'I thought you remembered everything?'

He seems off in his own little world and then shrugs. 'Not really my part of town this, though, man. Never a student, was I.'

'Come on, mate,' I say. 'Let's go and grab a bite.'

We cross the road and head for the Tesco, and once through its automatic doors Devon disappears down an aisle and I find the cabinet of reduced to clear items.

I stand in front of the chiller and appreciate the cooling air while scanning the shelves. As I try to make a decision, I feel a fog begin to envelop me. Maybe the thing is on the blink and slowly leaking some gas disagreeable to the human condition. I see myself being discovered, a few minutes from now, spaced out on the floor and surrounded by items I've reached for on my way down. Prawn mayonnaise. Bacon, lettuce and tomato. Egg and fucking cress.

It's like a strong sense of déjà vu or an out of body experience. Perhaps, an out of time experience. It isn't forwards I'm going, however, but backwards. The sounds around me lower and my vision fades in from the edges until I'm lost to the past.

It must've been five years ago. I was at home in Chorlton and getting ready to turn in, when I realised we were low on milk. Rather than get up early the next morning and make a run to the local Co-op before breakfast, I decided to throw on my jacket and trainers in the hope I might get there before they shut for the night. With ten minutes to spare, I slipped into the store and found more people inside than I'd passed on the streets. Late shoppers milled about among the lingering presence of assistants who just wanted to close up and go home.

There was a figure bent over the root vegetables who I was set to race past in my hurry to the dairy section, when suddenly he stood up straight and there before me was none other than our former singer and my onetime best pal, Pete Moran.

In his trusty old army jacket and dark sunglasses, with a potato raised to the light for inspection, he looked like some Travis Bickle Hamlet holding aloft the soiled skull of Yorick.

This wasn't the first time I'd seen Moran since the events at the Academy. We'd had a brief reunion about ten years after the band split and then there'd been other chance meetings over time. We were both married, both had kids. The days of the band were already long ago.

'The General!' he said. 'How are you, cock?'

His use of 'cock' no longer held the implied danger it had in our youth. It seemed, in the absence of a better word, flaccid.

'I'm good, mate,' I replied. 'What're you up to?'

'Searching for a spud that hasn't been around since the Elizabethan period. Look at the state of some of these bastards. This one's got Francis Drake's signature on it.'

He tossed a beige lump in my direction, and I juggled this unexpected missile from hand to hand before returning it to the shelf.

'You'd best hurry up,' I told him, 'They'll be closing soon.'

'Really?' He glanced at the watch on his wrist. 'Fuck me, I've been in here since nine.'

As with a lot of things that escaped the mouth of Pete Moran over the years, it was debatable just how true these words were, so I felt it best not to question them. Nor enquire what he had planned for the potato.

'How're things?' I asked, instead.

'All good, cock. All good,' he said with one eye on the spuds he was rummaging around in.

'Are you still over in Swinton?'

'Oh aye, still hanging about the old way, you know. Someone's got to keep the local busybodies full of gossip and innuendo.'

'What brings you down this end?'

'The bus, cock. I was passing on the 22 and saw this place was open, remembered I needed a few bits.'

After paying for our items, we stood outside on the pavement and watched as the staff pulled down the shutters. Moran leaned back against a tree, a cigarette in one hand and his carrier bags in the other, while I cradled my increasingly lukewarm carton of semi-skimmed.

Night was closing in around us, the nearby pubs emptying out. Streetlamps threw spotlights on a handful of inebriated stragglers in front of the bars across the road. If we'd chanced upon one another a few hours earlier, me and Moran would probably have been there with them.

'How's the business?' I asked him.

He looked away and blew out his cheeks, then took a drag of his cig before answering. 'Same as it ever was, you know. I'm currently between record companies. I get asked to produce a few things now and then, bits and bats, but what do I know about production? The only knob I can twiddle with any authority is my own.'

This kind of line would usually be accompanied by a knowing grin or cheeky wink, maybe an elbow to your ribs, but there was nothing. He was oddly subdued. Of late, I'd seen neither his name nor his face in the press. He'd not released any new music in a decade. There'd been no newspaper interviews, no rumours of an autobiography, no talk of a tour.

'Have you written any tunes, lately?'

'Nah, not really. My mind's spottier than a teenager's chin. I feel…' he waggled his fingers around the side of his head, '…constipated, I suppose. There's stuff in there, you know, but I can't seem to draw it out. What about you? Do you still write?'

'No, not for a long time now. Shopping lists, birthday cards, notes to school for the kids is about as far as I get these days.'

'What about the bass? You still play at all?'

'Sometimes I'll get together with a few of the guys from work for a jam, but even that's becoming a rare thing.'

'Shame, that. A fucking shame. You ever see anything of Devon? I haven't seen him in time.'

'Yeah, possibly too much, actually. He's the same as he was back in the day, just with a wife, two kids and even less hair.'

Moran smiled. 'Well, send him my best when you see him.'

The whereabouts of Incendiary Tract's fourth member, Steve Williamson, had gone unmentioned. Across the street, two men danced to a rhythm only they could hear while a third attempted to coax them into a waiting cab.

'Can you believe we're in our forties?' Moran said. 'How time flies. You know, I was in the bank the other day, just to close an old account I don't use anymore, and this manchild behind the counter was taken aback my signature was slightly different to one I used in 1994. Only a bloody pedant would've found fault. The cock!'

'What was wrong with it?'

'I dunno. Flatter, squigglier. Less care applied to it, basically.' He took another drag before continuing. 'That's pretty much me, you know, in ink form. Sometimes, I'll see myself in the mirror and think, who's this old fella staring at?' He paused for a moment, then went on. 'Speaking of old fellas, I saw your dad the other day, he's looking well.'

'Yeah, retirement really suits him. He's got time on his hands, a couple of grandkids to dote on and we go watching the rugby when we can. He's even got some money in his pocket with the mortgage paid off. He's thinking about going over to Canada to see our Lee.'

Neither of us could've known that within a year or so my old man would be gone. Nor that within five, Moran would join him.

'How're your lot?' I asked.

'They're alright, still waiting for me to get a so-called proper job and our Rob's ever the loveable knobhead.'

'How about Lauren?'

'She graduated a few years back.'

'That's great.' For such good news, Moran looked strangely sad about it.

'Yeah,' he said. 'I'm so proud of her. I just wish she was as proud of me.'

'I'm sure she is, mate.'

He gave a half-hearted shrug and stared down at his boots. They were sturdy, but scuffed, the shine long gone. 'I dunno,' Moran said. 'I think I'm a disappointment to her. I'm a disappointment to myself, you know. I'd like to be a better dad, I'd like to be a better husband, but I'm not sure I've got it in me, the capacity to change. It's like these fuckers,' he lifted up his hand to show me the part-smoked cigarette between his fingers he'd been taking a drag from after almost every sentence, 'I keep trying to give them up and I'll think I've done it, an' all. But then I'll look down and there's another one, almost down to the bloody dimp.'

As he'd not mentioned Kelly, I began to wonder if they were still together, but then he suggested we all meet up, our wives and kids. How much of this was an honest plan and how much was just him playing up to social conventions, I couldn't say, and never did find out. We were mid-conversation when he turned and ran. Bulging carrier bags swinging at his sides and shouted goodbyes trailing after him.

I thought perhaps he'd changed his mind, was trying to put as much distance between himself and the idea as possible, until I realised his bus had been approaching from behind me.

Apart from a brief sighting on Tib Street years later, that was the last I ever saw of Pete Moran.

A chin comes to rest on my shoulder, and I'm back in the present. Back in Tesco and staring into the reduced-to-clear section amid a stink of stale booze.

'Are you buying that butty or squeezing the fucker to death?'

I laugh at Devon and the half-squashed sandwich packet in my hand but can't control my volume. The sudden noise brings dirty looks from other customers and assistants stacking the shelves close by. The store's security guard peers out from behind a stand of health food bars. I notice Devon's armful of plastic wrapped snacks.

'What happened to getting something down the road?'

'Well, you know what they say, man,' he tells me, almost losing a grip on the goods clutched to his chest, 'if you can't beat 'em, eat 'em!'

'What've you got there?'

'Crumpets, potato cakes, you name it.'

'And where do you expect to toast them all?'

'I don't,' he says, looking deadly serious. 'I'm having them as nature intended.'

'What? Straight from the packet?'

'Yeah, man.'

'You're a fucking animal, Devon Bradshaw.'

'Just cutting out the middleman, man. Man. Man.' He's stuck in a loop and getting progressively louder. The guard, no longer concealed behind a display, is staring straight at us.

In our suits, we might seem like any other office types, but our collars are wide open, our ties long since removed uncoil in our pockets like waking vipers. It's a Tuesday evening, not even seven o'clock and the look the guard is giving us isn't a friendly one. We're rogue elements in this man's day.

I'm tempted to approach him and explain the situation, but also to ask, is he happy in his work? What's the pay like? Does he consider it a fair amount for what he does? I've begun to do this in the last week. Not the actual asking, just the thinking. More a questioning of myself. What would I do if the worst happened at the warehouse, and I ended up out of a job? What would the future hold for me? I'll see tram drivers, assistants in book or record shops, anyone doing their job and wonder, could I do that?

Devon decides to go and get another pack of crumpets, so I head to pay for my choice, two chicken and bacon sandwiches, one lightly squished. Outside Steve is already waiting on the pavement and we nod at each other and watch Lauren at the self-service tills through the glass. It doesn't take long before he voices the question that's been on my mind all day.

'How much do you think she knows?'

The expression on his face is one of, what? Concern? Discomfort? Both? It's probably the same expression I have on mine. I take a breath and try to put my thoughts into some kind of order.

'I doubt she would've organised all this if she knew what went on back then. I mean, I just think she wants to learn a bit more about a hidden part of her dad's life. That's all.'

How much I convince Steve is debatable, as is how much I've convinced myself.

'You don't think her mother might have let something slip?' he asks.

It's a difficult question to answer. If I never really knew Steve Williamson, then I certainly didn't know the then Kelly Lewis. She was a mate's girlfriend and then an old mate's wife. If I didn't know her back then, she's even more a mystery to me now. What would she tell her daughter in their moment of grief? I see Lauren framed in the Tesco window. At this distance, and with my poor eyesight, she could almost be her mother.

'Nah, mate. Kelly was a lot of things, but I can't imagine she wants the past dug up any more than we do.'

Steve looks over at me. 'You're probably right. Thanks, Jim.' He's still looking at me when he clears his throat and continues, 'I was sorry to hear about your father, by the way.'

I stare at him, and he must see the surprise on my face, so begins to explain.

'My mother keeps in touch with a few of her old friends and one of them lived on his street, and well, you know how news gets round.'

Though it's been four years now, I've still not come up with a suitable response for whenever anyone mentions my old man's passing. I feel even more uncomfortable talking about it to Steve, almost a stranger. It's odd to think how our lives had intersected before either of us were born – that our dads had drunk in the same pubs, that our mums had attended the same school – and then converged again as teenagers before our separate paths took each of us to differing ends. I redirect the conversation to his folks and ask about his mum, Joanne.

'She's doing great,' Steve replies. 'Enjoying her retirement with plenty of hobbies to keep her occupied, still always reading. Not my father, though. I think he's pretty bored. To be honest, I think he's been bored since the day he sold the business. They're healthy, which I'm grateful for. But I worry about what will happen when one of them goes. I'm not sure how the other will cope. I don't know if I'll even cope.'

I try to think of some nugget of comfort for him, something profound. But there's little about death that doesn't sound trite as soon as it leaves your lips, no combination of words that life's great thinkers have yet to already put together. Death itself is trite. The concept crushingly unoriginal.

'You just do, I suppose,' is all I manage to summon and before I can elaborate, Devon and Lauren emerge from the store.

'Onwards!' Devon points the way ahead with one arm while juggling his selection of foodstuffs with the other.

'Didn't you get a carrier bag?'

'No way, Jim, man. Think of the environment,' he replies, before adding with a wink, 'and the five pence I've just saved, know what I mean.'

'We're not eating on the hoof, are we?' I ask.

'We could always sit in All Saints Park,' Lauren says. 'It's literally on our way.'

25

Hello, you've reached the home of Peter Paul Moran. I'm not in right now or maybe I am, who can really say. If you're calling about the roof, then Tony, please ring me back before the weekend. If you're from the press, feel free not to fucking bother.

Pete Moran, 2013

There's not a cloud above us as we sit in the centre of the park and spread out across stone steps with our supplies. A month or so from now this area will be buzzing with excited students from all over the world, but today it's mostly deserted, and we eat in silence, each lost to our own thoughts.

Beyond the gates, traffic motors up and down Oxford Road and beyond that, on the other side of the busy street is Johnny Roadhouse. The long-standing music shop stirs a memory I'm not ready to think about just yet, and I make it through half my culinary purchase, then take the opportunity to call my wife.

I make my excuses and wander off, following the path to a patch of shade provided by tall trees. It's just after seven and Katie picks up on the third ring.

'Good evening, stranger,' she says. 'I was wondering when I might hear from you.'

'What can I say, best laid plans, eh love.'

'How's it going there?'

'Much as you'd expect, really. Though, I'm not actually at the wake. We sort of got hijacked by Pete's daughter and have ended up in town. She wants to hear some stories about her dad from back in the day.' I tell her that Devon is with us but don't feel like trying to explain about Steve.

'How is Devon?' she asks.

'Devon's Devon, as usual. I'll tell him you said hello.'

'Do more than that, arrange something with him for your birthday.'

In just over a month, I'll be forty-eight and what present will I receive? Socks? A convincing toupee? My P45? I should tell her about what's going on at the warehouse, the possible threat of unemployment. Instead, I ask how the kids are.

Katie takes a deep breath before she answers. 'Jack's been acting up again.'

Gone are the days when our son would limit his dirty deeds to investigating the phone sockets with his Meccano. Now he's branched out into other misdemeanours. Seemingly pointless acts of destruction, which he goes on to defend in an internet speak I can't claim to understand bar the sprinkling of swear words which I'm pretty sure he didn't fucking pick up from me.

'What is it now?' I ask.

'Nothing major, I suppose,' she replies. 'Mild tormenting of his sister and standard insubordination, but it's just not what I want to come home to after a day at work. The child minder had a list of complaints as long as my arm. If he's this bad now, Jim, what will he be like in a few years?'

Now does not seem the time to be dropping bombshells about work.

'Why did no one tell us it was this hard?' Katie continues. 'All those friends of ours who said how wonderful it would be. Was it just a conspiracy to drag us out on bloody play dates?'

'They can't hear you, can they?'

'The kids? Course they can't hear me, they're plugged into the matrix. I could say anything right now and they wouldn't look up. I could tell them I'm popping out to slaughter next door's labradoodle and all I'd get in return would be two nods and a pair of grunts.'

'You'll be glad of the little sods when we're old and infirm,' I tell her, 'When it's their turn to look after us. Just think of it, me and you, tucked up under a big blanket with matching ear horns.'

'Are you OK?' Katie asks.

I can hear the change in her voice, the sudden injection of concern. How to reply. I could say this whole day has dredged up so many thoughts from times I'd rather not dwell on, times

I'd banished from my mind, that I feel under attack from the past. I could say that, but instead, I say I'm fine.

'Are you sure? It's just you sound mawkish.'

'What,' I say, 'like Robin Williams?'

She laughs. I love her laugh, it's completely at odds with the rest of her personality. Katie is essentially a quiet, restrained individual, fond of dry humour. But when tickled by something funny, her volume gets cranked up to the max and she ends up sounding like a character from a *Carry On...* film.

'You're not overdoing it, are you?' she asks, when her guffawing subsides.

I look down at the bargain bin butty in my hand. I feel reduced myself. A man past his best. Cartwright and Co. certainly seem keen to put an end date on me.

'Not really,' I tell her. 'We've only had a few, and we're nearly done. I can't see us being out all that much longer. What are you up to, anyway?'

'There's a *Columbo* on,' my wife replies.

Somewhere in the world, no matter the time zone, local language or catastrophic events taking place there's always a *Columbo* on. This is how humanity has made it this far.

'It's only just started,' she tells me. 'William Shatner's in it.'

'Really? Are we too late for you to press record?'

'It's never too late, Jim. We're not in the nineties, anymore. I can fast forward, pause and rewind, you name it.'

'Someone should've paused William Shatner a long time ago.'

'Now, Jim. I know you don't mean that. Do you want me to save it til you get home?'

The idea sounds tempting and not just that of settling down on the sofa with Katie to watch Peter Falk in his creased raincoat, and almost as creased face, get to the bottom of a tricky whodunnit. I mean the pausing and rewinding. The chance to start over.

Behind the park's thick foliage, I can no longer see the others. But the rear gate and back street are only a stride or two away making for an easy escape route should I choose to take it. I could disappear into the surrounding area and not even the renowned TV detective would be able to track me down. Unless he had my home address.

'I could give you an emergency phone call?' my wife says with a hint of mischief in her question.

It's a tempting thought. Five minutes to go and get settled on the grass, only to jump up and put on a frantic display over some invented crisis. I'd indulge in a spot of frenzied pacing before heading onto Oxford Road to flag down a black cab. Goodbye 1992, hello ITV4.

'Nah, you're alright. It'll probably be on again next week.'

I tell Katie I'll see her later and return to the steps to sit back with the others and the rest of my sandwiches. Steve and Lauren have finished eating and each are occupied with their mobile phones while Devon is still chomping away. Try as I might not to think about Johnny Roadhouse, the spectre is right there, across the street. It's not a memory I'm particularly ready for but I decide to confront it, nonetheless.

It was my seventeenth birthday when I met my old man there – I'd headed into town after college while he'd managed to finish his shift early. It was part one of Pete's plan being put into action: my acquisition of a bass guitar. This would be September '91. Three years earlier, when I was fourteen, my mum had died, after which my dad had not just grief to contend with, but a house with only a single wage coming in.

Understandably, he was wary about splashing out on something that might well end up collecting dust in the corner a few months down the line, but I promised him it wouldn't be a waste of money, that this new interest of mine was not just some passing fad. We agreed it'd also represent my future Christmas present, and I negotiated a similar deal with my gran. The pot had been swelled further with cash I'd saved myself.

The instrument I came home with that day was second-hand and unwieldy, its dimensions similar to those of a coffee table and with a playing experience to match. Should I remove my hand from its neck, even for a second, the headstock would dip violently, making a bid for the floor and I'd be left to fumble after the thing. It wasn't flash and it wasn't pretty, but it was mine and over the next fifteen months, together with a battered amp, I found the right set up to tease a half-decent tone from it.

But not long after our trip to Johnny Roadhouse, my dad lost his job. He'd been at the firm about six months, and they needed to make cuts. It was a case of last in, first out and so he was back on the dole. The situation took a while to really deteriorate. Serious debt doesn't happen overnight. It's a slow process, one of accumulation. The drip, drip of payments being missed, some monthly, others quarterly, until you reach the point where you're drowning.

By the time the band had got round to playing gigs, about a year later, things were a mess. My father was still unemployed and owed money to just about everybody. I told Lauren I disliked playing on stage, but the truth was that when the four of us were up there in front of a crowd, the feeling was like nothing I've felt before or since. Being in front of all those people, and the nerves it brought, having something else to concentrate on, distracted my attention from the growing financial turmoil at home. It was my respite, a life raft for me to occupy before we walked off stage and I was dumped unceremoniously back in the drink.

26

Wednesday 9th December 1992
Incendiary Tract (in support of Sonic Youth)
Manchester Academy

Last Thursday morning – can you remember the last time anything actually happened on a THURSDAY? Not even Mrs Grist's memory goes THAT. FAR. BACK – this fair if sodden city of ours was rocked by a couple of EXPLOSIVE imports from over the IRA-ish Sea. On Wednesday, the Academy felt the full FORCE of a couple more. This time, from all the way across the Atlantic.

West coast indie-rockers PAVEMENT and New York noiseniks SONIC YOUTH were the main attractions, but for a handful of the

CURIOUS, front and centre as the doors opened, there was a third INCENDIARY ACT.

Regular readers may recall I haven't been entirely complimentary about THIS Swinton quartet in my recent missives. A little over two months ago, they made their entrance into the world, and it was a PAINFUL affair, not least on MY. POOR. EARDRUMS.

Three weeks later, they appeared to have, if anything, DEGRADED. Were they going for half-baked Joy Division tribute act or mere PARODY? Were they guilty of listening to TOO MUCH of Lord Tony Wilson's doom darlings or nowhere near ENOUGH?

But – and it's a BIG BUT, I CANNOT LIE – faced with a larger venue to fill and a far more prestigious bill to live up to, they appear to have taken ONE. GIANT. LEAP.

Whatever they've been up to since their last public DISPLAY, be it rummaging through fellow Swinton resident Shaun William Ryder's GARBAGE on the hunt for inspiration or loitering at a crossroads in a bid to sell at least one of their young SOULS, it appears to have worked.

Musically they have established their own PATCH of dusty Mancunian WASTELAND, constructing a sound that can move from the BRUTAL to the beautiful in a fraction of a second while teetering on the VERGE of falling apart.

As for their singer, he's not just FOUND a voice, he's found HIS voice (forgive me, dear reader, while I VOMIT! You might want to clean that up sharpish, Mrs Grist, before it soaks through this EXCUSE for a carpet). No longer is he trying to be someone ELSE. He, perhaps, wasn't TRYING at all. The words and emotion seemed DRAWN from him as if by a higher power. At times this was more

EXORCISM than performance – alas, of MAX VON SYDOW, there was no sign.

There is something undeniably INFECTIOUS about them, although I can't quite put my FINGER on it and, in the interests of public health, I'm not sure I would WANT to. Not without a pair of RUBBER gloves, at least. You may even wish to DOUBLE BAG.

Be that as it may, Incendiary Tract will be back at the Academy before Christmas, supporting the Ramones, and on this evidence so will I – IF, and it's a big IF, that loutish oaf on the door doesn't PULL the same TRICK again and claim MY NAME isn't on the list.

Not on the list? NOT. ON. THE. LIST? I AM THE LIST, BABY!

Mark E Moon
Chairman of the Bored
Editor, Mere Pseud Magazine

27

It's been a while, hasn't it? I'm actually working on something at the moment, you know. Hopefully, it's my second wind and not just a case of passing flatulence.

Pete Moran, 2019

We leave the park with a long overdue feed inside us and move on, and if past and present have merged too often already today, then the scene greeting us at the Academy is no different. The darkness of its tall glass entranceway brings to mind the recent pandemic years, while the posters advertising upcoming events – So Solid Crew, Anthrax – could've been in place since the nineties.

The area is almost lockdown quiet. Even across the road at Kro Bar, the pre- and post-gig destination for many a concertgoer, only small clusters sit out front enjoying the sun. Without students, it's like a seaside resort out of season.

For me, though, this part of the city was never really about education, it was always the music. So many evenings at the Academy's various venues, and club nights at nearby Jabez Clegg, the onetime beerhall just a street away. I was here so often in my youth, but then over time my visits became sporadic. Every weekend turned into every fortnight. Every fortnight into every month. Regular jaunts became rarities.

In recent years I've identified this end of town more with its hospitals. The new St. Mary's next to the ageing Manchester Royal Infirmary. In the former for the birth of our second child, in the latter for the final days of my father. One hand in my wife Katie's clenched fist, her grip tightening with each push as our youngest burst into the world. The other cradling my old man's bony, weakening fingers as he slipped from it.

He'd begun to feel unwell nine months earlier, experiencing breathing difficulties and chest pains. My dad was pushing seventy and knew it might be serious, might be cancer of a sort. He'd been a smoker, more on than off, and so was braced for this. We talked about it, and he told me it'd be OK. People get cancer every day, he'd said. They have treatment and they recover.

After his struggles in my teenage years, his life had recovered. It'd taken a long while, but he got to enjoy a second act. The mortgage was paid off and with a bit of money from one of his own deceased parents in the bank he went on holiday, bought a brand-new car, enjoyed the sort of things most people take for granted but which had been denied him up until then. It didn't last. He was diagnosed with mesothelioma, a form of fatal cancer caused by exposure to asbestos. Not smoking then but working. Working would kill him. The doctor gave him six to twelve months.

A woman from some association had come round and they went through his work life, searching to uncover where this exposure occurred. My dad's employment history was varied: he'd drove; he'd sold; he'd guarded other people's property; there'd been his spell in the army; a brief stint as a plumber's mate. The likely culprit though was a period in the early '60s he'd spent ripping up and laying woodblock flooring at a Manchester dancehall. This was only a year or so after he'd left school at fourteen. In another time, he might've been William Blake's 'The Chimney Sweeper', sold to some master. In another life, a canary down a fucking mine.

My dad's final week was spent inside a small, sterile room, his body shutting down, pain and the medication to counter it slowly taking over. The ability to communicate reduced to ragged, breathy phrases, one of which was to tell me he needed a piss.

This man, who'd carried so much on his shoulders and raised me on his own, now unable to do something as simple as pass urine under his own steam. There were usually nurses close by to take care of him, but when I'd gone out into the ward to find one there was nobody around. So, over forty years after he and my mum had balanced the infant me on a potty at home, there I was loosening his pyjama bottoms to direct this dying man's penis into a hospital bottle.

The next day was his last. It was July, less than a year after he'd started feeling unwell, but over fifty since asbestos fibres had entered his lungs.

Lauren stands peering into the gloom of the venue. 'My dad brought me here for my first gig,' she says, talking as much to the deserted Academy as to us. 'Sonic Youth, it was. I was only seventeen at the time.'

'What year was that?' I ask.

'2010. That would've been, what, eighteen years after you supported them?'

Christ, I think. Eighteen years. Imagine playing with the same people for eighteen bloody years. The same faces, the same traits and quirks, perhaps eclectic and amusing in the beginning, but patience and tolerance eroding over time. Sonic Youth had lasted for almost three decades, but we didn't even survive four live outings.

'I couldn't believe how lucky we were,' Devon says. 'Opening the bill for a band like that, I thought we'd made it.'

'It was pretty amazing,' I tell Lauren. 'I mean, the whole thing just came together. The bad review we'd had for the Boardwalk really affected us, your dad especially. I think I'd underestimated how serious he was about the band. For me, it'd been an outlet for my writing…'

'And a way to impress girls,' Steve interrupts.

'Well, to try to, anyhow,' I say with a smile. 'But getting slated like that gave us a kick up the arse. We worked hard for six or seven weeks and, like I said, it all came together. Even Mark E Moon changed his mind about us.'

The camera is in Lauren's hands, and we pose for a few more shots. When she's finished, I expect us all to head over to Kro Bar for a well-earned pint, but she remains looking back at the Academy and we wait with her.

'When was the last time you were here?' she asks us.

'Me and Sandra, that's my wife, were here in January,' Devon says. 'Soul II Soul were on. I've suggested gigs here to Jim over time, but he's always been washing his hair.'

I'm about to make the old, reliable gag about still having hair to wash, but something in his tone makes me stop. Is this just playful teasing taken up a notch by alcohol or is there a touch of resentment there?

The last gig I went to with Devon was just before Christmas, The Chameleons at the Ritz, a place where the only lingering memory for me was of vomit and you can steel your olfactory senses to put up with that kind of thing after a while. Unlike the mental scars of an onstage brawl.

The single time I'd been in the Academy in recent years was with Katie to see some American indie band and I'd felt safe to do so because they were so far removed from the type of music we used to play. There was also the fact my wife knew next to nothing about Incendiary Tract. I told her I'd been in a band in my youth with Pete and Devon, but always played it down, never mentioning the times we'd performed on the same stages as real-life rock stars.

'What about you, Steve?' Lauren asks.

'Not since '92,' he replies quietly.

There's a pause as we wait for her to ask about our final performance. Traffic moves up and down the street behind us. An occasional pedestrian ambles by. But when she speaks it's not the question I've been dreading. It's not even a question, at all. 'Me and my dad were here late last year,' she says. 'Seems like forever ago now, like.'

She's still facing away from us and brings her sleeve up to her eyes. 'I shouldn't have said what I did about him before, about my mam neither. I love the pair of them, it's just they make me angry with how they behave. They make bad decisions, they've always made bad decisions, and I literally can't stop myself judging them for it.'

Lauren turns and her eyes are ringed in red, she looks tired. I wonder how she'll judge this day in the weeks and months to come, whether it'll be seen as the cathartic experience she needed to go through or as a mess that should've been avoided by all.

'I'm angry with my mam for acting out the same patterns she just can't seem to see, like, and I'm angry with my dad for putting her in those positions in the first place. Most of all, though, I'm angry with him because he's dead. You don't die from a heart attack at his age. You shouldn't, anyway. I don't understand why he did the things he did. Why didn't he look after himself better?'

'Decisions never seem quite so foolish in the moment you make them,' Steve offers.

Devon stares at him and I wish he wouldn't.

'But I miss him already,' Lauren says as she starts to cry.

'I know,' Steve says, his hand on her shoulder. 'I know, but we all make mistakes. If you're lucky, they don't come back to bite you on the arse.'

I gesture over in the direction of Kro Bar, but none of us move. We wait on Lauren, who doesn't seem ready just yet. Something about the Academy still bothers her.

It's hard to believe only a short while ago we were in All Saints Park, and I was being offered a lifeline by Katie. I could be at home right now, with my wife and Lieutenant Columbo, instead of here, waiting for the inevitable unpleasantness. Waiting for Moran's daughter to enquire about one more thing.

Lauren stares back at the venue for a moment and then turns to us and I feel I know what she's going to ask before she does. Maybe, by thinking it, I've passed the thought into her mind.

'What about the other gig, though?'

Steve's eyes flick off up the street, on the lookout for a passing taxi he might jump into, and Devon appears ready to pounce should he show any sign of escaping.

'Other gig?' I say, trying to sound calm.

'Yeah, the Ramones one mentioned in the fanzine, like.'

She's about to reach into her bag, to open the tin and bring out *Mere Pseud Magazine,* to point at the line itself. Or does she have that other copy, the issue detailing our shame.

'Oh, that one.' My words stop the movement of her hands.

Any slim hope I had the topic wouldn't arise is now gone. I knew it was coming, and yet I've put no thought into a reply.

Perhaps a part of me wants the truth to come out so we can all move on. Then again, perhaps not. I try to cobble together a tale that might stand up to scrutiny and our former guitarist's words from earlier play over and over in my head, "how much do you think she knows?" But as I open my mouth to speak, Steve is already talking.

'To be honest, it was a bit of an anti-climax. We'd peaked the week before, on the Sonic Youth bill, and were unable to repeat that. I think the morning in the studio proved a step too far for us. "Creative differences" they'd call it these days, I suppose.'

Moran's daughter looks away for a second and I glance over to Steve. He meets my eyes and gives me a slight nod, a silent confirmation he has this in hand.

'And that was why you broke up?' Lauren asks.

'Pretty much, yes,' Steve continues. 'The Ramones gig was just a last hurrah, a chance to say goodbye. There may have been other factors, your father deciding I was a bourgeois prick because I wanted to go to university, being one of them.'

'He wasn't far wrong,' Devon says with a smirk, which quickly disappears after I fire him a hard stare.

For a time, Lauren doesn't speak as she processes this information and I hope it'll be enough. When she does finally respond, her voice is slow and measured with a question I'm even more unprepared to answer.

'So, it wasn't because of me, like?'

28

Saturday 12th December 1992

We had an appointment to speak with the press. A form of the press, anyway. The band had been approached about an interview. Though approached may not have been quite right, either.

After our set, the promoter had handed us a pack of cans and ushered us from the backstage area to join the crowd. We claimed a spot about halfway back, in easy reach of the bar. The cans did not last long, and a steady flow of alcohol was required to neutralise the last of the adrenaline pulsing through our bodies. Without instruments, few this far from the front would match us to the quartet onstage a short time before. In jeans and trainers, band Tees and checked shirts, we were just another gang of teenage music fans watching the next group on the bill.

Pavement came and went and as the road crew readied the headliner's equipment, I noticed a strange movement to our left. A familiar head bobbing up and down in a sea of faces, all of whom were facing the stage except this one, who stared straight at us.

This head – all black-rimmed glasses and art school haircut – would vanish, sucked under by the current drifting forwards, only to pop up that bit closer, before submerging once again. There had seemed a moment when I thought he might never resurface, that he may have gone under for good, but soon Mark E Moon waded out to stand beside us.

Pete had longed for a showdown after the savage Boardwalk review and here was his chance. We bristled as one, producing a united front against this outsider and Moon shrunk back. A stand-off occurred as the music between acts came to an end and we eyed the fanzine writer, daring him to speak, while the lights began to dim. There had been cheering and whistling, then in the distance appeared Sonic Youth.

Moon coughed to clear his throat and that was the last we heard from him as an electric howl filled the air, as though the audience's whistles had been harnessed and relayed back at them, louder in volume and harsher in frequency. All other sound was cut off. Moon's jaw opened and closed with extra effort as he tried to make himself heard, but we made out not a thing. Exasperated, but undeterred, he reached into the brown leather satchel over his shoulder, pulling out notebook and pen. He wrote a quick message and passed it over.

Interview? was all it said.

I exchanged a glance with Pete before he snatched the pad and biro, turning to scribble down a reply no one else could see.

Onstage, the feedback had been replaced by a low-pitched wail, wheezing and shifting, building slowly. We might have guessed this laboured bombast was a worn-out air raid siren or Time Lord's Tardis had we not seen the distant guitarist who conjured it.

When Pete was done, he handed the book over with a friendly nod, and Moon flicked to the page of his polite enquiry finding imprinted below, a large cartoon cock and balls.

As Moon moved away from us, I thought he might disappear back into the mass of fans and our moment had gone, but instead he set to work, attacking the page as a second guitar joined the first, adding its own contrasting layer. A rattle high and sharp, like that of an approaching fire truck ringing its bell in ceaseless alarm.

Pete was intrigued by what his rival was producing and tried to sneak a look, but found his view repeatedly blocked. Was Moon composing a diatribe against the arrogance of wannabee rock stars like us?

Two rivals wielded the same instrument of power to vastly differing ends, siren and alarm blending into fevered panic before the impending assault. My ears felt heavy and ready to burst.

Moon finished and presented the notebook to us like a summons, his face betraying no emotion. Inside, the drawing of male genitalia was no longer visible having been transformed into a space shuttle during lift-off. The testicles were giant circles of smoke, billowing at the base, its shaft an external tank with the main craft clinging to its side. A miniature Stars and Stripes flag was detailed on the vessel's wing and underneath were three words:

GODSPEED JOHN THOMAS

The crescendo that had built around us fell away, leaving only rumbling bass and laidback percussion. I looked at Pete, who nodded in agreement and as the female voice onstage sang out a question, our singer took back the pen and asked one of his own.
When?

In the van on our way home, there had been an argument. Pete, as leader, decided only he and I would meet Mark E Moon. Devon was not too bothered about missing out or did not make a show of it if he was, but Steve was furious, insisting he should come with us.

Pete waved him away and the pair continued in this vein for the next few days, blighting our time in Spirit Studios when we should have been concentrating on putting together a demo tape. I was shocked when our singer finally relented, giving Steve the details of our meeting with Moon. I was less shocked when I found out these details were wholly untrue.

At around midday, our guitarist would be standing outside Odyssey 7 near the Corn Exchange, checking his watch and with no way to contact us. Whereas an hour earlier, Pete and I had got off the bus and walked in the opposite direction towards Piccadilly Gardens and found Mark E Moon, leaning against the Our Price glass, reading a battered old paperback, and ignoring shoppers as they hurried past.

He was clad in a suit of double denim, jeans and jacket fraying at the edges and stonewashed far beyond any acceptable level of decency. Underneath, the T-shirt he had on bore spiky skulls and crossed-out proclamations amid a riot of colour. It was an outfit that seemed inadvisable on such a cold day. I wore at least two more layers and was frozen to my bones.

I could not fault his reading material, though, not that I had read or even heard of it. *A Season in Hell,* the book was called. Its title painfully apt for a Saturday in town during the run-up to Christmas.

'Alright, *cock*,' Pete said to him, the greater emphasis on the latter word no doubt adding a first point of the day to his mental scoreboard. 'Where'd you wanna do this, then?'

Moon led the way down Oldham Street to Stevenson Square and a warm booth in The Koffee Pot. We chose a table by its steamed windows and condensation drew a veil between us and the world outside. The same notebook came out of the same satchel as three days earlier, but this time was followed by a plastic rectangle with pull-out handle. His tape recorder. We ordered food and brews and then Moon pressed record.

'So, you guys are still pretty young to have played the stages you have. How old are you?'

'For anyone who asks,' Pete replied, without missing a beat, 'we're all over eighteen and have got the fake IDs to prove it.'

Another point for Pete and for the most part correct, though Devon was still seventeen and would be well into the next year.

Moon pushed the frames of his slipping spectacles back into place with his biro, giving the pair of us a once over, probably wondering if this first answer was to set the tone for the interview ahead.

He was not what I had been expecting, was far less manic than his written persona, and I thought I might ask him a few things as well. When had he got into writing? How did he come to start *Mere Pseud Magazine*? Who was this Mrs Grist he so often mentioned? Was she a real person, maybe his landlady or his mum, or just a figment of his imagination? Yet I was nervous and still wary of him, of the words he had already published about us and those he might in the future. I also did not want Pete to see me showing what he might consider a too-friendly tone toward this stranger.

'Your band name is very distinctive,' the fanzine writer continued. 'Where did that come from? Is it inspired by anything in particular?'

Conversation stopped as the waitress brought our drinks.

'Well, Mr Moon,' Pete said, lifting his mug, 'I'm glad you asked.'

If I thought he might relate the tale of Salman Rushdie's possible water infection, I would have been wrong. Any nod to the literary world was stripped away.

'Have you ever had that feeling when you're having a piss and it burns like fuck on its way out?'

Mark E Moon did not answer, and Pete felt free to carry on racking up mental points. 'That's the exact sensation I want people to experience when they hear us, you know. Pleasure and pain.'

This tempted General Smart Arse into an advance. 'Relief in the middle of a raging fire,' I added for my own opening point.

Our interviewer raised his eyebrows while his glasses slid down his nose, and Pete turned to me. 'It's 'Slash 'n' Burn', isn't it? Do you think that's where the Manics got that from?'

Moon left this unanswered and pressed on. 'What about the songs, who's the writer among you?'

'We both are,' I told him. This was my chance to get Moon talking about what I wanted. 'It's exciting, having things out there and being heard. I've written stuff before but hardly anyone ever read it.'

The comic I collaborated on at school had had a readership barely in the double figures. From that, the leap to crowds of hundreds at the Boardwalk and Academy was huge.

'I mean, I love writing, but if no one ever sees it it feels like half a job.

Pete swallowed a mouthful of tea and cleared his throat. 'If a bear shits in the woods and no one's round to catch a whiff, does it make a stink?'

I chalked up another point to my mate but remained focused on Moon. 'You must get a buzz from your fanzine,' I suggested. Being on sale in Piccadilly Records, being read by people on the bus...'

'Or on the crapper,' Pete cut in again and smirked.

Moon tried his best to ignore him, readjusting his spectacles this time with a sneakily raised middle finger.

Our food arrived, the waitress placing full plates in front of us, and Moon paused his tape machine to give it a break from knives and forks chipping away against crockery, and rampant teenage sarcasm.

When Moon had eaten a third of his omelette, he restarted the tape. 'You've just opened for Sonic Youth. Where next for Incendiary Tract?'

'We're raw,' I replied, while Pete was still chewing, 'we know that. It's still early days, but we've improved so much in the last few weeks. We'll see if we can get some interest from labels and keep practising, keep writing.'

'What do you do when you're not practising?'

'College and stuff,' Pete broke in, toast crumbs leaking from his mouth. 'Plus, we've both got part-time jobs.'

'And after college, are you looking to go to university?'

Half a bacon butty was in my gullet, leaving Pete to answer.

'Uni is a step too far for me. Our mam and dad left school at fourteen, so I know I'm lucky to even be able to go to college. I knew when I started that university wasn't an option and I'm not sure it is for James, either.'

We had both been so focused on the band that Pete and I never talked of higher education, yet I harboured a wish to progress on to something. I had read the prospectuses, acquired forms and the dates of open days, but that was as far as I got. The topic had yet to come up at home. It was a conversation neither me nor my dad wished to start because I think we both knew how it would end.

Next to me in the booth, Pete leant back, slipping his hands into jacket pockets. 'I'm not bright, you know. Not in a maths way, anyhow. Not in a science way. My talents aren't appreciated in that sort of environment. I'm not cut out to sit quietly and be told how things are. These college years have just been a bit of a buffer for me. A safety net to still be a kid before the real world gets its hands on me and I have to grow up and become an adult like my parents.'

'And do you want that?' Moon enquired. 'To follow your parents?'

Pete hands came out again and I wondered if they had anything in them, a lighter or coin to fiddle with as he talked, but they were empty.

'Well, I can't follow my old man. He was a miner, you know, up at Agecroft Colliery. Went on strike when it all kicked off. He was a different branch of union than the Yorkshire lot but was one of them that went out in support. Stayed out longer than some, not as long as others. He's militant, and I admire that.'

Pete sat forward and picked up his fork. 'That Poll Tax, the other year, that really pissed him off. He refused to pay and took me and our Rob on some trade union march in town. All placards and brass bands and stickers. It was fun, until further down the line you've got bailiffs at your door and letters threatening to send him down. Prison, you know. Actual jail time. I'd hear him and our mam argue about it all. He'd say if it wasn't for her and us, he'd have stayed out on strike until the end. Then she'd reply how principles are all very well when you've the bank balance to support them.'

With his fork, Pete skewered a blackened sausage. 'But then the pit shut down, and twenty years of his life were gone just like that. He was proud to be a miner. A union man, standing up for what he believed. Now he's just whatever, you know. This, that, whatever pays the bills.'

My dad had his own issues. Earlier in the year, his money troubles had reached crisis point. He was barely keeping a roof over our heads and the structural integrity of that roof was no better than his financial situation. Settle one bill and another went unpaid. Place one bucket and the rain would soon drip in elsewhere. Letters arrived which he would try and hide, but I knew where to find them – we only lived in a small terrace and any paperwork of his was always filed away in shoe boxes at the bottom of his wardrobe. When he was out, I would read these letters, searching for meaning in their brutal prose, noting the strategic use of block capitals and bright red ink, becoming lost in the terminology and the tone, the excess of syllables and economy of feeling:

Final reminder. Evidence of arrears.
Bailiff instructed to recover assets.
Anti-Poverty Unit. Means Enquiry report.
Commence proceedings for possession of secured property.

A woman from some association had come round and they went through his finances, what he owed and what he had, attempting to balance the two, but it did not help and there were mornings when my dad was due to appear in court. We had talked about it, and he told me it would be OK, and I had nodded in understanding. Yet I do not know if either of us truly believed what we expressed to the other.

He would put on the same suit he had worn for my mum's funeral and leave to get the bus and I would head off to college, thoughts of university far from my mind. I knew there were grants I could apply for and student loans, but the whole thing felt self-indulgent given the situation. It was difficult to escape the idea that, come evening, the house we had both left that morning might no longer be our home.

In the cafés background noise, I heard the low mumble of a radio and a song I recognised. One that reminded me of a flash of graffiti I had seen sprayed around Swinton:

NO HOLIDAYS IN THE SUN FOR THE LIVING DEAD

It summed up my father's existence or lack of it. He had barely done much of anything apart from worry since my mum had passed. He had lost his wife and then his job. He was fixed on survival and little else.

There were times I would come home from practice or a gig and know he had been out for a pint rather than sit in the house alone. I knew this not because of the smell on his breath or the flush in his face, but by his words. When he was at his lowest, when things got too much for him, the same notion would play on his mind. That if he had died instead of my mum, things would have been better. The policy the insurance company insisted only covered the main breadwinner would have paid out. There would have been no final demands. There would have been no court dates.

Sat in The Koffee Pot, I came to a decision. I would finish college, get my A-Levels, but park any plans about further studying. I would look for a full-time job, maybe expand my role at the cinema and move up to the projection booth. Writing could wait. I had years ahead of me to come back to it when the time was right and life was more settled. The band might even make a bob or two, as well. Maybe Pete was right, maybe music was the answer.

He was still talking to Moon about his parents and brandishing the charred sausage untouched on his fork.

'They argue, you know, but it's not nasty or anything. It's just about money. It's always money.'

Moon asked Pete if his mum worked.

'She's a cleaner. Does stuff all day round the house and then heads out to do it all again for someone else. Offices an' that. After hours, because God forbid some arsehole in a suit will have to watch a member of the working-class at toil. I think she feels no one sees her. No one appreciates what she does. I do, though. I see her.'

He put the fork down and slurped his brew gone cold.

'They're a funny pair, our mam and dad. He's an idealist, she's a worrier. His heads in the clouds and hers is in her hands. Together, they make one functioning human being. But our mam's the one who holds us all together, she's the practical one, she keeps things going. I dunno what we'd do if she wasn't there.'

Pete's attention seemed focused on the mug, but as he said that last part, I was sure his eyes flicked my way. We had never spoken about my mum. By the time Pete and I met, she had been gone over a year. We were teenage lads, and it was not the kind of thing that came up easily. Even if I was ready to speak to Pete about her, I would not open up in front of a stranger like Moon and the moment passed.

'Making music,' Pete said, 'writing songs, that's all I want to do. We've just been in the studio yesterday and cut a tune. I've never felt anything like it. The sense of achievement is immense. Being on stage an' all is great but it's over dead quick. Before you realise, the time's gone. It's an experience, you know, but it doesn't last.'

He raised his drink and finished it in one gulp. 'Recording a song, though, building something from scratch, three minutes that never previously existed and wouldn't now if we hadn't put it together. Then having it in your hands, this piece of work. I can't get over the fact we actually did it, I must've listened to the thing fifty times already. This thing that's mine, that's *ours*. Like you with your fanzine. A thing you've worked hard on and that no one can take away from you. That's what I want. Not a job like my dad's, that can be ripped from you in a heartbeat. And not like my mum's either, you know. Unseen. Unheard. I want people to see me. I want to be heard. And I think what I'm doing, what *we're* doing, is worth listening to. I really believe that.'

Pete pushed the empty mug away from him. 'But it's like James said, if what we're doing doesn't get out there, doesn't get attention, it's only half a job. And it'd be great to make some money from it, you know. Not loads, I'm not interested in being loaded or a big star. I just don't wanna be skint, that's all. I see what it does to my parents.'

Mark E Moon was silent, scribbling Pete's words down in his notebook, treating him like the adult he was close to becoming.

Maybe this was the first time someone had really seen Pete. Had looked beyond the caustic exterior. Had let him talk without cutting him off. Had believed he might have something to say. Yet with drinks done and food almost eaten, attention moving to our watches, the pricklier Pete was still only an errant word or two away, and Moon had a final question.

'Your first gig was a spot on a bill at the Students Union after another local band had to cancel at the last minute. How did…'

'Look, cock,' Pete said before he could finish, 'people get the shits from time to time, you know. I have, James has and I'm sure you have. Get over it, I'm sure they did.'

Moon went to readjust his glasses. 'But I was just going to…'

'No,' Pete leaned over the table and pressed stop on the tape recorder, 'you weren't.'

Moon collected his belongings and was headed for the door when Steve burst in, the two exchanging looks. With no way to get hold of us, our guitarist must have raced all over town, sticking his head in every greasy spoon along the way. He spotted us in the corner and marched over.

'You did this,' he wheezed between breaths, an accusing index finger aimed at our singer, '…on purpose…didn't you?'

'Dunno what you're talking about,' Pete protested with a shrug. 'Simple case of crossed wires, *cock*.' He slipped the last piece of toast into his mouth to hide a growing smile.

'You're a… fucking… prick, Moran.'

'You want to watch how you talk to people,' Pete said, sitting back with hands steepled over his full belly. 'Manners cost nothing. Unlike your Les Paul.'

Steve took a moment, either to compose a reply or calm down, but then stormed out the way he had come, almost bumping into the waitress carrying a large plate of scrambled eggs.

Back in the cold of Oldham Street, Pete and I walked towards Piccadilly Gardens. It was strange to feel I had headed out that morning intent on one course of action, gaining advice from Moon about writing, only to end up deciding to put all that on hold. I would still write songs for the band, so I was not stopping completely.

'What're you up to tonight?' Pete asked as we stood window shopping outside Vinyl Exchange. 'A few of us'll be out and about, if you fancy it.'

'No, I've got a shift at the cinema and then I'm just having a quiet one. I'm off to the rugby tomorrow with the old man and can't be rough for that.'

My dad had mentioned going to watch Swinton and I said yes without listening to the details. Who they were playing or whether it was home or away did not matter all that much to me because it was not the game I was going for – music and girls had moved ahead of the sport in my list of interests – I was going for my dad. If he had a vice, it was rugby league and our local team, but it was one he had been unable to indulge of late and not just because of his lack of funds.

The last game we had been to was the local clash with rivals Salford in the spring. It had taken place on Easter Monday, but any hopes of a resurrection were too late, the Lions were already relegated. We never realised it at the time, but it would not just be their final game in the top division, it would be their final game in Swinton.

The club had been in similar straits to my father and after the season ended their home ground at Station Road was sold to satisfy creditors. The Lions were uprooted and transplanted to Bury, a place they had no connection with, and we had not been to watch them since.

While an away game might mean a train journey over the Pennines, even a home fixture involved a two-bus trip out to Gigg Lane. It might not be Huddersfield or Featherstone, but it may as well have been. Long gone were the days when my dad could take his son on a short walk to see our side.

The situation in our house had calmed down in the past few weeks. My father was back in work and payments plans had been agreed but there remained a nagging fear that things might deteriorate again and the same fate which befell the Lions might still await us. Exile, from home and friends and happier times.

My old man had squirrelled away a bit of cash for a pre-Christmas treat and for eighty winter minutes he could forget everything outside the markings on the grass and stand on a terrace with his son like he used to, convincing himself that it would all be OK.

'You not working this evening, then?' I asked Pete. He had moved on from pot collecting to serving behind the bar.

'Nah, me and the landlord have come to an agreement, you know. I've got tonight off but doing extra hours over Christmas. Eve, Day, New Years, you name it.'

'Shit, mate. Just think of the money, though.'

'I am doing, cock, I tell you.'

We crossed Dale Street and were peering through the glass of Eastern Bloc Records when Pete decided to take a detour.

'I'm off for a nosey in there,' he said, pointing over the road. 'See you round, cock.'

Pete, darted in front of a slow-moving double decker and headed for Affleck's Palace and I went off to my bus stop and home.

29

Lockdown has been shite in many ways but on a deeply perverse level I've rather enjoyed not having to spend energy coming up with new ways to say no to people.
I've done a bit of reading; I've done a bit of writing. I've tried to grow as a human being, you know.
I even did a song using some program my daughter showed me on her laptop. It's called 'Always Bloody Londontown'. What's it like? Think part KLF, part Cooper Clarke. It's this sparse farty beat with me shouting the word 'London' over and over and over for seven and a half minutes.

Pete Moran, 2021

'So, it wasn't because of me, like?'

Outside the Academy, Lauren's question becomes entangled with the words of her father thirty years earlier. I'm still trying to align the two strands when Devon asks what gave her that idea.

'It's just...' she starts to explain, then falters a moment, '...I know me coming along when I did literally meant my mam never finished university. Not that she ever said so. I didn't even know she'd gone to uni; they'd always told me I was the first of the family who did. It was my granddad Martin who let it slip. Not on purpose, like, he just couldn't stop himself.'

It's easy to imagine Martin Moran's mouth running at a faster speed than his brain. He was a man of opinions – often X-rated ones aimed at southerners and the Conservative party – and not shy about sharing them. But did I know this about Kelly, that she never returned to Manchester Met to finish her course after giving birth? While I try and remember, her daughter continues.

'He felt awful afterwards, probably worse than I did. My nana Joan was ready to throttle him. But then last week, I just started to think, if me being born stopped my mam from going to uni, might it also have broken up my dad's band?'

None of us answer because we don't know how, leaving Lauren to fill the silence.

'You lot must've meant something to him otherwise why did he keep all that stuff? And if it was nothing to do with me, why did he never mention it? Why hide everything from me?'

That she might believe herself responsible for our demise hasn't until this point occurred to me. I've been too caught up in my own worries about the past to consider how it might look from her perspective. But the more I think on it the more I understand.

To count back nine months from her birthday would place her conception right in the middle of that tempestuous time. A time her father never thought to tell her about and that neither her mother nor her uncle had been willing to discuss.

Today isn't the witch hunt we all feared, at least, not from Lauren. She was never out to uncover some grand conspiracy and shame us for the crimes of our youth. She simply latched onto a theory in her grief, one which grew the more those close to her refused to talk about it, leaving her to seek out the three strangers who could give her the answer her family never would.

With nothing in the fanzines about our sit down with Mark E Moon, I don't feel the need to bring it up, but I wonder about that day. Pete clearly knew Kelly was pregnant and that the birth of the girl now stood before us would change everything for him. His buffer, as he called it, had been well and truly breached, the safety net ripped out from underneath him. He was thinking about his future, preparing to work extra hours at the pub as the real world was set to drag him kicking and screaming into its vortex. But did the news he was about to become a father at eighteen set off the chain of events that led to our end? The brawl on the Academy stage, the rumours about Kelly and Steve, Pete's unfaithfulness. Did that all stem from Lauren being conceived?

Maybe her arrival did derail Pete's life for a few years, but he still got where he wanted to be. He still made it. And what if Kelly hadn't been pregnant, but Pete had still been in that same nightclub with the same welcoming young woman who was not his girlfriend? Would the outcome really have been any different, could he have kept his dick in his pants? None of this is what a grieving daughter needs to hear.

'It wasn't because of you,' I tell her. 'Not at all. I mean, by the time anyone knew your mum was pregnant, the band had already split and there was no going back.'

Lauren stares at me and this time I don't see her mother in her, this time I see her father. Her eyes may look like Kelly's, but they move like Moran's, narrowing and searching, and I feel uncomfortable under her gaze. Can she see inside my soul? Can she see the truth of the matter? I'm grateful when Steve begins to speak and draws her attention.

'If anything,' he says, 'the reason we broke up was because me and your father just could not get along. To be honest, I was as much to blame as he was. We were two teenage lads going head-to-head with each other, ill-suited to being in the same room much less the same band.' He gives a shrug of resignation then continues. 'I was a bull-headed little prick and so was Pete. It was a number of issues, but none of them were that you were on your way. Like Jim said, by the time anyone knew about you, the band was over.'

Across Oxford Road, we sit inside Kro Bar lounging on a couple of worn two-seater sofas, our first drinks for some time on a low table in between. With the news her birth wasn't responsible for our break-up, Lauren had cried, relieved to have her fears allayed. She's quiet now but content, cradling a half pint in her hands and listening to Devon and I bicker back and forth about the selection of cakes on offer behind a nearby glass counter. I feel so glad to have got the day's first problem settled without any trouble, I'm close to ordering one.

'You've just eaten, you fat bastard,' Devon says after I suggest I'd like a slice of chocolate sponge to go with my pint.

'I can't help it,' I tell him. 'I'm hungry.'

'You'll put on weight and it's a slippery slope at your advanced age, man.'

'But not for a young buck like you though, eh, Devon? Didn't you say you'd buy me a kebab if we were still out.'

He shakes his head. 'That doesn't sound like something I'd say.'

'You are losing this famed memory of yours, aren't you, mate?'

Devon leans forward, squinting at me. 'Who are you, again?'

Lauren smiles at our antics, satisfied with all we've told her.

'Do any of you still play?' she asks.

'I've not picked up an electric guitar since,' Steve replies. 'I had an acoustic for a while, but what with work, kids and other distractions, there just isn't the hours these days.'

'My old kit's still in the garage,' Devon tells us. 'It's a different garage, of course, being up in Clifton now, but I go in there a couple of times a week and make a bit of noise.'

'What about you, Jim?'

'Nah, not anymore.'

I no longer even own a bass. In my late twenties, I'd had a brief musical revival, turning five numbers on the lottery into a black and white Fender Jazz, my dream instrument. I'd even threatened to help re-form a colleague's old punk band. But then time just slipped away. The bass had stood in the corner of the bedroom gathering dust and I was more likely to stub my toe on its hardcase than accumulate calluses on my fingers from its cable-like strings. When I finally gave in and sold it, I hadn't played the thing in over two years.

'What're you planning to do with the pictures?' I ask her.

She stares at the camera on the table and shrugs. 'I'm not sure, really. It just felt like something I should do. I could turn them into a project, or might just keep them for myself, like. I've literally not thought about anything past today.' She looks up. 'Thanks for indulging me, though. I know it's been strange, but I feels like it's helped.'

Under the circumstances, it's been a pleasant enough day, as pleasant as a day that starts out with a funeral can be. But the prospect of what'll happen once Lauren leaves hangs over the evening.

'I do have one last question, though,' she says and, for a second, I stop breathing. 'That first gig, at the Students Union. The fanzine says the other act had to cancel because they had diarrhoea and makes it sound suspicious. Did anything happen?'

'No,' Steve replies, 'not as far as I'm aware.'

'Me neither,' I add, after my entire body has unclenched.

Devon remains silent and hides behind his pint. He takes a mouthful from the glass and keeps his eyes on the golden liquid within.

'Devon?' she says, 'do you know anything about it?'

He swallows his beer and tries to stifle laugh. 'I couldn't tell you.'

'Come on,' Lauren says, 'what happened? Did someone slip that other band some laxatives?'

Devon puts his pint down. 'Your dad might've done. I've never been entirely sure. I know the idea was in his head, and the laxatives were in his pocket, but I was having no part of it. He never mentioned anything afterwards and I didn't want to ask.'

It's a tale Lauren's father had alluded to many times back then, but one I never wished to get to the bottom of either and there's now a Moran-like grin on her face. She seems happy to leave it at that and takes a sip of her beer before turning to Steve.

'So, when the band finished, you went off to study?'

'Yes. Economics in the Home Counties.'

'That's a very specific course,' I can't help but offer. All I get in reply is a heavy roll of Steve's blue eyes.

'And you two stayed friends,' Lauren directs at me and Devon.

With Pete off the scene, our drummer had stepped out from behind his kit and in beside me. He'd begun to let his hair grow and was no longer all that quiet, especially after a drink. With shared interests and similar temperaments, me and Devon had laid the groundwork for our burgeoning double act and easy friendship of over thirty years.

We get a final round in and Lauren texts her boyfriend to come and meet her.

'He's not in a band, is he?' Steve asks. 'You should steer clear of musicians, they're nothing but trouble.'

'No, he's a filmmaker, or that's what he's working towards anyhow.'

'Have you been seeing him long?' I ask.

'About a year.'

'And did Pete approve of him?'

She looks away with a cheerless expression. 'Do dads ever really approve of their daughter's boyfriends?'

When our drinks are almost finished, a young guy pokes his head in the door and Lauren stands up to hug him. He looks about fourteen.

'Christ,' Steve says. 'He's basically a sperm.'

'Everyone looks young to me, man.'

'Well, we are the oldest people in here,' I add.

Last goodbyes are exchanged and before she walks out of the bar Lauren Moran thanks us again for accompanying her down memory lane and we wave and watch her pass through the doors, heading out into an evening that is still warm and light.

Down to just the three of us, the mood becomes quiet. Devon's eyes are glued to Steve while our former guitarist stares out of the window behind me, and I'm reminded of the initial hostilities back at the crematorium. I find it hard to believe this is still in the same August day.

'Shall we have another pint?' Steve suggests, out of nowhere.

I'm surprised he wants to prolong this, but perhaps he knows he can't avoid it and wants to retain some level of control over the situation. Or maybe he's just going to make a run for it once he's stood up. With his long legs and a clear start, Devon would struggle to catch him.

'For the road, yeah,' Devon says in agreement.

Steve heads not toward the exit, but to the bar and I try, one last time, to avert whatever is coming.

'Don't do it, Devon.'

He raises his hands innocently. 'I'm not doing anything, man. Just having another drink.'

'Don't, mate.'

'I dunno what you mean.'

'Leave the past alone. It's not worth it. It never is.'

'Jim, man, it's worth it because we'll probably never see this lanky twat again and I want to know. It wasn't just your band, yours and Pete's, it was mine an' all. My band and my past and I've a right to know.'

Devon sits back, and I realise there'll be no changing his mind. He's waited a long time for this, he wants answers and that's that.

Steve returns with three glasses and once more there's silence. We each take a mouthful and I decide to break the tension with a harmless enquiry, one that shouldn't lead anywhere unpleasant.

'Did you manage to sort a train out, Steve?'

'Yes, I booked it back in the park. I'm on the 13:15 back to Euston. Time enough for a good lie-in and some breakfast. Are you working tomorrow?'

'No, I've got some leave I'm owed so I'll be doing much the same as you, but from the comfort of home.'

'Didn't turn out too bad in the end, did it?' Devon asks.

'No, it's been a decent day, considering,' Steve replies. 'How are you lads getting home?'

'I'll wander up and get the tram from St Peter's Square.'

'What about you, Devon?'

'Cab.'

I've never heard the word sound quite so threatening before and it lingers bluntly in the air. We each take a gulp from our drinks.

Devon returns his pint to the table with a dull, ominous thunk. 'While we're asking questions, I've got one of my own. That was quite the little speech you gave over the road, *Steven*.'

I glare at Devon and wonder where this'll end up.

Will he get what's he's searching for?

Or will he get what Lauren did, an approximation of the truth?

Would the full, unedited facts do any of us any good?

'Well, she's a nice kid. She doesn't need to know all the details.'

'That's very diplomatic of you, but it's the details I'm after, know what I mean. So, my question is this, did you fuck that girl's mum?'

'Leave it, Devon,' I say.

'I'm curious to know,' he says, turning to me, 'and I think we're owed some kind of explanation.'

There's a pause while Steve takes a deep breath and then a mouthful from his glass.

'No, Devon,' he says, calmly. 'I did not shag Kelly.'

The pair sit across from one another, each staring into the other's eyes. I may as well not be here.

'So, why'd Pete and pretty much everyone else in Swinton think you did?'

Steve looks away and shrugs. 'I can't answer that. All I can tell you is this, nothing happened between me and Kelly. Nothing whatsoever.'

Devon eyeballs him and Steve matches his gaze. The two face off until Devon begins to nod and reach for his pint. For all his insistence on a confrontation, he seems satisfied with this easy denial. The tension appears to have passed and I'm just starting to relax when Steve carries on talking.

'Not that I didn't have the opportunity, though.'

'Oh, really,' Devon sits forward again and it's Steve's turn to nod.

'That Sunday,' he says. 'Between the gigs. The day after she found Pete had cheated on her, she turned up at mine when my parents were out. She was all tarted-up and trying it on, but I was having none of it.'

'Well, of course not,' Devon remarks, not even attempting to hide his sarcasm.

I say nothing. All I can do is stare in surprise at Steve's words.

'It's true. I did *not* want to get involved with whatever bullshit those two had going on, so I sent her packing.'

'You're a proper gentleman, that's what you are.'

'Fuck off, Devon.'

I can't speak. I'm not even sure I'm still breathing.

'To be honest, I wish I had shagged her. I got blamed for it, so I might as well have fucking done it.'

Still, I say nothing and just continue to gawk at Steve.

He looks from Devon to me and, for a split-second, my eyes break away before glancing back at him. Now Steve is staring at me. Staring *right* at me and I hear Devon talking in the background but can't make out a word. My mind isn't interested in what he's saying and as me and Steve focus on each other I wonder if it's truly possible to see guilt on a person's face. Because if it is, that's precisely what Steve can see on mine.

30

Tuesday 15th December 1992

Outside was torrential. The proverbial cats and dogs coming down along with any number of other household pets. Gerbils, tortoises, the occasional budgerigar, all bouncing off the paving stones outside the house, and drip, dripping through the leak above my window into a bucket on the sill.

I should have been at college, but had not gone in. The weather, plus my mood, convinced me not to bother. I had woken up and gone through the pretence of getting ready, of having breakfast, of putting my bag in the hallway. Then I waited for my dad to leave for his still new job and returned to bed where I lay listening to the rain.

Our house was only small and there had been a time when it felt too small. A time when there always seemed to be a visitor, Cousin Lee or an auntie or my grandma. A time when music was playing, most often my mum's as she did the housework, The Carpenters, sixties girl groups or Motown. But then my mum died, and home to just me and my old man the place felt empty and quiet.

Her death had been a shock, a dose of unreal drama interrupting our Sunday evening watching a film. It began with a headache, a simple and mundane enough ailment, the kind of thing usually seen off with two paracetamol and a lie down. Instead, she had collapsed, and lost consciousness. A hurried emergency call was made and soon our street was filled with the distressing sound of a siren.

Curtains were pulled aside and faces peered out, neighbours came to stand on their paths. Our television was still on in the background, as the full horror of life played out in front of us. When they took her away in the ambulance, I never considered she might not come home.

My mum had worked as a nurse at the local children's hospital and if I was off school or it was a weekend, I sometimes went along with her. I would sit in the staffroom with my books or stroll around the ward, playing board games and talking to kids my age who were there as patients. I would return the next week and find that some of them were there no longer. My mum would tell me they had gone home. They were young, they got better, they went home. This made sense. But my mum was young as well, only forty-three, yet she went into hospital and a week later she was dead.

That my dad could lose his job, that the Lions could leave Swinton, that we could come so close to losing the house, all came down to money or lack of it. These were simple maths problems you might find in a textbook. If the numbers did not add up, if Mr Edwards didn't have x amount of money, then bills y and z could not be paid. But that an otherwise healthy women in her early forties might be fine one minute and then suffer a brain haemorrhage the next, this I found no explanation for.

After the funeral we had gone to my gran's house where I drifted among family and people I barely knew, anesthetised by a mug of room temperature lager given to me by Lee. My most vivid memory of that afternoon were two middle-aged women I had never seen before and never saw again, loitering by the spread, their plates loaded with triangular cut sandwiches. I remember the one whose face was ruddier than the other looking skywards and her words, 'the Lord moves in mysterious ways.'

'You can say that again, Ida,' her friend agreed between mouthfuls.

If Ida did repeat herself, I did not hear it. I was out in the backyard launching my empty mug at a brick wall. As a fourteen-year-old searching for answers about the justness of the universe, this was not what I wanted to hear.

Back home, I headed straight for my room and the picture of the Pope on my wall. God's number one on Earth.

Why was he up there?

This smiling, waving figure at a window. Benevolent, and a bit rum looking. Did I imagine him a surrogate grandfather? My real grandfathers were strangers to me. By the time I came along they were both dead men in cheap frames on our mantelpiece. Men I knew less about than I did John Paul II.

Why was he up there?

My mum was dead. But why? Why her and not somebody else? Why not Thatcher? She was much older than my mum and Margaret Thatcher did not spend her life caring for children. She stole their fucking milk.

Why was he up there?

I could not say. The conclusion I came to about fairness was there is none. Some people get to walk through life well above the surface and barely touched by its spray. The rest of us trudge through shit.

I had stared at the picture. Then torn it down and ripped it apart.

A little before twelve the doorbell rang. I was still in bed and ready to ignore the bloody thing, picturing some poor sod trying to hawk their wares out in the driving rain, but I got up and peeked through the curtains to see who it was.

Kelly Lewis. Up until that moment I would not have thought she knew where I lived, let alone turn up on our step. I threw on jeans and a T-shirt and went downstairs to open the door.

Kelly was short, dark-haired and a good eleven months older than me. I always thought she looked like the girl from Suede's 'The Drowners' video – full lips, intimidating eye shadow and wholly unattainable. Stood outside, without umbrella or hood, Kelly seemed as if she had almost been drowned herself.

She wore Doc Martens and a striped dress with an army jacket, one of Pete's. The pockets were dotted with badges he acquired at gigs we had been to; experiences we had both shared.

'It's not polite to leave a girl out in the rain, James,' Kelly said.

I could think of many reasons to shut the door, but only one to invite her in and it was not politeness. I led her through the hallway to our front room and then helped her remove her jacket. It must have doubled in weight with the morning's shower and was probably heavier than she was.

Try as I might, I could not stop myself from following the neckline of her dress as it dipped like a rollercoaster. My eyes were drawn to the droplets of rain on the upper parts of her breasts, and her nipples, erect from the cold, poking through her clothes. A pendant hung in the centre of her chest forming the final point of a Bermuda Triangle an inexperienced traveller just might get lost in.

I bent down to turn the gas fire on and felt my cheeks begin to blush before it had even begun to warm. 'I'll get you a towel,' I said and hurried out before the blood rushed anywhere else she might notice.

'Do you have anything to drink?' she called after me.

Nervously, I started to list beverages. 'Coffee. Water. Tea. Milk?'

'I was thinking of something a bit stronger, like.'

I rifled through kitchen cupboards, searching among bottles of cheap, supermarket spirits which had lain hidden for years, trying to find one remotely drinkable, while wondering, and yet knowing, just where all this would end up.

Three days before, during a night out in town, Kelly had caught Pete in the cubicle of some club toilets with her friend, Deborah Moore. The same Deborah Moore for whom I had long carried a torch. I was not even aware she was in Manchester. Deborah Moore had gone off to university in September and was studying in Sheffield. Had I known she was back, maybe I would have gone out that evening after all and how might events have unfolded then.

Pete knew I liked her. He had even encouraged me to do something about it before someone else made a move. This had been why I had not gone into college; it was not the weather that stopped me from leaving the house.

On the Monday, I had left my English class and been heading for the canteen when a lad called John Simpson, ignorant of my feelings towards Deborah Moore, had spilled the beans. In fact, it was more like vomit than a mere spillage. His mouth had opened, and the words came rushing out in a torrent as if they were something his body could not wait to expel. Words of bile and acid with unpleasant, yet familiar, chunks. Two other people had then confirmed the story to me, describing how Kelly ran out of the club in tears and Pete chased after her.

I returned to the front room with a towel and two mismatched glasses of a foul-smelling liquor. Having tested a mouthful in the kitchen, I discovered it did not taste any better either.

Kelly was standing with her back to me, inspecting the pictures and trinkets above our fireplace. Photos of me in my school uniform. My parents on their wedding day. One of us all on a rare holiday, an experience so long ago it felt as though it had happened to someone else.

I watched her and could not help but trace the outline of her underwear through the dress which clung to her like a second skin. When she turned around, I handed her the towel and looked away while she dried first her hair and face, then her legs. She swapped the towel for a glass, which she sipped at. Her brown eyes now seemed to be inspecting me.

'Have a seat,' I said, taking a gulp of the burning booze.

'I wouldn't want to soak your sofa,' she said. 'My dress must be ninety percent water.' She took another small drink before she smiled, inclined her head to one side and added, softly, 'do you think I should take it off?'

If I had ever imagined myself in such a position, faced with some question of deep morality, I might have pictured the two halves of my soul appearing on my shoulders, engaged in lively debate over just how I should answer. Angel me on one side, devil on the other. The reality, however, was very different. The angel me must have walked out the front door the same moment Kelly Lewis walked in.

'I suppose,' I said, slowly, 'that would depend on how wet you were underneath.'

It was a ridiculous line. The kind of thing only Roger Moore or a partially inebriated eighteen-year-old with a burgeoning erection might consider appropriate and as such, I was unable to look at her as I delivered it, so I never did see the sodden dress slide down her body, only heard it as it landed heavy and damp on the carpet.

*

Afterwards, we lay in silence under the duvet of my single bed, the gap between us growing larger while neither of us spoke. At some point one of us would have to say something or soon we would tumble off the edges.

The rain had stopped, and for that I was glad. It meant I no longer had to listen to the rhythmic drumbeat as it dripped into the bucket on the sill. It meant Kelly didn't have to hear it either, and I did not have to explain what it was.

My attention was at end of the bed and two bumps under the duvet. The cherry red Doc Martens which Kelly still wore. As we had made our way up the stairs, there passed an unspoken agreement that the time it would take to remove her footwear would be better spent doing other things. Had we bothered to unlace and remove the boots, we may have given more thought to what we were about to do. Had we taken those extra minutes we might not have even made it up the stairs, but stopped halfway, a couple of steps apart, laughing about our almost-mistake, how close we had come to jeopardizing what we both had. It could have been a moment we would look back on years later and cringe about; 'remember that time we almost…'

It was Kelly who spoke first. 'You've got a lot of posters,' she said.

All four of my walls and most of the ceiling were covered in glossy freebies from music papers and magazines plus others I had found in storage at the cinema. Promotional signage for new releases or advertisements for older films, rolled up and under varying layers of dust.

'It beats decorating,' I replied.

It beat decorating because decorating would have required money which we did not have. The house needed work, but with everything that had gone on, the place had fallen into a state. The roof leaked and there were window frames which were rotten.

The window in my room had a gap where the pane was broken, and the lower glass had slipped into the soft wood. This gap was only about a centimetre, but a centimetre was enough. It meant you could never really shut the world out. Howls of the wind would come through, as did those of dogs and the random shouts of neighbours or passers-by. My curtains were drawn so this and the bucket remained out of sight.

The walls had damp with areas where the paper was peeling back and others where loose plaster came away in chunks and powdered form. The heavy posters, when pinned tightly enough made an effective support to keep this from happening. They meant I did not have to look at these issues and I could convince myself that behind the posters might be a normal wall, with no weaknesses or damage. Just a wall, plainly decorated, but intact. I did not invite people into my room easily. A sense of shame always stopped me, yet a power greater than shame had allowed Kelly access.

Her focus was on a particular poster, a sizeable one of Nirvana's *Nevermind* album and its iconic image of the baby in water chasing a fish-hooked dollar bill. 'I'm pregnant,' she said, out of the blue.

I turned to stare at her, thinking she may have been making a joke and replied in kind. 'I don't think the process happens that fast.'

'Don't be a dick, James.' She was still staring at the poster.

Was this a shock? Not really. Despite only being eighteen, there was little in life which genuinely surprised me anymore. I had already learned to expect the unexpected. I thought back a few minutes to how much of her body I had seen. Was there any clue she was carrying a life inside her?

'Does he know?' I asked, unable to mention Pete's name.

'He knows, alright. He knows and he turns round and fucks someone else.'

Pieces fell into place. How my mate had acted at the interview with Mark E Moon. His talk of how the world was about to get its hands on him. Maybe it was the hands of a looming baby Pete had feared, with himself as that dollar bill. I moved the conversation in a different direction. 'I've never had sex with someone who was pregnant before.'

She moved onto her side to look at me. 'Have you ever had sex with anyone, before?

'Of course,' I replied a little too quickly, a little too forcefully.

'Alright,' she laughed. 'Keep your hair on.'

Being told to calm down, made me wonder just how her parents had reacted to this news and I asked how they had taken it. Any sign of amusement was erased from Kelly's face and she took a while to answer, during which I pictured a crib in her father's record room and her mother's response to another unexpected household addition.

'They haven't taken it either way because I've not been able to tell them. I dunno what to say.' Kelly twisted onto her back and closed her eyes. Her focus not on any point in the room, but on a time and place outside of it. 'I don't want to be a disappointment to them, but I've made a mistake and it's not one you can just apologise for and move on. They have this idea of me as the perfect daughter. The no trouble girl. They're dead proud of me. My exams results, my going to university. They want me to go further than them, James. Get educated. Get a good job. Have the chance they never did, but I've fucked it up. They've pinned their hopes and dreams on me doing well and worked hard to give me that chance. All their expectations are on me.' She looks my way again. 'Who'd be an only child, eh?'

My dad's expectations for me were virtually nil. We both knew he was unable to help me out, no matter how much he would like to.

'Are you gonna keep it?' I asked, unsure whether I meant adoption or abortion. Being on the sharp end of parenthood was not a concept I had thought much about.

Kelly shrugged her bare shoulders. 'It's not a question I expected to have to answer at my age, James. This isn't how I saw life turning out.' Her body shuddered and hands came up to cover her face. I was sure the next time she opened her eyes it would be to cry. 'I dunno what I'll do about uni,' she said. 'Manage, I suppose. I haven't really been thinking much beyond the next few weeks. I'll carry on until the summer and see what happens. Maybe take a year out and then go back, like. I hope so, anyway. I've put too much effort in to give it all up now.'

'What's it like?' I asked.

Her hands moved away from her face, her dark eyes looked into mine. 'Uni's great. It's big and new and not the same faces you've been seeing every day of your life so far. Not the same ideas or opinions, either. It's exciting. You start to feel like anything's possible. College is just a small town in comparison. You'll find out yourself when you get there.'

It was not the moment to explain I would be going nowhere. I had already begun to think about my revised future and how things would unfold, enquiring at the cinema about going full-time when I finished college and my idea about becoming a projectionist.

'What are you gonna tell Pete?' I asked, changing the subject.

'I reckon I'll tell him nothing and you'll probably do the same.' Her voice had gone harsh, but then lightened as she continued to speak. 'I didn't even think she liked him, you know, Debbie. I always thought you and her would get together. I thought she liked you. But then I thought she liked me an' all. Ten years of friendship and she does this. My best mate and my boyfriend. I probably shouldn't have come here, James. I think I half hoped you wouldn't be in.'

Kelly asked where our bathroom was and as she got up, I tried, and failed, not to stare at her naked form as she walked out of the room. I also tried not to think about what we had just done, but every time I looked up there on the wall there was that bloody baby. This tiny innocent creature, bobbing along in the water with its cherubic face.

Watching me.

Judging me.

I needed something to take my mind off the situation and reached under my bed for the stack of music papers I kept there, pulling out the week's *Melody Maker*. On the cover two indie stars were entwined above three thick red capitals:

S-E-X.

I folded it up and stuck the thing back where I had found it just as Kelly returned fully clothed. I did not even hear her go downstairs to collect her dress and jacket. Pete's jacket.

She lingered at the bottom of my bed. 'I'd best get going.'

'Right,' I replied, starting to get up. 'I'll see you out.'

'Don't worry about it,' she said. 'I know where your front door is. See you Friday.'

I was about to ask her why Friday when it dawned on me. Friday was our band's next gig, supporting the Ramones at the Academy and sharing a stage with my best friend, if that was what Pete Moran still was.

31

I've never spoken much about the drugs because it's painful to admit you've become a cliché. I'd always look at your Rock 'n' Roll addicts and think it showed a wholesale lack of imagination. Why drugs, you know? Why not get into to something really taboo, like collecting Gonks or radical left-wing thought?

It's a theory I've trotted out many times over the years and not everyone takes it in the spirit it's intended.

To get to the meat of the thing, early lockdown I found myself traipsing the barren wastelands at all hours and rocking up at some vestibule of Hell just off the ring road, where I waited for what felt like a week for this twitchy-eyed fuck to return from the gloom with a bag I'd made the mistake of already paying him for. Well, as I waited, I got to hearing things, see. Things I'd not like to account for under oath, you know. Let's just say it wasn't in the realm of Ginsberg experiencing Blake read 'Ah! Sun-flower' and leave it at that.

Pete Moran, 2021

With Kro Bar's sofas being so low and enveloping, I've time to watch the tall figure of Steve Williamson push himself upright. Long, spindly limbs move him into position like a spider ready to feed on targeted prey. But, before Steve's at his full height, before he's reached out to make a grab for me, his legs knock the table, toppling glasses and spilling his almost full pint onto my shins and feet.

Steve ignores this and clambers over the obstacle between us, knocking the drink out of my hand, and gripping me by my suit jacket collars, fabric scrunching tight in his fists. With eyes wide and teeth snarling, his beer and onion breath enter my nostrils while chilled ale pools in my best shoes.

As my glass shatters on the floor, I tense up in expectation of what? A headbutt? A bite on the nose? I can't remember the last time I was in a scrap. What should I do? I could knee him in the bollocks, or I could just take my punishment. It's been a long time coming, more than thirty years living with what I did. Past sins have a way of catching up with you, but I never thought it'd be my turn, never truly believed this moment would arrive.

I was eighteen and made a stupid mistake. One that cost me my band and my best friend. I should've done the same as Steve, I should've turned Kelly away and yet didn't. I was pissed off, with Pete and the world. At a time when life was supposed to be opening up for me, it felt like it was going in the opposite direction, closing in on itself. I was a quiet kid, a good kid, I worked hard, I studied hard, but it wasn't enough. I had anger and frustration inside me which I hid behind funny comments until, one day, I could hide them no longer.

Pete hurt me and he'd hurt Kelly, too. He'd betrayed us both and she was out for revenge, and I guess I was as well. I justified our tryst by believing we were two aggrieved souls balancing life's scales, not thinking ahead to any possible consequences. But here I am, all this time later and consequence has me by the lapels. Consequence is growling in my face. I close my eyes and brace for the inevitable impact.

More glassware tumbles and smashes, chair legs screech across a wooden floor. The hold upon me lessens. My eyelids open, and I see Devon's hands on Steve's arms, pulling him away. Good old Devon, I think. My partner in rhythm, my best mate. I relax and smile just as he throws the punch that knocks me sideways off the sofa.

I crash to the ground, dazed and unsure what just happened. The world has flipped. I'm on my back, laid out on the floor while my brain tries to adapt to its new surroundings. I hear shouting and swearing, threats of calls to the police and a hustle of movement. I twist myself round and catch sight of a face in the cake cabinet, a gaunt grey one staring back at me out of the glass. I believe it's my old man, wearied by life, shellshocked by grief. But it's not. It's me. An older version, ten or so years in the future.

I want to ask how the next decade will turn out, ask if it'll all be OK, but I'm grabbed from above and lifted and jostled against a nearby wall, my head almost bouncing off the chipped green paint. I've barely a second to gather myself before I'm hauled towards the exit, emerging onto Oxford Road as if propelled from a wild west saloon, the door halves swinging on their hinges as I'm launched through. I stumble down the steps and hit an unoccupied table, sending condiments flying left and right. I slump to the ground, my chin bloody from a sizeable lower lip gash, and watch Devon and Steve grapple with members of staff.

An audience is out front to witness this commotion. Couples on dates looking horrified and a gang of four lads, their faces animated by amusement and lager. This quartet seem familiar, standing close together with pints in hands. One of them I recognise, his Fred Perry polo and living room haircut give me a flashback.

I see James Edwards, straight from the summer of '92, enjoying life before events took a turn. Next to the young me is a young Devon and a young Steve and just visible behind them is another lad, laughing loudest and hardest of all. At first, I think it's a young Bob Dylan, but in the shadow of a passing double-decker, he changes and becomes Sabbath's "figure in black", the stencilled Pete Moran, a vandalised mural come alive, peeled away from that brick wall and here for me.

A hand rises out of his pocket, a forefinger aimed in my direction. His eyes ablaze and mouth opening slowly, readying a curse.

'Have him, grandad,' this apparition wails.

Devon breaks away from his tussle with a barman to respond. 'Who're you calling grandad, you fucking little prick?'

Something must've opened. A gap in the space time continuum, offering me a chance to put things right. I try to stand and communicate with my younger self. I want to tell him not to open the door, not to let her in. I want to tell him maybe there's a chance at a different future if he doesn't make the mistakes I did. I want to tell him to keep his dick in his pants, but can't seem to get his attention and why would he listen to an old bastard like me, anyway?

The lads jeer and laugh some more, an unopened bag of crisps spins through the air hitting Steve on the side of his head.

'Fucking students!' he roars back.

My former bandmates rail at the teenagers some more as we're escorted away from the bar and onto the pavement and this being the year 2022, their younger selves have mobile phones held out, recording our shame.

32

What advice would I give my younger self? It's a tough one, you know. For better or worse, the things I've done have made me the person I am and if I went back and told the eighteen-year-old me not to do certain things, I might end up being somebody else entirely.

Pete Moran, 2021

We begin the return journey in single file. Devon walks ahead, hands planted deep in his pockets and Steve follows a few metres behind. I trail our former guitarist by about double that distance. Our heads are bowed and not a word is exchanged. I stare at my shoes and the wet feet inside them.

It's been a long day, and the sky has at last begun to darken. We're well and truly in the "after" phase now. Everything is out in the open, all those secrets and ghosts. Our past loose in the present. How will I explain this to Katie? How will I explain it to the kids? How do I tell them we no longer see their "Uncle" Devon and "Auntie" Sandra and their two "cousins"? I could always say they've moved to Canada like my actual cousin. Fuck. Even Lee will find out and Pete's brother, too. Everyone will know my shame.

Ahead, I see Devon stop at a row of takeaways just past the Footage. His hands leave his pockets and after a quick count of coins he disappears into a kebab shop. Steve, upon catching him up doesn't go inside. I reach him and we stand ignoring each other again. No words. Not even a glance.

Devon's head leans out the doorway. 'What's the matter with you sorry pair of fuckers?'

'I'm out of cash,' Steve says, before he points to a sign taped up in the window, 'and you've chosen the only place in the modern world which doesn't take card.'

Devon turns to looks at me for the first time since he lamped me in my face. 'And what about you?' he asks.

'Same as,' is all I manage, in barely a whisper. He stares at me a moment longer, then ducks back inside to ask the bloke behind the counter for two extra forks.

Minutes later we're sitting in an Oxford Road bus shelter passing a kebab between us, the tray of chicken tikka and doner meat with everything gets lighter and lighter with each bus that rattles past. All Saints Park is at our backs and Johnny Roadhouse once more loitering in front. But our positioning has changed. Steve, the pariah only a few hours ago, is now the one to occupy the middle ground, overseeing a tentative peace.

'How's the lip, shagger?' he asks me.

'Split.'

'Well, be careful you don't get any chilli sauce in there or it'll sting like a motherfucker. And be thankful Devon here doesn't know how to throw a punch.'

Devon swallows down a strip of meat before replying. 'What can I say, man. I'm a lover not a fighter. Anyhow, Steve, I was impressed with the way you dealt with those children.'

'They weren't children. At the very least they were teenagers.'

'Either way, man. It was impressive.'

'"Fucking students"?' I ask Steve. 'Have you turned into your dad?'

'It is a distinct possibility.'

'Why? Does he dye his hair, as well?'

'Piss off, Devon.'

The tray goes left and right again before Steve has a question. 'So, Jim, are you going to tell us about it or what?'

'No,' I say. 'I'm not.'

'Come on. Give us something. Were her tits as great as they looked?'

'Steve, man,' says Devon. 'Don't be a twat.'

'I'm only saying what you're thinking.'

'Oh, really and can you tell what I'm thinking now,' he gives Steve a piercing glare.

'I don't believe I want to.'

A smiling couple step into the shelter, give the three of us a quick once over and then move on to the next stop. Between the blood and crumpled suits, the chilli sauce and kebab grease, we must look a sight.

The tray is in Devon's hands again but he's not eating. He leans round Steve to address me.

'Why'd you do it, man?'

I avoid his gaze and take a deep breath. 'I did it,' I tell him, 'because my best mate shagged the girl he knew I had a thing for.'

'You had a thing for Debbie Moore?' Steve asks.

'Yeah.'

'Well, I did not know that. Of course, it turns out there's a lot of things I didn't know back then. I have to say, Jim, I did not see any of this coming.'

'I remember the name,' Devon says, 'but I can't picture her face.'

'She was a mate of Kelly's,' Steve explains. 'Always hanging around the Lewis'. I'm sure she's friends with me on Facebook, do you want to have a look?'

'I don't,' I tell the pair, but neither pays me any mind.

'I do, man. I'd like to see just what this has been about all these years.'

Steve brings out his mobile, flashing the waistcoat now missing a button and after several taps on the screen, he hands his device to Devon in exchange for the tray.

'*That's* Debbie Moore?

Steve passes the tray to me then performs a few more swipes and presses on the phone in Devon's hand. 'And *that* is Debbie Moore circa early-nineties.'

'Fair enough,' Devon says. 'I can see the attraction, but I have to say, Jim, she was well out of your league. Do you want a look?'

'No, just leave me to my kebab.'

'It's not your kebab,' Steve points out, 'don't go scoffing it all.'

Devon is still looking at the screen. 'What I don't get, though,' he says to our former guitarist, 'is why Kelly told Pete it was you.'

'Fuck knows,' is Steve's answer. 'Maybe she didn't. Maybe she said it was someone in the band and Pete just assumed it was me. You know how it was between us, there was always something brewing.'

'And did you tell anyone this back then?'

Steve takes his device back and slips it into a pocket. 'I tried, but all the rumours just fit so well together for anyone to believe I might actually be telling the truth.'

As I listen to him, I needle the cut on my lip, pressing my tongue into it and reigniting the sharp pain. 'I'm sorry for all that,' I tell him, my eyes lowered and fixed on the tarmac. 'I mean, I fucked up and let you take the blame. It was a shithouse thing to do.'

'It was, James, and three decades too late though it is, I accept your apology.'

Another double decker trundles past followed by a black cab and a cyclist.

'Do you think things might've gone differently?' Devon asks.

'What?' Steve replies. 'If certain people hadn't put their cocks where they shouldn't have?'

'Yeah.'

Steve shakes his head. 'Not really. I was off to university no matter what. Whether you lads would have persevered with it, we'll never know.'

Devon stares back down the road, towards the Academy. He may be contemplating an alternative timeline where things didn't go to shit, where the band carried on and our teenage fantasies were fulfilled. Or he might be wondering about those lads we saw outside Kro Bar, our younger selves. After a time, he turns back to us. 'Sorry about the punch, Jim. I just got carried away.'

'That's alright, mate. I deserved it.'

'Nah, man. I shouldn't have done it. I'm not sure why all this has bothered me so much. I thought I'd put it behind me but seeing this twat's big ugly head again brought it all back.'

'Less of the ugly, please,' Steve puts in.

'I'm sorry for today, Steve. Sorry for being a, a...'

'A twat?'

'Yeah, sorry man.'

'You also are forgiven.'

Devon stretches his legs out in front of him, slips his hands into his pockets and leans back against the shelter. 'I think I was jealous of you lads, going to college an' all that, know what I mean. The decision had already been made for me. I was told I needed to earn my keep. My dad had sorted out this apprenticeship with a fella he knew and that was that.'

Devon brings out his Rizlas and tobacco pouch and begins to roll up. 'I was supposed to be grateful and, don't get me wrong, I am these days, but at the time it was a different story. One minute I was in school and the next I'm training to be a plumber. Out of the classroom and straight down a U-bend in about twenty-four hours. It's hardly the stuff of dreams. I had money in my pocket, but I wanted something more. I felt like I was missing out.'

He puts his newly made cig to his mouth and lights up. 'All my hopes went into the band. It was my dream, and it was happening for a while. But then it was gone, pretty much overnight, and I never had a clue why. I was gutted when it ended.' He takes another drag and exhales. 'It's silly, I know. An hour ago, I was fuming about it but now I know the truth, I'm alright. This morning, before I left, I was alright. Today has just dredged a lot of shit back up.'

'Did Clyde not think of getting you in at the Post Office back then?' Steve asks.

'No and I can't blame him for that. I love my kids, but I'm not sure I'd want to work with them either. No, he had his job for life sorting letters for Her Majesty and I was to be a plumber. He wanted me to have a skill, one that was always gonna be needed, one that didn't require a boss. I didn't see it at the time because you don't do you, know what I mean, but he was right. Work for yourself. Be your own boss. Make your own rules.'

'And how is he, your dad?' Steve asks.

'He's good, man. The sad thing is, we only really started getting along after my mum passed. We talked properly for the first time. Before that all we did was swap words, trade information. Trivia, cliches, nothing you'd describe as deep. But I understand him a lot more these days. As a father. As a man. We went over to Jamaica the other year for the first time – me, him and my sister – we met this old cousin of his who said he was a right terror when he was a lad. I found that hard to believe.'

'How is Louise?'

'Married, *Steven*.'

Devon's sister still lives in Swinton. She has a job at the civic centre and a seven-year-old girl.

'I was just making polite conversation.'

'You forget we know how your polite conversation about women usually ends.'

'I probably deserve that. Did you get to any cricket while you were there?'

'Nah, thankfully there was none on.'

'Why thankfully?' Steve asks.

Devon shrugs. 'Because sport begins and ends with football, for me, always has, always will. I never managed to get into cricket. Maybe it was all that carry on between Pete and him, back in the day. Do you remember the pair of them every time England lost a wicket? It pissed me off.'

'And did you discuss this with Clyde on your little voyage of discovery?'

'Did I bollocks. I said we talked, Steve. I never said we ironed out every grievance we've ever held.' Devon takes a moment and another drag. 'I doubt he wasn't doing it on purpose, I doubt he even knew it bothered me. And, who knows, if we'd got on better at the time it probably wouldn't have. We might've had a laugh about it, but we didn't, so there you go.' The cigarette moves again to Devon's mouth, but then stops. 'Pete annoyed me, an' all. All that acting up of his. The letter, the laxatives. That Irish shit he used to pull. Could you imagine if I'd gone round telling everyone I was Jamaican?'

'Pete was a prick,' I state, 'but he was our prick.'

The almost empty tray is in Steve's hands. 'Well, Devon, at least you can speak to your father about some things,' he says. 'I can't with mine, not really. Not without it ending in an argument. You couldn't even call it trading information, we trade resentments. Him that I went my own way and never took over the business and me that he's never found a way past that fact.'

'Has he said that?' I ask.

'No, but he doesn't have to. It's always there in the background. Never mentioned, but never forgotten. It just takes different forms, that's all. He likes to question my choices, second guess my entire life. The car I drive. How we're raising the girls. Nowadays, of course, it's Brexit and wearing masks.'

'Please, Steve,' I say, 'Not today. I'd rather get back to talking about death. It's a lot more palatable.'

'You're right and I don't want to talk about that shite either.' He flicks crumbs off his trousers, smooths down his jacket, lingers over the spot on his waistcoat where once a polished button had been stitched. 'It's odd really. To be honest, I didn't even want to come up here today. Yesterday, actually. I got the train after I finished work. But right up until I was in my seat waiting to leave Euston, I had half a mind to backdoor it. Even this morning at the hotel, I was tempted to stay in bed. Order room service and watch TV, spend the day in a complimentary robe. But I'm glad I didn't, it's been nice to leave everything behind for a while. To have my mind otherwise occupied.'

I know how he feels. I've been so preoccupied with imminent doom, the thought of future doom has been kept at bay.

'Are things not good at home, then?' I say and try to remember what Steve has said about his immediate family, but don't recall anything.

'I can't give a simple yes or no answer, Jim,' he sighs. 'I'm not sure it helps my parents live just down the road from us now. And when I say down the road, I mean just that. They're on the same fucking street. As nice as it is to have them close, especially during lockdown, there's such a thing as too close. It's like being eighteen, again, and I wanted to get away then. Get away and get on, that's what he could never understand.'

'Get on to what?' Devon asks. 'Adopting a permanent telephone voice?'

I laugh and despite Steve's mood he's not far behind me in smiling. 'That's something else my father enjoys pulling me up on. He never tires of telling me how much I sound like a southerner.'

'I'm sure there are worse things than sounding like a southerner,' I remark.

'You could always sound like Pete,' Devon suggests.

'Well, I'm glad I escaped that,' Steve grins. 'I did admire him, though. Pete, that is. Stubborn bastard that he was. Imagine having the balls to go on *Top of the Pops* with that voice. Fuck me, he could make Bob Dylan sound decongested. Are you happy with life, Jim?'

I'm startled by Steve's sudden tangent. Am I happy with life? It's a difficult question to answer without delving back into the past or fearing the future. I wonder, instead, about the lives of those I've spent the day with.

I think of Steve and our last months at college and how I allowed him to be punished for a mistake I made. I heard the rumours and let them spread. I saw Steve in the corridor and ignored him because I knew he was innocent. Why did I find it so easy to let him take the blame? If Devon was jealous of us, then did I in turn envy Steve? His big house? His Les Paul? His chance at further education? That his parents and mine had started out on similar paths only for life to split them off, to send his on a trajectory upwards and mine on a spiral down. I might say that I wasn't jealous but deep within me, in that place where my teenage self will forever reside, how sure could I be that it was true?

I think of my mate Devon and what those early years must've been like for him, a kid from differing cultures looking to work out just who he was, attempting to fit in living in a place where he stood out – the very opposite of Pete, who sought attention where Devon didn't. We've had a lot of big conversations of late, about our kids, the death of parents, health scares, but it seems silly we've known each other so long yet never really spoken that seriously about race. We've addressed our differences only through jokes. Perhaps we lacked a shared incident which would've forced us to talk about it. Had the events of early lockdown – the murder of George Floyd and the protests – happened at a time when we were able to sit down face to face over a pint maybe we would've done rather than simply exchanging texts of shock.

But there are many conversations I've never had. There are things I would've said to my mum. Things I should've said to my dad. There's at least one thing I need to say to my wife. And then there's Lauren. I feel guilty about how my actions no doubt added to the disfunction of her parent's relationship. If not quite so much damage had been done back then, might they have been able to repair their problems, might things have gone easier for them all? I feel sad that Kelly never made it back to university, that her dreams fell by the wayside. I've apologised to Steve, maybe I should apologise to her, as well.

But how do I see *my* life right now?

'Home life is great,' I say, finally. 'My working one less so.' The idea of becoming a projectionist at the cinema went unfulfilled. Those already in the position were firmly entrenched, but I'd stayed on after college before trying my hand at other jobs, and then the position at Cartwright and Sons warehouse had come up and the next two decades and more had gone by in a flash.

'They want rid of me,' I state.

'The warehouse?' Devon asks and I nod.

'Why?' enquires Steve.

'Health stuff. They're threatening to medically retire me.'

'What's the matter with you? You look well enough.'

'He's got a dodgy back,' Devon tells him.

'From what?' Steve asks.

'From twenty-plus years of manual labour.' I reply too quickly, hearing the tinge of anger in my voice.

'What're you gonna do?' Devon asks.

'I don't know.' After a quarter of a century in the same place the idea of starting elsewhere and at the bottom is a frightening one.

'Have you thought about retraining?' Steve asks.

'I wouldn't know what as.'

'Whatever happened to your writing? You used to always have a pen in your hand.'

I shrug. 'Once college finished that was it. I haven't written anything since. I wouldn't know where to begin again or what to what to write about.'

'Maybe, you should write about this,' Devon suggests.

'What?' I ask. 'Three men and a kebab?'

'Nah, you twat. About the band. About Pete.'

'Who'd want to read about us, mate?'

'Probably no one, but it's a start, you know what I mean?'

'People do love a tell-all about some star,' Steve offers, 'that or a celebrity cookbook.'

'What about that project Lauren mentioned?' Devon says. 'About her dad. You could write some stuff to go along with the photos.'

'I doubt anyone would be all that interested.'

'You never know,' Steve offers, 'but if you do write about the band, a few words of advice. You might want to leave out the part where you fucked your best mate's girlfriend.'

'Cheers for that, mate.'

Steve then performs a throat clearing that is a little too dramatic for our bus stop locale. 'Actually, while we're all being so very candid,' he says, 'I have a confession to make.'

'What?' Devon asks, excited at the thought of some more gossip.

Steve looks away and begins laughing to himself.

'Come on,' I say. 'Don't be a tease.'

'Let's just say I've got myself into a situation at work?'

'A situation? Have you had your hand in the petty cash?'

'Petty cash, Jim? What year do you think this is?'

'What then?'

'No, Steve, man,' Devon says, having already guessed. 'Tell me you haven't.'

'I wish that I could.'

'What?' I ask, now sensing the answer myself.

'You know that phrase, "live every day as if it's your last"? Well, I don't think it should apply to the office Christmas party.'

'How old is she?' Devon asks.

'Hang on a minute,' I say, 'you've just been giving me shit about something I did a lifetime ago, as a kid, and you're banging your secretary?'

'I never said that I wasn't a hypocrite, and she is not my secretary.'

'Is this your "foolish decision"?' I ask. 'The mistake that's coming back to bite you on the arse, like you told Lauren.' Suddenly all his furtive mobile activity explains itself. 'Is that who's been calling you all day?'

His hand goes nervously to his hair. 'Err, yes.'

'What are you telling us for, man?'

'Because I need to tell someone, and I probably won't see you arseholes for another thirty years.'

'How old is she?'

'It doesn't matter how old she is, Devon.'

'Come on, Steve,' I say. 'Tell us how old she is?'

'Is this why you dye your hair?'

'Fuck off, Devon.'

'You do though, don't you?'

'Fine, fine. Yes, that's who keeps calling me. She's thirty-four and yes, I dye my hair. Are you satisfied?

'I think the question, Steve, is are *you* satisfied?'

He crosses his arms in front of his chest, defensively, and then adds a shrug. His body is doing everything it can to force out an answer. He reminds me of my son trying to explain away some act of naughty behaviour.

'I don't know, really,' Steve says. 'I can't put it into words. It's not one thing. It's stupid and I know that. I've taken a wrong turn I can't seem to find my way back from.'

'I imagine,' Devon points out, 'that's not gonna cut it with your missus.'

Steve ignores him and turns to me. 'Look at us, James, confronting our guilt. We're growing as human beings. Unlike Devon, here, who's still a short arse.'

'Piss off, you lanky twat.'

There's a pause while I stand up to put our empty kebab tray in a bin. I stare back down the road and think about what I saw outside Kro Bar. Our younger selves. Only they couldn't have been, could they? Not really. It must've been my tired brain or the punch or just my shitty eyesight. I wonder what the others saw, but don't wish to ask in case they think I've a concussion. They might insist on dragging me to A&E and that would really cap the day off.

'Would you want to be eighteen, again?' I ask instead, leaning against the bus shelter.

'No,' Steve answers, without even taking a moment. 'To be honest, I'd much rather be mid-twenties. Bit of money behind me and a better idea of how everything works. Eighteen is a mugs game. You think you're cock of the world, but in reality, you know fuck all. It's just a ton of spunk building up and pressing in on your brain, forcing you to make a right cunt of yourself.'

'That's very philosophical coming from the almost fifty-year-old man who's banging his secretary,' I tell him.

'She is *not* my secretary. She works in a completely different department and, if anything, she may actually be higher up in the company than I am.'

'You little tart!' Devon laughs. 'Are you shagging your way up the corporate ladder?'

'I don't think I know what I'm doing,' Steve replies.

Ready to go our separate ways – Steve to his hotel, Devon into a taxi home to Clifton and me for my tram – we head back along Oxford Road and pass under the ring road. Now lit up, this shadowy entrance doesn't look half as foreboding as it did a short while ago. Whatever we uncovered was not as bad as I'd expected.

It's after ten and there are very few people about. The street is quiet, but Tesco still open, the store glowing like an urban oasis.

'Have you ever been back to Swinton?' Devon asks Steve as we walk.

'Back to?' Steve replies. 'I never *lived* in Swinton.'

'You what?'

'Worsley, Devon. I lived in Worsley.'

Devon is finishing up his cigarette. 'All this time and you're still pulling this bollocks, eh Williamson?'

'It was Worsley.'

'It was not fucking Worsley.'

I look down at my best shoes, worn and scuffed from their long life and our recent brawl. The socks still damp inside them.

'Higher Worsley, wasn't it Steve?' I offer.

'Exactly, Jim. Higher Worsley.'

'Piss off,' Devon says. 'If it was anything it was Swinton South.'

'Swinton South?' Steve asks. 'You've just made that up, haven't you?'

'It's no more or less made up than Higher fucking Worsley.'

Steve laughs. 'Are we going to keep in touch?'

'I dunno,' I say. 'Should we?'

'Well, we possess each other's secrets now, don't we?'

'All apart from Devon's. Come on, mate. There must be something you've held back all these years. A skeleton in your closet, a secret child? The missing persons buried under your patio?'

'Nah, Jim, not a thing,' he says. 'Sorry to disappoint you.'

'Shall I add you on Facebook?' Steve asks. 'I could have nose into your private life, see if I can find anything incriminating.'

'Yeah, sure, man.'

'Are you on there, Jim?'
'Nah, mate. I'd rather have a turd pressed into my eyeballs.'

33

What do I think about it? That's an easy one. I don't think about it.
I don't.
Look, cock, we both know what you're up to here, I've been dealing with your type since before you were a tickle in your daddy's gilded balls.
Your type, yes.
Over-educated and under-inspired.
You're trying to goad me into writing this article for you by spouting something mildly controversial as fuel for today's opinion sphincter industrial complex. Well, seeing as I'm in a good mood, I'll oblige, but just this once. Have you got a pencil?
Even better, let's begin. The moneyed classes… are the least… interesting… people in… history. Did you get all that?
Nice one, cock. Mind how you go.

Pete Moran, 2022

We part on the corner of Portland Street, email addresses swapped, and threats traded to do all this again sometime, though hopefully no one else will have to die for that to happen.

As I reach St Peter's Square, a tram bound for Chorlton lingers at the platform in the distance, but the memory of my last dash for a Metrolink, plus booze and the third of a kebab lying heavy in my stomach persuade me to let this one go. Well before I reach the steps, it glides away slowly to south Manchester, and I sit down on a metal bench and wait.

After the disaster at the Academy, it'd taken over a decade to finally run into Moran. I'd seen his name and face on the television or in the papers, had heard his voice on the radio in interviews and songs but any idea we'd meet again in the flesh had long been abandoned. The world had moved on from that December night and our lives had taken different turns. The thought of whether I even wanted to see him had not entered my mind, so I didn't quite know how to feel when I finally did.

I was out with Katie in the Northern Quarter. That area had only just begun to open up with new bars and the two of us were on a midweek date. We'd been together a while, but marriage and children were still off in our future.

Partway through the night I'd excused myself to go to the toilet and there I stood, reading the posters and flyers on the wall when there was a creak from behind me and a burst of noise flooded in from the bar area. The door shut and I heard footsteps on the tile floor and a fly unzipping before some thunderbolt struck the metal.

Seconds later came a voice. *His* voice.

'Am I hosing this trough down or is it hosing me?'

Sung words floating through the air towards me as a pale-yellow urinal cake made a similar journey in the piss below.

I didn't need to turn, but turn I did and there, grinning over at me, was Pete Moran. Bar the addition of sunglasses, he hadn't changed much from when he'd disappeared into the night ten years earlier after the Academy brawl. He still had the same super-charged hair, the same big smile, and was still dressing in the same clothing he had as a youth. But he'd moved on from bastardising other people's lyrics to his own.

'Alright, cock,' he said. 'This where you've been hanging out, is it?'

As I'd had a pint or two and was in a giddy mood, I nodded to the penis in my hand. 'Are you talking to me or him?'

Moran began to roar, and the sound of his laughter echoed in the enclosed space. His head was thrown back and where his head went his body followed as he leaned further and further the wrong way, limbo-style. I watched my old friend and wondered if his flexibility would fail him and he'd end up flat on the floor, pissing skywards like a human water feature. Eventually his amusement died off and Moran realigned himself into an upright position.

For a moment the pair of us were silent as we stared at the walls in front of us. A man is rarely more vulnerable than when he's stood at a urinal, back to the world and most treasured possession in his hand. It was the perfect spot to be reunited. We could neither embrace as long-lost brothers, nor start knocking lumps out of each other. Our eighteen-year-old selves had both done things we weren't proud of, but neither of us were those kids any longer.

Back in the bar with Katie, Moran had sat with us for a few drinks while customers turned to catch a glimpse of this local boy made good. One who had followed his dream of making music while refusing to compromise. Of the difficult artist Moran was portrayed to be, there was no sign. He was charming and witty, asking after my old man and cousin, then regaling Katie with stories from our teenage years. He told us what a lovely couple we made, how beautiful our offspring would be and brought out pictures from his wallet of his daughter, Lauren, almost nine at that point. He was every inch the proud father.

But as pleasant as that meeting had been, as nice as it was to talk of our shared pasts and separate presents, a thought niggled at me. Whether Moran knew as much about my indiscretion as I did about his.

It's Wednesday, the morning after. My secret is free, and the world hasn't ruptured. When I got home last night I'd stayed up with Katie for a few hours and talked. I told her about work, about medical retirement, about my fears.

She was shocked. 'They can't do that.'

She was angry. 'After all the years you've given them.'

She was understanding. 'We'll manage.'

'Whatever happens,' Katie said, just before we turned the lights off, 'it'll be OK.'

I'm not sure I can ever put such a positive spin on the things ahead of us. I've seen how a life can change with no warning. I've too many scars that may never heal.

Tomorrow at the warehouse I've another meeting with upstairs about my hours. Next week they want 65%, and 80% the week after and then back to full hours. I don't know what I think about work, apart from that I shouldn't think about it today as I know it'll set my mind off about so much.

About working up chimneys, down pits, or with a poison.

About being handed a gun and sent onto the streets of a near-neighbour to fulfil the whims of your so-called betters.

About going out to work while many stay home because your role is so fucking vital right until the time you ask for something in return. A little loyalty, or compassion, or a decent wage.

It's a train of thought I like to alight at the first available station as it winds me the fuck up.

For today, I'm at home. Katie's at the nail salon, the kids are with the child minder, and I sit at the kitchen table with a mug of coffee, my laptop and a blank open page. There are things I need to get out, things it might be wiser to type onto that empty space rather than push to the back of my mind. Writing. I think about writing. I make a second cup of coffee and think about it all some more.

I think about yesterday and all those days long ago. The post-practice games of pool. The gigs. The arguments. 'The End'. I could probably find any number of things to do other than write. There's a stack of books waiting to be read. A list of chores to be performed. No doubt, there's even a *Columbo* on.

I think about Moran and his life cut short. The last time we spoke he'd been frustrated at his failures as a family man and with the career that'd stalled. Pete never wanted millions or to be a big star, but could he have had success on a wider scale, been more than just an industry footnote? How might things have gone for him had his next act been allowed to play out?

As teenagers, we'd both had dreams. Then, circumstances had lessoned our grip on those dreams. I'd taken a hand away to juggle life. But then life had required a second hand and I'd taken that away too, hoping the distance would remain the same, only to watch it grow with each passing year.

Pete had kept his dream within reach. One white-knuckled fist tight on its shirttails. He'd fought to hold on until success was his but couldn't stop fighting when he had it. That fist had never unclenched. Maybe for fear the dream might once again begin to drift.

The page is still blank as the screensavers kick in. From a night-time city smeared with neon, to a mountain region reflected in calm water, to drab grey ruins under a blue sky. Out of the ruins I start to see modern concrete and that exit ramp on the Mancunian Way. At first, I think it incomplete and useless, but then I see it as something more. Not a slip road to nowhere, but a path veering towards endless possibilities. I also see the safety barrier blocking it off.

My fingertips touch the keyboard, though I believe my hands are on that barrier, heated by the sun as an electrical charge warms my laptop. The metal burns and I pull away, the flakes of a cheap paint job in my palms.

There were times when I might've found the way again, be it night school or online training, but then steady cash in formerly empty pockets is a seductive thing and the freedom money brings is itself a trap. My old man, though, was stuck in a different trap. He sacrificed and grafted to hold on to the house, but now it's home to someone else.

When we cleared the two-bedroom terrace, I found all my dad's papers. The records of financial dealings he kept in musty shoeboxes in his wardrobe, certificates of marriage and death, pictures of him and my mum, a woman I never had the chance to really know. I also found, under the bed in my old room, a stack of forgotten diaries. That was four years ago, and I've been unable to throw them away or read them. But I've no need to read them, I already know the words they contain. I didn't only write them, I lived them. But now my life needs rewriting.

I take another mouthful of coffee and look at the mug I'm holding, another memento from the house, an old one of my fathers with the Lions rugby emblem on the side. After all this time the team are still no closer to returning to Swinton, their destiny to drift rootless around Greater Manchester. Bury, Salford, Whitefield, Salford, Leigh, Whitefield, Sale. It's not a fate I wish to share, and I drain the mug and put it down.

There's that tired old saying about how sometimes you need to go back before you can move forward and it is tired, but there's truth in there as well; sometimes you need a bit of a run-up to things first, and there's a leap I need to make. Some ghosts of the past have been exorcised but it's the future that scares me now.

It's not just the starting at the bottom rung of a new job I fear. It's the not having a ladder to even climb onto. Who, after all, will employ a forty-seven-year-old with ongoing back problems? I don't want to be unemployed. I worry about the effect that'll have on my kids as I can never forget the effect it had on me. The things I held in. The damage that doesn't show.

You look well, I think and that slip road appears in front of me again.

I return my hands to the laptop and that scorching barrier blocking my way. Cars and lorries hurtle along behind me, the momentum of ring road traffic clawing at my back. I look up at the open blue sky.

Fuck it, I think, and I'm over and running.

Acknowledgements

I'd like to thank the following people:

To the early readers, Jeff Wraith, Chris Grogan and Adrian Hemstalk, for giving their time.

To Graham Ennis of When Skies Are Grey fanzine for being my first editor, Ian Cusack for advice on publishing, and Paul Connery for proofing.

To my Royal Mail colleagues – especially Simon Barley, Mark Ormrod and Mike Tomlinson – for indulging my nonsense, and Abdul Saleh for Keeping Me Moving.

To John Hubbert and Mike Smith for the beers, company and laughs.

To my parents, Paul and Frances, who both loved to read but are no longer around to see this become reality, and my brother, Simon.

And to Nicola Mostyn, who inspires and amuses me daily.

Printed in Great Britain
by Amazon